TREASURE LIES WAITING
FOR ONE LUCKY READER . . .

Hidden in the pages of THE DREAM PAL-
ACE are the clues to five questions. It will
take a clear eye, a brave heart, and a dedicated mind to find the answers . . . but they
are answers well worth finding, for a gold
wizard and $500 await one successful reader.
Will *you* be the adventurer who solves the
secret of

THE

DREAM PALACE

BRYNNE STEPHENS

THE
DREAM
PALACE

BAEN
FANTASY
BOOKS

DEDICATION
For my parents, Raymond and Viola,
and for Michael, my One True Love.

THE DREAM PALACE

Copyright © 1986 by Brynne Stephens

A Baen Books Original

Baen Publishing Enterprises
260 Fifth Avenue
New York, N.Y. 10001

First printing, March 1986

ISBN: 0-671-65557-4

Cover art by Stephen Hickman

Printed in the United States of America

Distributed by
SIMON & SCHUSTER
TRADE PUBLISHING GROUP
1230 Avenue of the Americas
New York. N.Y. 10020

THE
DREAM PALACE

OFFICIAL CONTEST RULES

A. **Entries.** Complete the Official Entry Form on following page and attach it to any 8½″ × 11″ paper(s) on which you have *printed* or *typed* your answers to the following five questions:

1. Who cast the spell?
2. How was the spell cast?
3. When was the spell cast?
4. Why was the spell cast?
5. How can the spell be broken?

Print or type your name, address and telephone number in the upper right corner of each sheet. Answer all five questions completely and mail entry to: DREAM PALACE, P.O. Box 458168, Cincinnati, OH 45245.

You may enter more than once, but each entry must be accompanied by an Official Entry Form plus a 50¢ processing fee* (cash, check or money order payable to Dream Palace). Official Entry Forms may not be copied or mechanically reproduced. Entries must be in English, legibly *printed or typed only* and must be received by December 31, 1986.

B. **Judging.** Contest answers in the author's own words are sealed in a bank vault. All entries will be reviewed under the supervision of Penultimate Promotions, an independent judging organization, whose decisions will be final. If more than one entry, or no entry, has the correct answers to all questions, contest winner will be the entrant who, in the opinion of the author, has best expressed the correct an-

---

*Processing fee not required for Canadian residents only.

swer to question 5, using the fewest words. The best answer to question 5 will be the one that is closest in meaning, logic and style of expression to the actual words the author has used, which will be found in the bank vault. The author's decision will be final.

C. **Prize Winner.** Contest winner will be notified by mail on or before February 27, 1987 and, upon verification, will be awarded $500 and a gold pendant of a wizard. Winner, and parent or legal guardian if a minor, will be required to sign and return an Affidavit of Eligibility and Release within 14 days of receipt, or prize may be awarded to another contestant. Taxes on prizes are winner's responsibility. For name of winner, send a stamped, self-addressed envelope to: DREAM PALACE WINNER, P.O. Box 312, Milford, OH 45150. Requests received after March 15, 1987 will not be fulfilled.

D. **Author's Answers.** For a copy of the author's contest answers, check appropriate box on Entry Form and send 50¢ for postage and handling to: DREAM PALACE, P.O. BOX 458168, Cincinnati, OH 45245. Requests for this answer insert, which can become a permanent part of your book for future reference, will be fulfilled after January 15, 1987 but not later than March 15, 1987.

E. **Eligibility.** Contest open only to residents of the U.S. and Canada (excluding residents of Quebec Province), except the author and author's family, judges and employees and their immediate families of Baen Publishing Enterprises, Simon & Schuster, its subsidiaries, advertising agencies and Penultimate Promotions. *Contest is void in Florida and Vermont* and wherever prohibited or restricted by law. Subject to all federal, state and local regulations. Awards will be made to parent or legal guardian of a winning minor.

Official Entry Form

Mail To: DREAM PALACE CONTEST
 P.O. BOX 458168
 Cincinnati, OH 45245

Use this form to enter contest and/or request author's solution. Check appropriate box(es) below and *print or type all information requested*.

☐ *Please enter me in the contest*. I am enclosing the following:
 a) My answers to the 5 questions (see back of this form) on one or more 8½″ × 11″ sheets; plus . . .
 b) 50¢ processing fee.*

☐ *Please send me the author's answer insert* (available after January 15, 1987). I am enclosing 50¢ for postage and handling.

Note: To enter contest *and* obtain author's solution insert, enclose $1.00 cash, check or money order payable to "DREAM PALACE."

Name of Entrant_____

Address_____

City_____ State_____ Zip _____

Telephone ( ) _____

To Be Eligible For Contest Prize . . .
clearly *print or type* your answers to the following 5 questions on one or more 8½″ × 11″ sheets. Be sure your name, address and phone number are on the upper right corner of each sheet.

---

*Processing fee not required for Canadian residents only.

Question 1: Who cast the spell?

Question 2: How was the spell cast?

Question 3: When was the spell cast?

Question 4: Why was the spell cast?

Question 5: How can the spell be broken?

Important: If more than one entry, or no entry, has the correct answers to all five questions, contest winner will be the entrant who, in the opinion of the author has best expressed the correct answer to *question 5* using the fewest words. The best answer to question 5 will be the one that is closest in meaning, logic and style of expression to the actual words the author has used, which will be found in the bank vault. The author's decision will be final.

NOTE: This Official Entry Form may not be copied or mechanically reproduced and must accompany all entries and requests. Be sure to enclose appropriate fee. Residents of Florida, Vermont and the province of Quebec, Canada, are not eligible. See Official Contest Rules for complete details. *This entry must be received by December 31, 1986.*

Important Note: Requests will not be honored unless all applicable fees and postage have been paid. No responsibility will be assumed for any late, lost or misdirected mail. Entries become the property of Baen Publishing Enterprises and will not be acknowledged or returned. No correspondence regarding this contest will be entered into, acknowledged or returned.

INTRODUCTION

Welcome to *The Dream Palace*! The journey you are about to begin is full of magic and beauty, exotic places and interesting characters. There is a mystery, five questions to be answered, and a chance to win a very special prize. There is also danger. Not everyone you will meet wishes you well. Your quest will involve choices, some trivial and some that will mean the difference between life and death.

You will follow the adventures of two best friends: Kym and Watkin. Their choices are yours. Every so often you will see these choices at the bottom of the page. If you have no interest in questing, you may ignore them and read the book as you would any other.

If, however, you have an adventurous soul, then the rules of the game are simple. When you come to a choice at the bottom of a page, a number is given for each decision. For example, you might see: *To go east, see #10. To go west, see #11.* Turn to page 238—to the section marked "Instructions"—find the number for your choice, and follow the directions.

Some of the choices are dangerous, and if you choose wrong, the characters can be killed. When this happens, you must go back to the beginning of the book and start again.

There are clues scattered about the book, both in the text and in the "Instructions." Putting them together will allow you to solve the mystery and answer the five questions, making you eligible for the prize.

Good Questing, and good luck!

ACKNOWLEDGEMENTS

The experimental nature of this book created a lot of difficulties and frustrations for me, which I duly passed on to my ever-supportive friends and family. I'd like to thank the following people for their patience, ideas, support, and much-needed *nudzhing*: Michael Reaves, Betsy Mitchell, Jim Baen, Steve, Dianne, Dal, and Stephani Perry, Candace Monteiro, Avon Swofford, Cherie Wilkerson, Marc, Elaine, and Gloria Zicree, Pat Russell, Cynthia Lindblad, Patrick and Jerry Byrne, T.H. White, The Voyager Inn in Van Nuys, CA, and my daughter Mallory, who chewed up only the pages that really *needed* rewriting.

"Friendship is love without wings."
—LORD BYRON
quoting an unknown source.

Prologue

The night is filled with laughter and music, people dancing and having fun. There is mead, strong ale, and cask upon cask of bad valley wine, which is never opened until everyone is too merry to care what they drink. The crowd is on its second cask, and is very merry indeed, which is a rare thing in this particular village. The villagers' lives are mostly quiet and dull, and the appearance of a lone carnival wagon has given them a reason to celebrate for the first time in far too long.

The wagon in question sits in the center of the dusty village square, beside a tiny, trickling stream. Once brightly painted, the wagon is now chipped and peeling. The cracked wooden wheels do not look sturdy enough to hold the wagon's weight, and maybe they are not—the wagon lists to one side. It still carries an air of reckless gaiety, however, and all who see it have to smile.

The inside of the wagon is just as ramshackle, and just as gay. Seated on soft cushions in the middle of the bright, threadbare rug are three men deep in conversation. All are tall; two are slender, and one is young.

Watkin, the one who isn't slender, refills the mead cups and settles his muscular, bearlike body deeper into the cushion with a sigh. "By the stars, man, you've been everywhere! Is there anything you haven't done or seen?"

The man in question smiles. He is the wagon's owner, and is dressed as brightly and shabbily as befits that title. He wears worn red cloth breeches, scuffed boots, and a clean but tattered black velvet tunic with patches of every color and texture imaginable.

He is surprisingly young, with long dark hair that falls almost to his shoulders, and his black beard is thick and soft. His face is thin and handsome, its solemn intelligence belied by the friendly wrinkles bracketing his eyes and the dimples hidden in his beard.

"There are two things I have never experienced," he says, his voice a pleasant rumble. "I have never been on a Quest, and I have not yet found my True Love."

"There's no such thing," says the third man. He sits half hidden in shadow, hunched over his thin knees as though trying to curl into himself. Usually given to moroseness, Kym doesn't take well to mead—or it to him. Added to that is the sad fact that the gaiety and good-fellowship outside depresses him—mostly because it never includes him.

"No such thing as a Quest?" asks Watkin, with a hearty laugh. Mead agrees very well with *him*.

The wagon's owner smiles. "I think our friend was referring to true love. And I think that he is wrong. It does exist."

"Not for everyone," Kym says, his voice a rough whisper.

The man in the patchwork shirt smiles to himself. "You have to know how to look for it, my friend."

Watkin sits up straight, so suddenly that he spills his mead. "Kym, that's it, boy!" He grabs his quiet friend in a rough bear hug. "We will go on a Quest to find our true loves."

Kym looks at Watkin incredulously. "We will do no such thing!"

Watkin grabs Kym and pulls him to his feet. He is impulsive, and once he gets hold of an idea he rarely lets it go. "Of course we will! We are not happy here, and none of the maids will have us. Do you want to die a lonely old man?"

Kym shakes his head. "Watkin, the maids here will not have us because we are neither fair nor clever, rich nor young. What makes you think that maids anywhere else will have us?"

Watkin gives Kym a shake, rattling his teeth. "We will win them through bravery!" He hugs Kym tightly, squeezing the breath out of him, then releases him suddenly with a slap on the back that sends him sprawling back down onto the cushions.

"I don't think I could survive a Quest," Kym mutters, showing a rare flash of humor. "Besides, where would we go?"

"I know a place."

Both Kym and Watkin turn at the intensity in the young man's voice.

They sit back down and listen, spellbound, while he tells them all he knows about a place people call the Dream Palace.

"What is known isn't much," he tells them. "It is a fabulous place, the site of a great love and a great tragedy. It is shrouded in mystery, and there will be a great reward for the one who can solve the puzzle."

It takes a while, but Kym is soon convinced of the viability of a Quest, and he agrees to accompany Watkin and search for love. Once it is settled, Watkin decides that they should leave in the morning, and announces that they should go and pack.

They make their goodnights and start to leave, but at the door of the old wagon Watkin tells Kym to go ahead home, and turns back inside.

The young man smiles up at Watkin. "Have you lost something?" he asks.

"Yes, my head." Watkin chuckles.

The man laughs, and waits for an explanation.

"I think that I will need some help on this Quest. Oh, not for me, of course—for Kym. What if he meets his true love, and she doesn't love him back? I need something to ensure that the lass will fall for the right man." Watkin twists his hat anxiously.

The young man nods in sympathy. "It would be a terrible thing if a man's true love refused to have him. I have something that will help." Reaching into a small, ornate chest set to one side of the table, he pulls out a lovely locket on a fine satin ribbon. When your true love wears this—"

"*Kym's* true love!" Watkin interrupts.

The young man smiles to himself. "Of course. When *Kym's* true love wears this, she will fall irrevocably in love with the man who placed it around her neck." He hands the locket to Watkin.

"Irrevocably?" he asks, placing the locket carefully in the pocket of his homespun shirt.

"Well, irrevocably as long as she wears the locket," the wagon's owner explains. "I have two more things that may help you," the young man offers. "A glowbubble to provide light—be careful not to break it—and a key. I do not know what it opens, but it may prove useful."

Watkin hesitates to take the cloth sack containing the treasures. "I have nothing with which to pay you for these."

With a smile, the young man pushes the sack into Watkin's hand. "If your Quest is successful, come and find me. We will tap a cask of ale, and the stories you will have to tell will be payment enough."

Watkin laughs, and bows, and rushes home to tell Kym about everything the young man has given him—everything but the locket, that is.

Kym listens patiently as Watkin spills the sack open and shows off the treasures he has been given. As soon as his friend is asleep, however, Kym dresses and slips quietly out of the house and makes his way to the cockeyed wagon.

The young man sits just where they left him, and he has set out two cups of calmberry tea, as though he knew Kym would be back. He gestures for Kym to sit, and fills his cup. "I am glad that you returned. I have some things to aid you on your Quest."

Uneasily, Kym folds his long body onto the cushion he has so recently left. Picking up the hot teacup, he clears his throat. "Thank you," he says, simply.

The dark-haired man holds out his hand, and Kym can see two ordinary objects resting on his palm. One is a small silver whistle, the other a plain red stone. He takes them curiously.

"The stone is a truth stone," the man explains. "If a person holds the stone while speaking, he may speak nothing but truth. The whistle is just a whistle, but you may find a use for it."

Kym thanks the man, then shifts about uncomfortably. He clears his throat and sips at his tea.

Kym is a shy man, not comfortable with himself or his world. Had he more wit, he would surely be a poet. As it is, he spins dreams too big for him, but though he is aware that the fit is wrong, he does not know how to fix it. So he dreams on, hoping that someday something—either himself or his world—will change.

That time has come, and he is afraid.

It takes Kym a moment to gather courage enough to speak, and when he does, he is embarrassed. "I need help," he begins, not meeting the other man's eyes. "I thank you for what you have already given me, but there is something else that I want—*need* to buy from you."

The young man refills his cup and waits.

"I am afraid," Kym whispers. Clearing his throat again, he forces himself to go on. "I am afraid that if I do find my true love, she will not love me. I want a spell to make me strong and brave and clever."

The young wizard, for that is what he is, smiles softly. "I will give you a Spell For Being," he tells Kym.

"For being what?" asks Kym, not sure he wants to know.

"For being anything you want." He holds up a small velvet pouch, tied at the neck with a silver cord. "Sprinkle this powder on yourself and wish, and you can be anything."

Kym reaches for the small bag. "Anything?"

"Yes. Even a tree, a cloud, or a mythical beast— whatever you can dream, you can be."

Kym considers the little pouch, unsure. "I do not think that I can afford this."

"You have paid the price with the courage it took to ask me for it. Go now. Your friend Watkin will want an early start tomorrow."

Not knowing what to say, Kym stands and walks toward the door. As he is ducking through the small opening, the wizard calls to him once more.

"Kym, the powder will work on anyone, but it is you who must make the wish. Make it carefully."

"This will ensure that I am worthy of my true love,"

Kym says, wondering. He bows slightly and goes through the door.

The young wizard smiles. "It will, but not in the way you think. Good luck on your Quest."

1: The Newly-Crowned Queen

Morning, not far away when Kym finally gets to sleep, comes quickly. Before he is barely awake Watkin is at him to hurry, and in the time it takes for Kym to bathe and eat, Watkin has packed a small knapsack for him and they are off.

It is a crisp day in early autumn, and the ground is covered with withered leaves that crunch underfoot as the travellers make their way to adventure. Kicking amiably through the leaves, Watkin keeps up a steady stream of conversation.

"I think this plan's a good one, lad, and there are no two men better able than us to make it go!" Turning to his companion, Watkin gives him a hearty thump on the back, making him stumble.

Watkin is a jolly bear of a man, proud of his strength, simple in his ways, and loving to his friends—especially this friend. While his companion is very different from himself in both look and outlook, Watkin has great affection for him, although he must continually remind himself to be somewhat less rough in expressing it.

9

Steadying him with one strong hand, Watkin repeats his remark. Getting his feet back under him, Kym nods in agreement.

Kym is also tall, but willow slender where Watkin is broad. He could be muscular if he wanted—the capability is there, but Kym has no idea how to use it. Instead, he has learned to project an air of dark moodiness—one of the things he hopes to change on this Quest.

He answers Watkin thoughtfully. "The plan is a good one, yes, but are we, I wonder, the ones to see it through?"

Watkin laughs, his bellow shaking a few of the more stubborn leaves loose from the branches overhead. "Of course we are! Who better?" He gathers Kym in a great one-armed hug. (Kym has never liked this horseplay, but has neither the heart nor the courage to say so out loud.) "Who better? The maids in our own village may not think much of us, but that is because they are small-town girls, and shallow. They care only for youth and beauty. On our travels we will meet sophisticated women, women who can appreciate a man for what he is inside. We will impress everyone with our bravery and skill, and win ourselves two young and beautiful wives. What could be simpler?"

Kym can think of a great many things that could be simpler, including just turning around and going home, but as usual he says nothing. Watkin is his only friend, and the huge man's never-failing optimism attracts Kym like a bright flame attracts a moth—although, unlike the moth, he knows the likely consequences of flirting with fire. Besides, their home is a wretchedly plain and lonely place, and leaving it isn't terribly hard.

Also, Kym hopes that this Quest will give him a chance to drop all of his protective poses, and let what he feels is his true personality come through. He has no illusions as to any great inner talent, but he has never hurt a living soul, and he thinks—or at least hopes—that somewhere inside he possesses the cleverness and caring to attract the love of a special woman. And if he doesn't, then the young wizard's spell will give it to him.

Watkin, watching as his friend once again sinks into reverie, pats the smaller man on the back—gently. "Everything is going to be just as we want it, Kym, my boy. We'll have it all, and we will have fought the good fight to get it!"

Kym nods in agreement as they continue down the road. He doesn't smile—he rarely does—but to one who knows him, the set of his shoulders and the lift of his chin show that he is, if not happy, then happier.

They travel on in silence for most of the day, stopping several times to eat and rest. Kym debates with himself whether or not to tell Watkin of the Spell For Being that he carries, but he doesn't know how. Watkin is so heartily sure that they'll win wives on their own merit that Kym is a little ashamed at needing magical help.

Not that magic is unheard of for everyday folk. On the contrary, there are spells for everything. Wizards, both male and female, create and sell the spells, and they are available to almost everyone.

Right now Kym wishes he had a Spell for Traveller's Aid—an incantation that lets a person take strides two or three times longer than their usual gait. His legs are already aching, and he and Watkin are barely out of sight of their village.

As they top the first of many hills, Kym looks back in the direction from which they've come for one last sight of his village.

It sits nestled in a small valley, looking snug and safe and warm, and Kym knows that this is just an illusion. Looking at Watkin's broad shoulders and amiable face, Kym is reassured. He squares his shoulders and lengthens his strides to match those of his larger friend. After a few moments his thighs ache, though, so he continues on in his usual loose-limbed stride, for the first time actually glad he's on his way.

The pair travel easily, walking until they are comfortably tired, and resting often. The farther they get from their own village, the more hospitable the countryside becomes. There are whistleberries, apple trees, and wild pig grass, which is tough but flavorful, plus several other varieties of easily accessible food.

In one small hamlet a young mother feeds them some wonderful spicy soup and homemade bread, in return for their promise to deliver a message to her sister in the next village. Kym and Watkin agree, and on reaching the next place and delivering the message are given more hot soup, and an even hotter proposition from the sister, who is a widow. They decline politely and continue on their way.

If either of them still harbors doubts as to the wisdom of their Quest, neither brings them up. Despite Kym's general reserve, and the fact that the two have been friends since childhood, they never run out of things to discuss, and their silences are companionable. The crisp weather makes sleeping outside under the warm blankets they carry very pleasant, and there are even enough streams and lakes to provide daily baths for the fastidious Kym.

There are no more towns for quite a while, however, and one morning, upon awakening, the pair have to agree that they are ready to see some people besides each other. They bathe, break their fast in silence, and travel for most of the day without speaking, other than to murmur cautions as to dangerous insects, loose stones on the path, the windblown remnants of old Trespassers Will Be Transformed spells, and other such nuisances.

As night draws near it grows colder, making each exhalation a fleeting cloud. The air is fogged as Watkin and Kym climb yet another steep hill, the fourth or fifth in a row. The land all around them is marked by these ungentle rises. The travellers climb them grimly, silent save for their panting breaths. A Quest is a poetic thing in the planning, but the actual questing can be extremely prosaic.

Watkin stops and leans against a handy tree. Taking a bright red handkerchief from his pocket, he wipes impatiently at his slightly less red face. "I don't know why I let you talk me into this, lad!" he gasps, and carefully places the soaked rag back in his pocket, lest some wizard find it and use his perspiration to cast a spell.

Kym, unaware that his friend has stopped, turns in disbelief. "*I*? But it was *you*—" He cuts his protest short as he realizes that Watkin is teasing him. The only child of rather taciturn parents, Kym is not used to being teased. He always reacts as though the remark were meant literally, and always curses himself for doing so. At a loss as to how he should respond, Kym waits.

After a bit, Watkin, turned from mopping at his face to grumbling at his fate, notices Kym's silent attention. Hot and tired, and very hungry, another man might have snapped out a rude remark. Watkin, however, for all his size and bluster, is a gentle man, never cruel to small children or helpless creatures. He considers Kym to be something between the two. Lumbering to his feet, he hefts his pack up onto his bearlike shoulders.

As he turns to struggle onward, he is stopped in his tracks by a sudden breeze, carrying with it an unmistakable smell—a small so strong that he can almost feel its velvet softness wrap around his skin. "Bubbleberry pie!" Watkin shouts, hardly daring to believe.

Kym looks up, startled. "What?"

"Bubbleberry pie!" Watkin repeats, dancing around in a little circle, nose held high in the air to catch every last whiff of the heavenly smell. "The single most wonderful pie in the world! My poor old mother, bless her dear departed soul, used to bake it on festival days. The crust was so tender, so light, and just the color of new gold. And the center! Oh, my friend, it was a tiny taste of paradise!" He stops suddenly and sniffs cautiously about. Wetting a finger in his mouth, he holds it carefully aloft, then groans. "The wind is changing! Hurry, before we lose the scent!" Grabbing his confused companion by the arm, Watkin hurries off in the direction of the smell.

At the crest of the next hill they stop, amazed. Down below them there is indeed a festival. Brightly colored tents are scattered about, each crowned with a snapping pennant. People dressed in fine silks and brocades wander among the tents eating, drinking, and greeting friends. Children run in packs like furless puppies, playing games of chance and skill, and begging coins for sweets from indulgent parents.

Watkin starts off at a quick trot down the hill, then notices that Kym isn't following. "Well?" he asks with exaggerated courtesy. "Shall we?"

Kym regards Watkin suspiciously. "Your mother isn't dead!"

Watkin laughs and repeats his offer. "Shall we?"

If you want to go with Watkin, go to page 15. If not, see #1. "Instructions" begin on page 238.

Kym hesitates, still suspicious. "Have we the time? I mean to say, what of the Quest?" Standing perfectly still, Kym gives the impression of shifting nervously from foot to foot.

Watkin laughs and grabs Kym's arm. "My boy, the only thing I'm in quest of just now is bubbleberry pie!" With a hearty tug and a playful slap on the back for Kym, Watkin starts off down the hill. Sighing a little, Kym follows.

The fairground is hot and dusty, and somewhat less glamorous then it looked from above. A multitude of people dressed in heavy fabrics on a hot day can give rise to a startling array of smells. Add to this the various food aromas, and the presence of a number of kinds of livestock, and you have a very heady atmosphere. Undaunted, Watkin has found his way to a pie vendor, and has purchased two steaming pies. Balancing them carefully on his enormous hands, he wends his way slowly through the crowd to where Kym leans queasily against a tent post.

"You're looking kind of peaked, friend! This will make you feel better!" Watkin thrusts the pie under Kym's quivering nose.

Kym looks down in horror at the bubbling pastry. Slightly larger than Watkin's hand, its sweet smell is startlingly strong. Bright red juice bubbles at the rim, and up through a small tear in the crust. Kym's stomach shifts uneasily, and he shakes his head quickly, afraid to open his mouth. Watkin leans closer, peering worriedly into his friend's greenish face. He shrugs, lifting the first pie to his mouth. "Oh well, we'll find you some dry bread and strong ale to settle you. I'll just get these pies eaten and out of your way—hey!"

Before Watkin can get so much as a bite of the first pie, he is hit hard from behind and both pies land in the dust at his feet. Rising to his full height, Watkin turns and grabs the collar of the unfortunate fool who cost him his treat. Pulling in a great lungful of air for a bellowing lecture on manners, Watkin lets it out again, sheepishly, as he sees that he holds not a drunken man, but a small, wriggling girl. He gives a look of surprise to Kym, who is still clinging weakly to the tent pole.

The child, who seems to be no more than twelve or thirteen, is totally unafraid. Grasping Watkin's huge wrist with both little hands, she attempts to sink one of her slippered feet into his stomach.

"Whoa, there!" Watkin stretches his arm farther, one hand spread over his stomach to protect it from further attack. "We'll have none of that!" he says, trying to be stern, and gives the girl a little shake.

"And I'll have none of *this*! Put me down!" she demands, imperious as only a little girl can be. Watkin laughs. "Oh no, my girl! Not until you apologize—and pay me—for making me lose my pies!"

She glances down at the ruined pies and smiles charmingly. "You were in my way!" Then, as Watkin shakes her a little more: "All right! I beg your pardon for running into you. But I have nothing to repay you with." Watkin sets her gently on her feet, still holding tightly to her collar. They both look up at a weak word from Kym.

"Information," he repeats, through clenched teeth. "What town is this, and why the celebration? And where can I find fresh air?"

The girl studies Kym intently, then turns to Watkin. "Your friend looks sick," she observes. "But come, I know a place!" And she starts off at a run.

Kym and Watkin follow the child as best they can through the bright, noisy crowd. Kym holds a hand over his nose and mouth to filter out the overpowering smells. (Watkin had offered his handkerchief for this purpose, but Kym, after taking one look at the crumpled, still-damp cloth, quickly declined.) At length, after dodging lords and ladies, being stepped on and bumped into by everyone else, and trying to keep a careful eye out as to where they place their feet, the travellers find themselves at the far end of the fairgrounds. They stand beside a long row of hedges, in a small grove of leafy trees. It's shady and cool, and best of all, upwind of the festival. The child is at first nowhere to be seen, but she appears presently, flushed and excited, holding her apron like a sack at her waist with one hand and two nearly full tankards in the other.

"Here we are! Sit yourselves down. I've brought good things to eat!" So saying, she settles herself down on the soft grass, and looks inquiringly at Watkin and Kym. Startled by her abrupt change from defiance to motherliness, they obey.

There's bread and cheese, cold strong ale, a meat pastry, and to his delight, a bubbleberry pie for Watkin. They learn that the child's name is Kirri, and that her mother, Aviane, is the palace cook. As they finish the meal and stretch out to rest, Kirri offers to tell them all about the town and the festival.

If you'd rather take a nap than listen to Kirri's tale, see #2.

Too sleepy to be really interested anymore, Watkin is also too polite to hurt the girl's feelings. "Yes, tell us a story, girl—it's just the thing after a hearty meal!"

Disregarding Kym's doubtful glance, Kirri begins her tale in her high, clear voice. She has more the air of a scullery maid imparting a bit of gossip than a child reciting her town's history.

"A long time ago. this town was settled by King Rayner. He ruled a long time—not too well, but not too badly, either. When he was real old—last year, I think—he brought a beautiful young girl to his palace, and—well, everyone says she's beautiful, although I really can't see why. I think she's a bit plain. Um, he told all of his people that after he died, this girl, Rayanne, was to be queen. And he did."

Kym, interested in spite of himself, turns to look at the child, who is shredding a starflower, quite pleased with herself. "Did what?" he asks.

"Who?" says Kirri, already off on another train of thought.

"The king," Kym prompts, a little impatiently. He hasn't Watkin's patience with children. Or anybody else.

"Oh! Died. He died a cycle ago, and now Rayanne's been crowned today, and she's the queen, and that's why there's a festival, although my mother says that it's rude to have a party to celebrate somebody who's benefitting from someone else's bad fortune. Have you a wife?"

"No," Kym answers, glaring at Watkin, whose last snore sounded suspiciously like a snort of laughter. "We're on a Quest for one." It occurs to Kym that this is not the sort of thing one safely confides to a mischievous girl of twelve or thirteen, and is proven right a second later when Kirri jumps to her feet.

"Well, that's easy to fix! My mother isn't married,

and neither is the queen! You stay right here—I'll go and get them!" With that, she is off into the crowd, darting among the festive throng like a small fish among brightly colored sea fronds.

"Wait!" Kym jumps to his feet, ready to chase her. He stumbles as Watkin reaches out and wraps a huge hand around Kym's ankle.

"Let her go." His voice is muffled under the hat lying across his face.

"But she's bringing back the queen!" Kym struggles for a moment to free his foot, but realizes quickly how undignified his struggling must look, and stands still. Watkin releases him and sits up, stretching lazily.

"Of course she's not. D'ye think the queen has nothing better to do on her festival day than chase after a waif? Or the queen's cook, for that matter? She'll be back, after a suitably long time, with a message that the queen and her mother are too busy to come—and maybe a treat or two." Secure in his knowledge of the ways of children's minds, Watkin settles back into the fragrant grass and pulls his hat down over his face.

Kirri is back in a moment, breathless and excited. "My lady the queen can't come to you (Watkin winks broadly at Kym) but she bids you join her for dinner tonight. Come, I'll show you!"

If you wish to follow Kirri, see #3. If not, see #4.

Watkin, sitting up again, exchanges a startled look with Kym, as Kirri stands waiting. With arms folded, tapping one foot on the ground—a pose that she most probably learned from her mother—she manages to look even more charming and elfin than before. "Well, come along; you can't go to dinner like that. First you've got to get cleaned up! Hurry, you don't want to be late!" Kirri scolds.

Watkin looks at her thoughtfully. "Are you having us on, girl? Why would the queen wish to dine with such as us?"

Kirri meets his gaze, wide eyes full of innocent surprise. "Well, of *course* the queen would want to dine with you! I told her all about what great travellers you are, and about your quest!" As she speaks, Kirri begins to walk slowly backwards, forcing Kym and Watkin to follow. "I know you must have wondrous stories to tell. The queen *loves* stories. I tell them to her all the time, but mine are just made up. She's looking forward to hearing *real* tales, and so is the rest of the court. It's usually rather quiet here. Oh! Here we are!"

They have stopped before a gap in the hedges, and Kym and Watkin can see a small door set in the wall behind the shrubbery. Kirri steps forward to open it, but as she reaches for the latch, Watkin gently takes her small hand in his. She turns to find him squatting beside her, suddenly at eye level. "Girl, you wouldn't be teasing two weary travellers, would you?"

Kirri shakes her head. "I swear by my mother's heart. Through this door is the bathing house, where you can get yourselves ready. Go ahead!"

If you wish to go ahead, see page 21. If not, see #5.

Exchanging a glance and a shrug, Watkin and Kym go through the door—and into an ambush! The two men get a brief impression of flying bodies as they are tackled and borne to the ground. They hear Kirri scream as they are buried amidst a tangle of arms and legs, while they struggle fruitlessly. For the second time that day, Watkin fills his lungs to bellow, and finds himself looking into the startled face of a child. It is a young boy this time, about the same age as Kirri, and just as elfin. Startled at finding himself looking at a stranger, the boy shouts a command, and Watkin and Kym are released, helped to their feet, and brushed off.

The still-startled boy bows gravely to the two men, and tugs his disheveled forelock. "Your pardon, sir. I thought you were someone else. Forgive me."

Watkin nods, still a little out of breath. "And who is it that I should be thankful I'm not?" At the boy's puzzled look, he rephrases the question. "For who were you lying in wait?"

"Whom," Kym corrects.

"That's what I'm asking," says Watkin, for the first time showing signs of testiness.

The boy shuffles one foot in the dust. "We were waiting for the stableboy." Kirri, standing nearby, turns a bright scarlet as he continues. "We were going to throw him in the bathhouse and hold his head under water until he swears to stay away from Kirri."

Watkin and Kym exchange amused glances and then turn to Kirri, who is standing with her hands behind her back and her head lowered. She looks up at the boy and shakes her head. "Oh, Tal! He's just friendly!"

Tal glares, hands on hips. "Let him be friendly with someone else's girl! It's a lucky thing that dueling is forbidden to anyone younger than three trines, or I'd give him what for!"

Watkin, who has witnessed many a grown man fight

for a woman, throws back his head and laughs. He stops abruptly when Tal buries a small but determined fist in his large, soft stomach.

"It isn't funny!" shouts Tal, struggling as Watkin grabs him in a bear hug. Watkin sets the angry young boy back on his feet, ignoring the circle of his friends who stand shifting uneasily from foot to foot, ready to rush to Tal's defense.

"There now, I meant no offense," Watkin soothes. "But don't you think ye're a bit young for all of this?"

Tal shakes his head defiantly. "We may be half grown in body, but our hearts and souls know love when it comes. Children feel more deeply than their parents are willing to credit." Kirri, blushing but solemn, steps to his side and their fingers entwine.

Watkin looks once again at Kym and clears his throat, embarrassed—but also touched. Kirri breaks the moment by rushing forward, her usual bossines restored.

"We have no time for this! Into the bathhouse, you've got to get presentable for the queen!"

And so they do, with a good deal of hilarious, roughhousing help from the boys. When Watkin and Kym finish, they find that Kirri, banished during their baths, is nowhere to be found. What they do find are two paths leading from the bathhouse, one dirt, one stone.

To take the dirt path, see #6. For the stone one, see page 23.

After careful consideration and thoughtful discussion, Kym and Watkin set off down the path made of stone. There is no further sign of Kirri.

"Where d'ye suppose the little witch has gone?" Watkin asks.

"Most likely to make sure that whatever hideous joke is to be sprung on us is ready," Kym replies gloomily. He fancies himself a dignified fellow, and has never understood that it's exactly that air of false dignity that attracts practical jokers.

Watkin puts a friendly arm around Kym's hunched shoulders. "Now, now, I'm sure the lass means no harm. And maybe there *is* no joke—it could be that we really *are* to dine with the queen!" He slaps Kym's shoulder in boisterous camaraderie.

Kym turns a sour look on Watkin, not bothering to answer. Sometimes Watkin can be so gullible, he thinks. Of course, as large as he is, not many are willing to risk making him angry. It's easy to be good-natured when everyone is afraid to cross you.

The path they are on twists and turns through a carefully sculptured landscape. Exotic shrubs and dwarf trees litter the ground with fragrant leaves, and tall, flowering plants catch the sunlight until they almost seem to glow with a light of their own. At length, Kym and Watkin come to a door. It is old and scratched, and standing partly ajar. The path here turns to dirt and continues on around the stone building in which the door is set. From within the building they hear laughter.

If you wish to enter, see page 24. If not, see #6.

Slowly, sweeping Kym behind him with one huge hand, Watkin cautiously pushes open the wooden door with the other. When no evil befalls them, the two men step gingerly into the room.

And find themselves blinded by the light of a thousand candles. There is absolute silence as a hundred curious people turn to stare.

They are in a huge dining hall, which is dominated by a long wooden table, polished to a glassy sheen. Intricately carved high-backed chairs, upholstered in rich brocade, line the table. Each chair, except for two, holds an elegantly dressed man or woman. Small, bored-looking pages stand behind each place, and two young girls wander about, keeping the hundreds of candles lit. One of the girls looks up and winks as she goes by, and Kym and Watkin are startled to realize that it is Kirri.

At the far end of the table, with an empty chair on either side of her, sits the queen. At least, Watkin and Kym assume she is the queen. This is a fairly safe assumption as she is the only person in the room wearing a crown. As the silence stretches on, she rises and beckons to the two intimidated men standing by the door.

Watkin pulls Kym around in front of him and gives the smaller man a gentle push, while holding tightly to the back of Kym's tunic.

"Leave off!" Kym mutteres, stumbling a few steps forward, and trying unobtrusively and unsuccessfully to remove Watkin's enormous fist from his clothing. Watkin nudges him again, and Kym swats at him. In this fashion they slowly make their way to the head of the table, and the queen.

The young queen rises to her feet, studying the decidedly odd progress of the two scruffy but clean young men. She notes the difference in size and build, and the comical struggle going on between them. They actually seem to be afraid of her! An impulsive young woman, and rarely wrong in her decisions, the queen decides immediately that she likes these two. She suppresses a smile as they reach her place and execute a pair of identically clumsy bows.

"Welcome! I am Rayanne, queen of this valley. I have heard that you are travellers, on a great Quest. Will you join my table, and tell us of your journey?" With a sweep of one slender hand, Rayanne indicates the chairs to either side of her.

Watkin, waiting for Kym to answer, is startled when he doesn't, and so gives his friend a sharp elbow in the ribs. He is privately amused at the way Kym freezes up in front of women. In this case the reaction is certainly justified, but since Watkin has seen Kym act this same way in front of kitchen maids and tavern whores, he is less than charitable. It doesn't occur to Watkin to question the fact that he, himself, might have spoken instead.

Feeling Watkin's sharp jab in his side, Kym realizes with a start that he has been just standing there, staring open-mouthed for at least ten seconds. Gathering his shaky wits about him, he endeavors to bow once more before the queen, and stumbles a bit as he places his back foot carelessly and turns his ankle.

"If it pleases your majesty, my fellow traveller and I would be most honored to join your table." Watkin ducks quickly as Kym, indicating his friend with a sweeping motion, nearly hits him in the eye.

A sigh runs around the table as Watkin and Kym are seated. The people of the valley like to consider themselves terribly jaded, but the truth is that they are simple and kindhearted folk, and Kym's stumbling performance was painful to watch.

Pages come forth with platters of meat almost as big as they are, tankards of foamy ale, and thick mead. There is fresh fruit, hot and cold spiced vegetables, and a delicious soft bread baked with honey that Queen Rayanne remarks is made from her mother's recipe. After dinner is eaten and the thin silver goblets at each place are filled with sweet sherry, Queen Rayanne holds up her hand for silence and turns to Kym, on her right.

"Tell us, sir, of your travels and your quest," she requests. Her voice is soft and clear, and Kym, aware that he should be answering, finds himself held motionless by the depth of her green eyes. So caught is he by her beauty, he doesn't feel it at all when Watkin kicks him under the table, twice.

Realizing with an inner smile that she is going to get nothing out of Kym but moony stares, Rayanne turns to Watkin, and repeats the request.

Watkin clears his throat and shifts to a more comfortable position. He is not unimpressed by her beauty, but if there's one thing Watkin loves more than a beautiful woman, it's a beautiful woman who asks him to talk about himself.

If you wish to share the reason for the quest with the assembled company, see page 27. If you would rather thank them for their hospitality and be on your way, see #7.

"We are on a Quest, my lady," Watkin begins, "with a very important goal. Maybe the most important there is." Watkin pauses for effect, enjoying the attention. He glances down the table out of the corner of his eye, making sure that everyone is listening. They are. Satisfied, he continues. "Our goal, you see, the thing for which we are searching, is nothing less than—true love." He lowers his head modestly, as though the significance of this is too much even for him.

The assembled company reacts appropriately, murmuring gently, with soft, throat-catching gasps from a few of the more sensitive ladies. They hush instantly when Watkin clears his throat once more, signalling that he is about to continue. Before he can, a little voice speaks up from behind one of the carven chairbacks—a page who has gotten temporarily carried away.

"Were there no ladies who would have you where you come from?"

Watkin turns a slow, deep red, as a ripple of unsuccessfully suppressed laughter floats past him. "There were plenty who would have us—" Watkin begins, but he is startled into silence as Kym speaks up.

"No, child," Kym says, his voice soft and solemn, yet sad. "We are neither fair nor clever, and we have no riches or special talents. Although not yet old, neither are we very young, and in the place from which we came, a kind heart and simple soul are not considered things of very much value."

The room is quiet as all at the table consider this. Young lovers and old couples exchange soft smiles, grateful for having found each other. Unmarried men search their souls to see if this is not the case with them, and the unspoken-for women wonder if they, too, are guilty of such thought. Surveying the table, Rayanne thinks that most of them are.

Smiling warmly at Kym, she leans forward slightly,

folding her small, elegant hands around the stem of her sherry glass. "And have you a plan to carry out this quest?"

Kym, made shy once more by her scrutiny, looks helplessly at Watkin.

The larger man shakes his head. "No, my lady, we've no definite plan. But since staying where we were was fruitless, our luck can only change for the better, as far as women are concerned."

A feminine voice speaks up hesitantly from the gathered company. "Have you considered a love-spell?" The lady belonging to the voice blushes furiously as Kym turns and glares at her.

"We would not win a wife through trickery, or have one against her will. We seek to win the love of good women through bravery and what cleverness we have."

Undaunted, another voice speaks up, this one male and very old. "Have you heard of the place they call the Dream Palace?"

A gasp runs around the table, and several people try to shush the old man. He is straight and tall, and wears a key on a chain around his neck. Kym and Watkin both take note of the fearful glances directed at the young queen, and of her tight mouth and white face.

"We will not speak of this," she orders quietly. "In any case, we do not have time. It is late, and I suggest we all go to bed." She turns to her two guests of honor. "Will you accept our hospitality for the night?"

If you wish to accept, go to page 29. If not, see #8.

Watkin gets heavily to his feet and, bowing, answers for them both. "We would be honored, my lady. Thank you." As the rest of the guests get quietly to their feet and begin to depart, Rayanne directs a nearby page to escort the travellers to their room. Allowing them each to kiss her hand, she gives them a warm good night and leaves, surrounded by her ladies.

Watkin takes a last deep draught of mead, hesitates, and then, shrugging, picks up both the mead cup and the decanter and gestures to the boy to lead the way. Kym starts to follow, then stops to pick up another cup, and hurries after Watkin and the page.

They walk down many twisting corridors lit by clean-burning wall sconces, and finally stop before a large painted door. The scene depicted is an ordinary one—a dragon being charmed by a wizard. The craftsmanship is only fair, but the colors are pleasantly bright.

The little page opens the door and bows Kym and Watkin through it, then scampers off down the hall. Watkin smiles as the child disappears around a corner, then turns and surveys the room.

It is large and well-appointed; extravagantly so, by Watkin's standards. There is a huge canopied bed, with wooden posts in the shape of griffins rampant. The canopy is a rich satin brocade, as is the coverlet. The wardrobe and washstand, as well as two large chairs, are also done in the griffin motif, with a satin brocade for upholstery. There are no carpets on the floors, nor any rushes, but the flagstones are warm and clean.

In one corner stands an enormous brass tub with claw feet and rolled edges. It looks big enough to hold not only Watkin, but a companion as well. Dangling from the ceiling beside the tub is a velvet pull cord with a gold tassel on the end.

Watkin surveys all of this with delight. Although he

has always lived in simple surroundings, he is not in the least intimidated by luxury.

It is not so with Kym, however. The tall, thin man stands in the center of the room, holding his disheveled pack in one slender hand, looking around the room morosely. The rich appointments just remind him of how poor his life has been so far, and how unlikely it is that he will ever actually live in a place even half as nice as this. He sighs.

Watkin smiles to himself at Kym's obvious line of thought. "Come now, lad, it isn't that bad," he says, teasing. "Not as nice as sleeping under the moons and stars, but we can manage for one night! I know what will cheer you up! A good hot bath!"

Kym sighs again, attracted by the thought, but unwilling to be jollied. "I've had a bath today," he says, moving a step closer to the tub. "I don't think I need another." Watkin laughs, a hearty roar.

"That was for clean! This is for pleasure. Peel out of those fine garments, and I'll ring for hot water!" Kym makes no move to comply until Watkin gives the pull cord an enthusiastic tug.

By the time Kym has struggled out of his boots, stockings, and tunic, there is a loud knock at the door. Watkin sweeps the heavy door open and laughingly bids someone enter. Kym, struggling with his breeches' knotted laces, looks up in irritation, then lets out a squeak and grabs for his shirt.

Bustling about the brass tub are two young maids. They have brought two enormous casks of water, set up on wheeled dollies with hinges for tipping the steaming water into the tub. This being done, the young women have tucked their skirts efficiently up around their knees and climbed into the tub.

Kym stares at them aghast, his shirt clutched modestly to his pale chest. It is a moment before he can speak, and when he does, his voice cracks. "W-what are you doing?"

The maids, surrounded by curls of scented steam, exchange puzzled looks. "You called for a bath," the smaller of the two begins helpfully. "We're here to give you one," finishes her blonde partner.

Kym looks from the women to Watkin, jaw hanging loose. "Well—I've changed my mind." To his chagrin, Kym feels himself blushing. He curls one set of toes over the other, clutches the shirt more securely in front of himself, and looks away.

The maids giggle. "Now don't be embarrassed—this is our job! We bathe everyone—men, women, and children alike. There's nothing to fear."

Seeing Kym's pleading look, Watkin takes over. "Where we come from, ladies, folk bathe alone. To do otherwise is, well, not done." He shrugs and smiles disarmingly, as if to show that he himself finds this a silly custom, but what can one do?

The two women smile understandingly and climb out of the tub. The smaller of the two apologizes for embarrassing Kym, and with another round of giggles, they depart. Watkin gestures toward the tub. "Be my guest!" he tells his comrade.

If you wish to bathe, see page 32. If not, see #9.

Turning his back on the vastly amused Watkin, Kym gingerly steps out of the rest of his clothing and into the tub. He closes his eyes in pure ecstasy as he realizes that the tub is deep enough for him to submerge up to the chin, keeping even his knees under water. He barely stirs as Watkin presses a cold cup of honeyed mead into one limp hand.

"There now, see? Doesn't that make you feel so much better?" Watkin inquires. Kym nods sleepily, then starts violently as a loud knock sounds on the room's heavy wooden door. Watkin grins. "I'll bet it's those two bath maids, come back to lend you a hand!" Kym sits straight up, a look of terror on his face as he grabs for his shirt and once more clutches it to his chest.

Watkin strides to the door and throws it open, a courtly bow half started. In the doorway stands an old man—a very tall old man. He is taller even than Watkin, and thinner than Kym. His white hair and beard are carefully groomed, and his clothing is of the best fabrics tailored in the latest fashion. He is neat and trim, and moves with a startling grace for his obviously advanced age. He returns Watkin's courtly half bow, causing a small flash as the golden key he wears on a chain around his neck catches the light.

"Good evening. I am Doren, Keeper of the Wine." He smiles charmingly. His voice is low and throaty. "I thought you might be interested in the tale I have to tell."

"We are somewhat fatigued," Watkin begins, only to be interrupted.

"The tale concerns something that I think you will find fascinating. I have come to tell you everything that is known about the place they call the Dream Palace."

If you are interested, see page 33. If not, see #9.

11: The Winekeeper's Maze

Watkin smiles, not quite as charmingly as Doren, but with great sincerity. "We are very interested, sir," Watkin replies, turning to Kym for confirmation. Kym, sitting bolt upright in the tub with his shirt clutched to his chest, unaware that half of it has fallen into the cooling water, nods silently.

In a few minutes Doren is settled in a comfortable armchair, long legs stretched toward the fire, mead cup in hand. Kym, all puckered from the bath and dressed in one of Watkin's shirts, sits with Watkin on the over-stuffed couch with the other cup in hand, while Watkin holds the bottle.

Taking a long draught to wet his throat, Doren begins his tale. "A long time ago, before Queen Rayanne was a queen, she was betrothed to a man called the Scarlet Prince. He was a bit of a rake, and no good at all for her, but it was a wise match in the political sense. They seemed happy—until the prince got a better offer. Lord Darna, a local lord with a very rich protectorate, offered one of his three beautiful daughters to the prince in marriage. Not much is known about these girls, for their father kept them very sheltered, but their names are Loria, Auriane, and Celia. It was the Princess Auriane that the prince was promised."

Doren pauses, recrosses his ankles, and takes another sip of mead. "Lord Darna and his wife, Lady Alsinor, decided to throw a grand ball to announce the betrothal, and maybe to find husbands for the other two girls as well. No one knows, because the ball never happened."

"Why not?" ask Kym and Watkin, in perfect unison. They glare briefly at each other, then turn again to Doren.

"I'll get to that in a moment. Where was I? Oh, yes," he continues. "Invitations were sent out. That silly Alsinor even sent one to Rayanne, though of course the poor child declined. A few guests arrived from far away a few days before the ball, and everything seemed to be going fine, when suddenly a host of messenger boys descended on us, canceling the invitations! Odd about those boys, they all looked exactly alike . . . probably conjured. Well, Alsinor is a bit flighty, so we all assumed that she'd maybe forgotten some unimportant little detail like the caterers or the orchestra, and that the ball would be held at a later date. But it never was."

Kym and Watkin both start to speak, look at each other, and start again. Watkin claps a large hand over Kym's mouth and asks the question alone. "Why not?"

Doren smiles, the same charming smile as before, but with an air of mystery attached. "Why not, indeed? That's what we all wondered. The guests who arrived early never left, and their kin started to worry, so we gathered up a search party and set off to find out what happened." Doren pauses for another sip of mead.

Before he can continue there is a loud pounding on

the door, followed by a demanding male voice. "Doren! This is the Captain of the Guard! I know you're in there, and you know you're not supposed to be spreading your foolish tales!"

If you wish to turn Doren in, see #10. If not, see #11.

Doren leaps from his chair with surprising agility. Watkin runs to the door and braces it with his shoulder, just in case the captain of the guard should prove very determined to get in. Kym stands in the middle of the room unsure of what to do, looking momentarily bewildered at the frantic gestures being directed toward him by both Watkin and Doren. Their meaning dawns on him suddenly; he draws himself to his full height and walks over to the door.

"Doren! I know you're in there! Open this door, or I shall have to break it open!" the captain yells. Kym reaches the door, shoulders unconsciously falling into their habitual protective droop at the man's powerful voice. When he speaks, the quaver in his own voice isn't pretended. "There's no one here but my friend and myself! Go away." He looks to Watkin, who nods approvingly.

"I beg your pardon, but I shall have to see for myself that the winekeeper isn't in there. Open the door!"

Kym squares his shoulders. "No!"

"Very well. Then I shall have to break it open!"

Kym is beginning to feel brave. "You and what army?" he taunts.

Watkin and Doren are making frantic hand signals again, warning Kym to stop this line of conversation. Kym, however, takes their agitated arm-waving for encouragement and goes on.

"You probably couldn't even break this door with a Spell for Stubborn Locks!"

The captain is outraged. "Oh, yeah?"

Kym is smug. "Yeah!"

"Well, it just so happens that I have a Spell for Stubborn Locks, so stand back!"

Watkin grabs Kym in one strong arm, and places a large hand over his mouth. "What did you do that for? Never mind. What are we going to do?" Kym makes a muffled series of explanatory noises, which Watkin ignores. Outside, they can hear the captain of the guard chanting in a self-important voice.

Doren smiles, looking not in the least perturbed. "I have been studying this castle for years, gentlemen. It has many secrets—most of them useful!" So saying, the tall old man steps behind a tapestry. There's a quiet creaking noise, followed immediately by a loud poof! and a billow of blue smoke, as the captain's spell takes effect on the door. Kym and Watkin stand motionless as the captain makes his way, choking and gasping, through the acrid cloud.

"There, then! See? And you said I couldn't do it!" The captain's smug sentence trails off a little at the end as he realizes that he is looking at the queen's two guests, who seem to be alone. "All right, where is he?"

Kym and Watkin look extremely innocent, and shrug in unison.

"Who?" Watkin says.

"Whom," Kym mistakenly corrects.

The confused captain looks once around the room, then shrugs. "I thought I heard the winekeeper's voice. Guess not." He cheers slightly at the sight of the empty doorway. "I'd better go get you a new door. That spell is marvelous!" He pauses in front of Kym. "In the future, I'd mind how I speak to members of the military!" With that, the captain leaves.

Kym and Watkin rush to the tapestry and pull it aside, and to their surprise, find nothing there but a blank stone wall.

✸A little later, as they are getting ready for bed, here in a strange place so far away from anything familiar, Kym starts to feel a little nostalgic. Their home isn't the most exciting or beautiful place in the world, but it does have some nice points. He smiles in memory.

"Watkin, remember the stream that wound through the middle of the green at home?"

Watkin, already in bed, answers sleepily. "The one with the leeches in it?"

Kym frowns. "There weren't that many. And they were small."

Watkin grunts. In agreement or dissent Kym can't tell, so he tries again.

"Well then, remember the tavern maid at the Griffin's Wart? She was a beauty." Kym had never been brave enough to speak to her, but he wishes he had.

Watkin snorts. "She was hardly a maid, and she had a mustache thicker than mine! What is all this?" He turns over and sits up with a groan, looking to where Kym sits dreamily on the edge of the bed, nightshirt half on and half off, staring into space.

He comes back to himself with a start as Watkin pokes him with one foot. Kym shrugs. "I am a little bit, well, homesick."

Watkin smiles at Kym's uncertainty. When they started the quest, Kym was his usual moody self, never saying much, creeping around being dignified and mysterious. Those mannerisms seem to have vanished lately, and Watkin has the feeling that he's seeing the real Kym. He likes this one better. "You're just fidgety at being under a roof after all those nights under the moons and stars. And I know just the thing to do!" He climbs out of bed and picks up his breeches. "Let's go exploring! A little adventure will make you feel better!" As Kym watches doubtfully, Watkin strides over to the nearest tapestry and pulls it aside. "All castles have secret passageways, right?" Watkin states.

Kym peers over the larger man's shoulder doubtfully. Exploring dark spidery passages is not Kym's idea of fun.

Ignoring the waves of doubt emanating from behind

him, Watkin squats down and begins to search the spaces where the wall stones are joined. The mortar in most of the cracks is weak and crumbling, attesting to the age of the castle and the dampness of the climate.

Unsure of exactly what he is looking for, Watkin scrapes at the loose mortar, and presses randomly on the cracked wall stones. He swears as Kym, leaning forward suddenly, loses his balance and nearly falls on him. "Careful there!" Watkin growls. "What are you doing?"

Kym's voice is squeaky with excitement. "Look!" He reaches a long, thin finger over Watkin's shoulder and points to a spot a few inches in front of Watkin's nose. Watkin peers closely at the place and frowns. He is about to turn away when his eye is caught by a tiny flash of gold. Looking closer, he sees that it is a gold chain, caught between the stones! Watkin presses on the intersection, and to their great surprise, a part of the wall swings inward, revealing a secret passageway!

Watkin turns to his partner truimphantly. "Shall we?"

If you want to explore the passageway, see page 40. If not, see #12.

Kym hesitates, not liking the look of the dark, dusty passage leading off to who knows where. He searches the gloom with squinted eyes, and is rewarded with another glint of gold. Reaching out carefully, Kym catches the source of the shine, and tugs gently. With two quick steps, he and Watkin are standing back in their room looking down at the chain lying in Kym's hand. Attached to the chain is a tiny golden key.

Watkin makes a sound of delight as he recognizes the pendant. "This belongs to the old man!" Kym nods, excited.

"If we find him, maybe we can find out more about the Dream Palace. Maybe we can learn something of use to our Quest!"

Watkin agrees. "Let's go!" He takes two quick steps forward, then Kym reaches out and grabs his arm.

"Wait! It's awfully dark in there. Don't you think we should bring a light with us?" Kym peers fearfully past Watkin at the long, shadowy passageway, sure that he can see things moving back in there.

Watkin goes to his knapsack and carefully lifts out the glowbubble. Lightspells aren't usually too fragile, but Watkin has a healthy respect for things he doesn't understand—especially magical things. Shielding the little light with one enormous hand, Watkin approaches the passageway and steps carefully into the gloom. At the last second, Kym grabs his arm again.

"Wait! Won't the light attract . . . things?" Kym gestures vaguely into the passageway. Watkin stops, considering.

You can still back out—see #12. To use Watkin's glowbubble, see page 41. To go on without the glowbubble, see # 13.

Almost tiptoeing, Watkin creeps quietly into the dark tunnel. The floor is a jumble of uneven cobblestones. The glowbubble throws eerie shadows on the narrow stone walls, and from the far end of the tunnel he and Kym can hear faint scrabbling noises.

Kym creeps a little closer to Watkin, taking comfort in the other's broad, solid back. Not for the first time, Kym wishes that he were larger and more fearsome. He glances over his shoulder, and the little hairs on the back of his neck rise. The doorway through which they've come has silently closed.

He tugs urgently at Watkin's shirt, afraid to make any sound that might attract the attention of . . . whatever.

Watkin, still moving very slowly, staring intently at something up ahead, swats at Kym's hand.

Stumbling slightly, Kym turns back to Watkin and peers cautiously over his friend's shoulder, and immediately forgets the closed door behind them, lost in dread at the two open ones in front.

Watkin stops, with Kym huddled close behind him, and they both stare mesmerized at the decidedly sinister sight up ahead.

At the end of the tunnel are two ramps. The ramp slanting downward leads to a corridor which is straight and very narrow, too narrow for Watkin's massive shoulders to pass. At the end of the corridor is a weirdly flickering yellow light, and a sound like a thousand people whispering. The ramp up shows a sharp curve in the tunnel, and all that can be seen of what's beyond the curve is a deep, steady, red glow.

Watkin turns to Kym. "Which way?"

To take the ramp down, see page 42. For the ramp up, see #14.

Kym points silently to the left. At least this tunnel is lighted, however strangely.

Turning sideways, Watkin inches into the narrow tunnel, for once even his usual jovial humor squelched by the eerie environment. The stones so close to his chest and back are uncomfortably warm, and he has the feeling that they are moving closer together, soon to press him and his friend like flowers in a book. The mental picture of himself and Kym as flowers brings a quick, lopsided smile to Watkin's face, but it dies quickly as they get closer to the echoing noises at the far end of the tunnel.

Kym sidles along next to his larger friend, trying his best to avoid touching the walls, which seem to be getting hotter. The loud whispering noise has grown to a roar, and is beginning to sound somewhat familiar. As they reach the three-pronged fork at the end of the tunnel, the sound suddenly becomes clear—they've somehow found their way to the castle kitchens! The flickering and the roaring are made by the huge fireplaces where the castle cooks do their cooking!

Watkin and Kym exchange sheepish looks and relax their tensely hunched shoulders. Watkin is about to make a wry remark when he is interrupted by a truly ominous sound—the throaty bark of the kitchen dogs! Kym tries futilely to get out of Watkin's way as the half-wild dogs charge down the narrow tunnel at them, teeth bared and fur standing in stiff bristles on their necks.

Kym looks frantically at Watkin. "Which way?"

To go left, see #15. To go right, see #16. To go straight ahead, see #17. To use Kym's whistle, see #18.

Watkin charges straight ahead, swinging the glow-bubble at the startled dogs. The animals quickly fall back, letting the two frightened travellers pass by, which they do at a very high speed.

This tunnel is much darker than the one they just left, and cooler. It descends gently as they go on. The men stop and lean gratefully on the stone walls, the cool dampness a relief. From all around them comes the tranquil sound of water dripping, as the condensation from the ceiling falls like slow rain.

Kym mops at his sweaty forehead with the tail of his shirt, wondering seriously if any quest—even one as important as a quest for true love—is worth all of the trouble they've gotten into so far. Maybe where they started from wasn't so bad after all. He thinks a little more, and comes to the conclusion that their home village is, in fact, a wretched hole, and anything would be better than going back. He straightens his shoulders and takes the glowbubble from Watkin. "Let's go on," he commands, leading the way.

Watkin, unaware of his friend's train of thought, regards Kym with mild astonishment as he begins striding purposefully down the wet tunnel. Smiling a little to himself, Watkin follows.

At the end of the tunnel they come to a curious stairwell. There is a set of stone steps leading up into a musty tunnel, and a set of precarious-looking wooden steps leading down into an even mustier-smelling cavern.

Watkin smiles as Kym starts deliberately up the stone steps.

If you want to follow, see page 44. If not, see #19.

To Watkin's surprise, they find themselves in a room that is light and airy. Moonlight streams in through the openwork windows, flooding the room with cold white light. The corners are obscured by inky shadows that look solid enough to touch. Watkin looks around, wrinkling his nose at the musty smell that permeates the walls themselves. There are odd wooden constructions scattered neatly about the room, each one a tall, stout vertical stick with a thick rod attached at the top, forming a "T". Noticing the size and color of the many feathers carpeting the floor, Watkin begins to move slowly toward the exit.

Kym watches Watkin tiptoeing around the room, and sighs happily to himself. He's decided to throw himself wholeheartedly into this quest, and the decision feels good. He's been the quiet, retiring type for far too long, and now maybe it's time he started to live a little. Delighted with himself and the world in general, Kym throws both arms out wide in a gesture of joyous abandon.

"Kym, no!" Watkin hisses, but it's too late. Kym's impulsive gesture has already disturbed the room's occupants—great horned snow owls. Enraged by the sudden movement, the owls swoop down from their night perches hidden in the dark recesses of the room and attack with cunning fury.

Protecting their heads as best they can, Kym and Watkin try to find their way out, but get hopelessly confused. Backed into a corner, Kym spies two possible means of escape—a wooden ladder leading up, and a ramp descending into the dark.

To go up, see #20. To go down, see page 45.

In desperation Kym throws himself down the ramp, with Watkin right behind him. They suffer through a long, sliding descent, not without a few splinters, and come to a sudden, crashing halt at the bottom.

Sitting up painfully, Kym and Watkin take stock of their surroundings. They are in a dark stone alcove. The walls glow faintly with a mossy phosphorescence. The smell here is somewhat different from that in the owl chamber, but in its own way just as strong.

Watkin takes quick mental stock of his bruised body and, finding nothing broken, gets gingerly to his feet. There are owl feathers stuck in his hair. "Well," he says to Kym, who is still huddled at the foot of the ramp, "now what?"

Kym lifts his head slowly and gazes miserably up at Watkin. He'd love to be able to take charge and lead the way confidently to a safe place, but all he can think of is how cold, damp, and uncomfortable he is, and how badly he wants to go home. Having enough pride left not to admit this, however, Kym struggles manfully to his feet and takes a good look around.

The surroundings are not very promising. Behind the two men is a ramp leading up, and ahead of them is a long, mildewy tunnel. Off to the left, a rope ladder dangles from a trapdoor in the ceiling. The open trapdoor is lit with a glowing red light.

Kym and Watkin exchange glances and shrugs. Kym, determined to somehow become master of his own fate, starts purposefully down the mildewed tunnel. Watkin stops him. "Are you sure you wouldn't rather go up the ladder?"

If you would, see page 46. If not, see #21.

Kym strides to the foot of the ladder and squints up at the red glow filtering down through the trapdoor. The strange light has an almost watery quality to it—he can see wavering patterns on the stones surrounding the opening as the light shifts in vaguely hypnotic rhythms.

Watkin stands quietly behind Kym, also looking up the ladder at the weird lightplay. Unlike Kym, he finds it threatening rather than mesmerizing. Although he's not really much of a fighter, being far too gentle in nature to become entangled in the brawls men of his size and build often attract, Watkin is no stranger to defending himself. Looking up at the shimmering glow, he feels the preternatural tingle that tells him he's probably going to have to defend himself if they go up the ladder. But against what? Looking down the mildewed tunnel, its walls limned in glowing moss, he feels an even stronger dread. Unknown to him, his thoughts echo those of his smaller friend—Watkin suddenly wishes very much that he were home.

As though hearing Watkin's thought, Kym turns from his intense scrutiny of the view at the top of the ladder and smiles with shaky reassurance at the apprehensive look on the other's face. Rather pleased to be the one doing the reassuring for once, Kym's smile widens and he pats Watkin clumsily on the shoulder.

"It's all right, Watkin," he says gently, with just a trace of embarrassment. "We'll find our way safely out of here and into some nice, soft beds."

Watkin nods. "But which way is safe?"

To explore the tunnel, see #21. To climb the ladder see #22.

The tunnel is bathed in a sullen red glow, liquid and eerie. From somewhere in the shadows Kym and Watkin can hear a sound like that a small lake makes, lapping against its shore. The air has a sharp, tangy scent to it, strong and maddeningly familiar.

Moving forward slowly, they find that the flooring under their feet is old, rotted wood, creaking and giving a little with each footfall. Treading carefully, they try to stay as close to the sweating walls as possible, where the floor seems to be strongest.

Unnerved by the familiar smell and soft, liquid sounds, Watkin stops and holds up the glowbubble, hoping to learn more about their surroundings. He and Kym look at each other, puzzled by what they see.

The walls are lined with thin pipes coming from beneath the floor, each pipe ending in a spigot, and none crossing another.

"Maybe this is the hook-up for one of those indoor privies," Watkin suggests. Both he and Kym have heard rumors of indoor plumbing, but neither has ever seen it, or really understands how it works. They suspect it is magic.

Kym shakes his head. "No, why would the pipes empty onto the floor? And what are the signs for?"

Under each spigot is a sign. Not being able to read, Kym and Watkin stare in confused fascination at the lettering. One sign says "Rose," the one next to it, "Burgundy."

Watkin shrugs, looking around in bewilderment. In doing so he shifts the glowbubble, revealing two trapdoors set side by side in the middle of the floor. One has a ring set in its center, the other hasn't. Watkin holds the glowbubble higher, further illuminating the trapdoors, and also showing a curve in the tunnel ahead.

"What d'ye think of this?" Watkin asks, nudging the trapdoor ring with the toe of his boot.

Kym shrugs and shakes his head, then goes back to studying the incomprehensible lettering under each spigot. "Chablis," "Claret," "Port"—they make no sense to him. Moving slowly down the line he comes upon a spigot with a sign that bears much more lettering than the rest. Drips of colorless liquid fall slowly from the it, splashing lazily on the floor. Steeling himself against the possibility that his sudden hunch is wrong, he puts a hesitant finger under the dribbling flow and lets one cold drop fall on his hand. Nothing happens. Catching several more fat drops, Kym brings them to his nose and sniffs. The familiar smell is suddenly clear, as is the purpose of the tunnel.

"Watkin!" he calls. Kym is inordinately pleased at having solved this mystery by himself. "I know what this place is."

Watkin moves closer, avoiding the trapdoors. "What is it, then?"

"A winery!" Kym exclaims, flushed with triumph. He passes his hand under the dripping spigot and waggles his wet fingers at his friend.

Watkin laughs. "So it is! And to celebrate the end of the mystery, I say we have a taste!"

Kym looks doubtful. "Wouldn't you rather try to find our way out of here?" He indicates the trapdoors.

For the trapdoor with ring, see #23. For the one without, see #24. To "have a taste," see #25. To continue through the tunnel, see page 49.

Watkin thinks a moment, then shakes his head. "On thinking about it, I don't think I want to do any of those things, lad. Let's just follow this tunnel and see where it leads."

Kym agrees, and with a last puzzled look at the strange winery, he follows his friend into the dark, curving tunnel.

The tunnel twists and turns, now rising, now descending, until the weary pair are beginning to feel as though their whole lives have been spent tiredly searching for the way out. Kym reflects that maybe, in a way, they have been.

Just as he's ready to give up and admit defeat, he spies a crack of light up ahead. With a small joyful sound, he picks up his pace, pulling the for once silent Watkin behind him. The rough cobbled floor seems to get worse as they get closer to the thin bit of light, and soon the two are clutching at each other to keep from falling.

At last they reach the light, and find that it is coming from a crack in what appears to be a blank stone wall. A careful search turns up no evidence of a hidden spring mechanism, or other clever device. The only indication that this is not an ordinary stone wall is the tiny keyhole set in the center.

Looking back over his shoulder, Kym is startled to see that the view is exactly the same as that from where they started. They have, in fact, come full circle. If that is the case, then there must be a way in—there was, after all, a way out. Kym bends over to inspect the keyhole more closely, and as he does, there is a small clink as something falls out of his pocket. Kym picks it up, and finds himself looking at the key given to him by the young wizard in the carnival wagon. To his and Watkin's astonishment, it fits the lock perfectly; soon they're back in their room.

With great effort, Watkin pulls off his boots and wiggles his tired toes. Glancing at Kym, Watkin sees that his smaller friend has collapsed on the bed fully clothed and is already snoring. Smiling gently, an expression that makes his rough face almost handsome, Watkin rises tiredly to his feet and tiptoes to Kym's side of the ornate bed. Trying not to disturb him, Watkin tugs gently at the sleeping man's boots. The right one slides off easily, but the left proves stubborn, and Watkin, not the most delicate of men, inadvertently awakens Kym, who mumbles something sleepily.

"What?" Watkin whispers.

"So ends our first adventure," Kym repeats, with several long pauses and sleepy sighs between words.

Watkin smiles again. "Yes, so it ends—and us no wiser than before." He chuckles, thinking that that's not quite right. He, Watkin, may be no wiser about the world, but he has learned a few things about his friend. Gone are Kym's aloofness and brooding air. He may not be as mysterious as Watkin had once thought, but he is certainly much more likeable. Watkin's expression softens, and he quickly hides it as Kym turns over and opens his eyes.

"Do you think we'll find it, Watkin?" he asks sleepily.

"Find what?"

Kym pauses. "True love," he whispers.

Watkin looks down at Kym, thinking what an unlikely pair they make, and nods. "If it's out there to be found, lad, we'll find it," he says softly.

Kym nods vaguely, turns over, and burrows deeper ito the feather pillows.

"I'm glad it's you, on this Quest," Kym says, his voice muffled by the pillows and by sleep.

Watkin ducks his head, embarrassed by the moment, and roughly pulls the down coverlet up over Kym's limp form.

"So am I, lad," he whispers. "Go to sleep." Watkin settles deeper into the soft bed as the glowbubble's light begins to fade. Having served its purpose, its gentle light now dies, clothing the room in velvet shadows. By the time the last pinpoint of light has winked out forever, Watkin, too, is asleep.

III: *The Desolate Land*

The day dawns bright, clear, and all too quickly for Watkin and Kym. They awaken to discover that sometime during the night their wash basin has been filled—probably by magic. Pre-timed Water Out of Air spells are all the rage this season. After a quick wash, the men venture forth in search of breakfast.

Queen Rayanne's court seems to be made up of late sleepers, however, and Watkin and Kym have to fend for themselves in the large, drafty kitchen. Kym finds some leftover bread and cheese in the cold pantry, and Watkin manages to locate a half-filled cask of cold ale. They eat quickly and very quietly, wary of attracting the attention of the kitchen dogs.

As they clean up after themselves, Kym takes a moment to think wistfully how nice it would be if he knew how to write. He feels that it would be polite to leave a note of gratitude for the queen's hospitality, but he doesn't know where the scribe sleeps and isn't really up to searching for him. He is impatient to continue their Quest, as is Watkin. Waiting for everyone to wake up so they can deliver their thanks in person could take

53

hours, so with a last quick brush at the crumbs on the table, they set off.

It takes a frustratingly long time to find their way out of the castle. Twice they end up in front of the door to the room they had occupied, making Kym suspect the presence of the popular Spell for Containing Wandering Guests. It hasn't been cast very well, obviously, for on their third try they find the front door and step out into the sunshine.

★The landscape they find themselves travelling through begins to change from rolling hills to lush forest. The air is filled with the smell of green growing things and rich earth, as well as the fragrances of a dozen different flowers. Birds chirp improvised melodies, with fat bumblebees providing the bass counterpoint.

As they wander along Kym picks out several varieties of berry bushes heavy with ripe fruit, and Watkin catches sight of a rabbit and one or two other brands of small creature, some edible and some not. There are also deathberry bushes, tanglevines, and marshy patches of ground that might be catchswamps. The travellers pick their way carefully through the forest, mindful of the dangers as they enjoy the beauty.

A slight rustling among the groundbriars lining the faint trail they are following alerts them to the possibility of danger from a terrifyingly unpredictable species— their own.

Before they can think of a likely plan of action in case of attack, the groundbriars erupt in a frenzy of rustling and shaking, and in a scant second Kym and Watkin find themselves surrounded by a ragtag army of men, all wearing masks.

Kym steps closer to Watkin as one of the band, a small plump man with beady eyes peering out from behind his mask, steps forward and regards them with satisfaction.

"Welcome to the Desolate Land, gentlemen," he says. His voice is thin and reedy. "And would you care to tell us why you're trespassing on our territory?"

Kym looks at the smaller man, startled into ignoring the question. "Desolate Land? But this place is beautiful, and full of wildlife!"

One of the band raises what looks like a wooden spear, although it has a few green shoots still sprouting from its tip. "Don't be speaking until you're spoken to!" he growls.

Watkin spreads his hands in a friendly gesture. "Certainly, whatever you—"

"And you neither!" the man interrupts, brandishing his unlikely looking weapon. His waving of the spear trails off weakly as the smaller, beady-eyed man turns and steps in front of him.

"And who's the leader here?" he asks, his thin voice sounding not nearly as menacing as he hopes.

The spear holder looks at his feet, mumbling his reply.

"You are."

"That's right," the leader agrees with satisfaction. "So I'll be giving the orders." He turns and stalks back to his captives—a comical feat, since his legs are short, skinny, and somewhat bowed. "Now then, you are in our custody, and it's up to me to decide your fate." Enjoying himself, the leader struts back and forth in front of Kym and Watkin, a gait even more ridiculous than his stalk. He parades in silence for a few moments, receding chin cupped in the palm of one hand. Abruptly he stops, having come to a decision. "You're to be executed."

Kym and Watkin stare at the man in open-mouthed surprise. One of the outlaws steps hesitantly forward and whispers in the leader's ear. The leader looks doubt-

ful, but after a second is apparently convinced. He
turns to the captives and clears his throat. "Ahem,
unless, I mean, you surrender."

*To surrender, see page 57. If you'd rather fight, see
#26.*

Kym and Watkin exchange glances, shrug, then raise their hands over their heads.

The leader chortles in glee, then, remembering his dignity (such as it is), extends his hand to Watkin. "Well! Now that you've surrendered there's no need for all of this martial nonsense—give me your hands and pledge yourselves friends!"

A little startled by his sudden change in status from prisoner to friend, Watkin slowly lowers his arms and takes the other man's hand. "Friends!" he declares, then watches as Kym does the same.

The leader turns back to his uninterested-looking troops. "Back to the camp!" he orders. Turning back to Kym and Watkin, he links an arm through each of theirs as they follow the ragged band of men through the forest.

"So," the leader begins chattily, "what brings you to our part of the forest?"

"Oh, we're just passing through," Watkin says. He glances at Kym over the top of their diminutive host's balding head, and gives him a warning look.

Kym nods, agreeing not to state their intentions until they know more about these men. "Why do you call this the Desolate Land?" he asks, as much because he really is interested as to change the subject.

"Ah, now, that's a long story," the leader says, "and we'll tell you all about it over a hot meal. For now, let us speak of you!"

Watkin nods amiably. "Well, my name is Watkin, and my friend's name is Kym—" He stops in surprise as the entire troop of men, the leader included, turns and begins making frantic hand motions and loud shushing sounds. The leader shakes his head and waves both arms, as though suffering a seizure. "Don't say your names!" he hisses, looking back over his shoulder as though afraid of being overheard.

Watkin looks from one man to the next, and the fear on their faces tells him that this is more than just some local superstition. "But why not?" he asks.

The leader looks back over his shoulder once more, and now he has the air of one being pursued. He grabs Kym and Watkin by their arms and pulls, tugging Kym forward but not budging Watkin. "I'll be telling you everything when we reach the camp, but we've got to hurry!" He tugs again at Watkin's arms, and this time Watkin allows himself to be pulled along.

The group, which had seemed jolly before, is now silent as they hurry through the forest. What was beautiful now seems sinister as Kym and Watkin flee from the unknown terror that inspired the sudden flight. What possible harm could there be in stating a name? Or even two names? After what seems like hours of furtive dashing through the groundbriars, the company begins to slow.

Ahead of them is a grove of giant trees surrounded by a thick wall woven of tanglevines and groundbriars. As they near it, a small patch of the wall begins to shake violently and, to the travellers' surprise, opens like a door. Two men stick their heads out. "Hey!" they yell, sounding more pleased than surprised. Gesturing for Kym and Watkin to follow, the leader squeezes through the opening, careful not to come in contact with the tanglevines. The men peer doubtfully back at Watkin, eyeing the man's huge body in contrast to the tiny door. Their leader beckons encouragingly, with an apologetic smile.

Watkin surveys the door, then gallantly bows and sweeps a brawny arm before Kym, indicating that the smaller man should go first. Squaring his skinny shoulders, Kym slips easily through the opening. Holding his breath and trying to make his large frame as compact as possible, Watkin closes his eyes and follows. There is a general sigh of relief when he makes it safely through.

Once inside the tanglevine wall, they can see that it completely encloses a small tree camp. The thick branches of the trees support an entire community of ill-made shelters. Off to one side of where the travellers stand are two huts in the process of being built. Men and women wearing masks work diligently at weaving crooked thatched walls, while masked children play in the clearing with a bitch and her puppies. The dogs, all six of them, are also masked.

Their arrival has by now been noticed by the population of the encampment, and the group is soon surrounded by people laughing, hugging, and smacking each other on the back. As Watkin watches, several people embrace the leader, each one smacking him on the back and saying "Hey!" Assuming this to be a local greeting, and wanting to show his willingness to learn the customs, Watkin waits until the next man greets him, at which point he smacks the man heartily on the back and says "Hey!"

The leader turns to Watkin. "What?"

Watkin smiles. "I said 'Hey!' "

"Yes, I heard you. What do you want?"

Watkin raises his eyebrows in surprise. "I don't want anything! I just said 'Hey!' "

The leader glares at Watkin, exasperated. "Yes, I heard you! What—"

"Wait!" Kym hastily steps between the two men and holds up his hands for silence. "I think, I mean it seems to me that maybe we have a misunderstanding here." He looks appealingly at both men.

Watkin agrees. "All I said was 'Hey!' "

The leader nods. "That's what I'm trying to tell you! 'Hey' is what folks here call me."

Watkin nods, enlightened. "I see! 'Hey' is your name."

Hey jumps forward, shushing Watkin in a panic. "No! No, that's not my name!" He shouts up at the empty sky, as though someone were hovering there. "Hey is not my name!"

Unnoticed by their host, Watkin jabs Kym in the ribs and shakes his head slowly while rolling his eyes heavenward. Kym frowns and smacks Watkin's elbow away from his side. He steps closer to the man whose name may or may not be Hey. "Excuse me, but we're a bit confused."

Hey nods sadly. "Yes, it is all a bit much. Come with me. I'll try to make some sense of it." He turns to the assembled group and makes a vague gesture. The group ignores him and goes on with their conversations. Hey shrugs and sets off toward the dangling rope ladder suspended from the nearest tree, muttering and shaking his head.

Watkin catches Kym's arm, hesitating. "Are we sure we want to get involved with this bunch?" Kym shrugs.

If you'd rather not, see #27. Adventurous types, see page 61.

"We're already here, we may as well stay. It would be rude to leave," Kym says.

Watkin smiles. "And you would die of curiosity if we didn't see this through."

Kym returns the smile, a little sheepishly, and nods.

As they climb the rope ladder, Hey calls impatiently to them from the branch just above their heads. On it is a small thatched lean-to, its opening covered with a bit of bright tapestry.

When Kym and Watkin climb safely onto the branch, Hey turns to the tapestry. "Wife! We've guests. Come out and greet them!"

The tapestry shivers slightly, and then a small hand pushes it a fraction of an inch to one side. Looking closely, Watkin can see a pair of big blue eyes peering out of the shadows cast by the doorway.

Hey smiles. "Come on out, Wife!" He lowers his voice. "They won't say anything, I promise you." He looks meaningfully at Kym and Watkin, who nod their heads vigorously, completely bewildered.

The curtain is slowly moved aside, and out steps a young, pretty, and very pregnant girl. With eyes lowered behind her mask, she moves daintily to her husband's side, delicate blonde curls bouncing with every step. Hey enfolds her in a bear hug, and suddenly his aggressive heartiness doesn't look quite so silly. He looks up at Kym and Watkin with eyes whose soft expression manages to camouflage their beadiness. "This is my wife. She's, ahem, shy."

Watkin smiles his most charming smile at the woman, and removes his battered hat. Kym attempts a courtly bow and very nearly succeeds in achieving the desired effect. Hey's wife smiles shyly, showing a deep dimple to one side of her mouth.

"I didn't get your name, madame," Watkin says, as though they were standing in the courtyard of a fine townhouse instead of in a tree camp surrounded by a tanglevine fence.

Hey's wife lets out a squeak and scoots back into the hut. Hey sighs. "Now you've frightened her!" He runs into the hut after his wife.

"All I did was ask her name!" Watkin calls after him. The entire camp falls silent, as everyone stops to stare, aghast. Before Watkin or Kym can move, they are surrounded by the remaining population of the camp. The inhabitants do not look friendly. A half dozen of the men take firm hold of the bewildered pair and pull them off the branch where they stand. "I should have guessed it!" exclaims the man with the sprouted spear. "I thought they was spies!"

"Were," Kym corrects, zealous in his belief that good grammar is important in *every* situation.

"Were what?" someone growls.

"Spies. We *were* spies."

"I knew it!" yells the man with the spear, advancing threateningly toward Kym.

"No, wait a minute!" shouts Watkin, trying to throw off the arms restraining him.

"What's going on here?" demands Hey as he pushes his way through the crowd.

"These men are spies for *Her*!" cries a tall man with a mustache.

"No we're not!" says Watkin. "We don't even know who 'her' is!"

"Who *she* is—" Kym starts, only to be forcefully inerrupted by his friend.

"You keep quiet!" Watkin bellows. "Now," he says, a little more quietly, "will someone please explain all of this? What is so terrible about asking a person's name?"

Hey studies Kym and Watkin for a moment, then nods. "Let them go, boys. I'm sure they're no spies. It's time for a cold drink and a long talk. You, go and get the ale and the cups."

"Sure thing, Hey," says the tall man with the mustache, who is standing behind the leader. He turns and trots off to the largest treehut.

The men restraining Watkin and Kym let go of them with muttered apologies, then the entire company makes its way to a long trestle table hidden in the branches of the largest tree in the center of the camp. The table is ringed with tanglevines, and more of the treacherous weed is woven into the backs of the chairs.

Kym and Watkin are shown to places to the right and left of the head of the table, and given thick clay goblets filled with cool ale. Watkin's goblet leans a little to the left.

It takes a few minutes for everyone to get settled. Working out seating arrangements is far more difficult when one has to climb halfway around a tree to change his seat. And even in a treehouse, no one wants to sit below the salt.

The man at the head of the table clears his throat. "Think carefully, friends. Knowing our tale makes our enemy yours, and a formidable enemy she is. Shall I go on?"

If you want to hear the tale, see page 64. If not, cover your ears.

Once again Kym and Watkin exhange glances, then both shrug. A Quest is meant to be dangerous. Otherwise, it wouldn't be such a momentous thing. "Tell us," Watkin says, "and your enemy will be ours."

Hey smiles, then puts on a serious expression and clears his throat. "Well, I imagine you'll be wondering about the masks."

Kym and Watkin nod.

"We're renegades," the leader states proudly. "Tax renegades. The masks are so we're not recognized."

Kym is puzzled. "But who would recognize you here? Do you hide your faces from each other?"

"Yes! And our names! In fact, we change them every third Twoday after doublemoon, just in case. But we're not hiding only from each other. The one we're really hiding from is—" His voice drops to a bare whisper. "—the Princess Elvina."

A sudden hush falls over the table as everyone holds their breath and looks fearfully around. Kym and Watkin also look, although they're not sure for what. After a few seconds in which nothing happens, there is a general sigh of relief, and everyone relaxes. Hey continues. "The woman in question is a powerful magician. To cast a spell on a person, all she needs is a likeness of their face, their true given name written by her own hand, or a bit of their body fluids." He pauses for a bit of ale. "Now, this woman hates everything and everyone."

"Why?" interrupts Kym.

"Because she is very beautiful."

"That doesn't make sense," says Kym. "I've known several beautiful women—well, been acquainted with them—and they can be just as nice as normal people."

Hey sets his goblet down with a bang and glares at Kym. "*As* I was saying, she will not put up with competition from anyone or anything. About a year ago, she conjured up some terrible creatures, the Shadowbats and the Nightspiders. She set them to destroying the countryside. She taxed her subjects until we were all too poor to buy healing spells, and she cast "Sow's Ears out of Silk Purses" spells on all of the women, and a few of the prettier boys. It was terrible. All she had to do was—"

"Write your name, or draw your face! That's why you don't use your names, or show your faces!" exclaims Kym, carried away by his clever deductive reasoning.

"That's right!" says Hey, all signs of his former heartiness gone. His tone is serious, and a little sad. "My wife and I left our village when my wife became, uh, shy." The leader assumes a very casual tone. "Another trick of Elvina's was to steal babies by using her Sightcrystal to spy on new mothers, to learn their babies' birth names. A spell cast on a child will last for life—especially a love spell. Elvina wanted all of the children to love her."

"She loves children?" Watkin asks, his tender heart willing to see some good in the princess.

"No. She's trying to make sure she'll never be assassinated." Hey shakes his head sadly. "All of us are here to escape from her spells. But even here we're not safe. This camp is just at the limit of her Sight. We never know if she's spying on us or not The tanglevine helps a little; once cut, it tangles spells the same as it tangles the thoughts of those it snares when alive. It's not much, but it's all the protection we have."

"But that's terrible!" Kym says. "How can you live like this? Something's got to be done about this woman!"

All eyes turn to Kym.

"Have you any ideas?" someone asks.

Kym shakes his head. "No," he says, anger making him uncharacteristically bold. "But we'll think of something." He turns to Watkin. "Won't we?"

Watkin looks up, his face terrible. "Anyone who would

enslave small children deserves what she gets!" he declares. "As Kym and I happen to be on a Quest anyway, and one of the purposes of a Quest is to defeat evil, we'll find a way to defeat this princess!"

A hearty cheer goes up, and is cut off raggedly as everyone remembers who might be listening in with her Sightcrystal. Hey calls for attention. "This calls for a feast!" he announces. His wife catches his eye and shakes her head. "Oh. Well then, this calls for a hunt! To celebrate our two champions, I propose that we hunt—" He pauses for dramatic effect, all of his former jocularity returned. "—the willowpig!"

Several groans greet this pronouncement. "Are you sure we couldn't celebrate just as well by hunting rabbit?" someone asks.

Hey glares behind his mask. "No! Get the hunting gear and we'll set off!" So ordering, Hey kisses his wife on the head and, beckoning to Watkin and Kym, sets off toward the door in the tanglevine wall.

After a few moments of waiting, the rest of the male population of the community assembles at the gate. Kym and Watkin are each handed a long pike with a colorful pennant attached to the handle. All of the men carry similar weapons, except for Hey, who carries a long, intricately twisted horn. "Now then," Hey says. "The willowpig is a clever and vicious animal. It lives among the fronds of the giant willow trees and attacks anything that moves—sometimes even things that don't. They are very difficult to catch, but—" A showman at heart, Hey delights in the dramatic pause. "—they are very easily hypnotized!"

Kym frowns. "But how does one hypnotize a beast that is both clever and vicious?"

"And attacks anything that moves," adds Watkin.

"And sometimes things that don't!" the two friends say in unison, pleased with themselves.

"That is what I am about to tell you," Hey says, the very soul of patience. "Through years of excruciatingly dangerous trial and error, our forefathers developed a foolproof method of mesmerizing the willowpig.

As he speaks, Hey wiggles through the gap in the tanglevine wall, and the rest of the company follows. He continues his lecture as the men make they way to the stand of willows where their quarry lives, ignoring the grumbling and muttering from the reluctant party trooping along behind him. Mostly he speaks of his forefathers, having gotten a little off the track in answering a question for Kym.

Therefore, when the hunting party reaches their destination, the willow grove, at least two of the hunters have no idea what they are supposed to do. Drawing himself up to his inconsequential height, Hey remedies that. "Now," he says, taking a self-important tone, "here's what we do."

Several hours later, as the hunting party takes a short rest, Kym and Watkin are not only exhausted, and very hungry, they are also extremely embarrassed for their host. Not only have they not caught any willowpigs, but with the method that they are using, it is unlikely that they ever will.

"All right, you men," Hey calls. "Let's get back to it!"

Kym and Watkin join in the general whining and moaning that accompanies this command. As soon as everyone is on their feet, the men make a loose circle around the nearest willow tree. Standing at arms length from one another, and all holding their long, pennanted pikes, they begin the arduous (and rather hopeless) process of mesmerization.

While Hey keeps the rhythm with his horn, the men begin to dance, Kym quietly chanting the steps to himself so that he doesn't lose his place. "Right foot, left foot, squat, jump! Kick, kick, hop, again. Right foot, left foot . . ." His voice trails off as he concentrates on not being left behind, or getting too far ahead. With each hop the men tighten the circle by a fraction of an inch, trapping the supposedly mesmerized willowpig between them and the trunk of the tree. Unfortunately, the willows are of gigantic proportions, and even though the hunt is several hours old, they are nowhere near the trunk—or the willowpig!

Watkin has just decided to give up when he hears a sudden rustling to his right. The men are well into the hanging fronds of the tree by now, and it is difficult to see more than a few inches on any side. The air has a strange green quality to it, and when the fronds are swayed by the hunters' passing, the scene takes on an eerie underwater feeling.

Moving slowly, Watkin parts the thick curtain of foliage and peers to his right, to where Kym should be. His body automatically keeps time with the sour, barely rhythmic blasts from Hey's horn. "Kym?" he calls, not daring to raise his voice just in case there really is a willowpig about. "Kym, can you hear me?"

Kym can hear him. He cannot, however, answer, because on untangling himself from a stubborn knot of vines (causing the rustling that Watkin heard), he finds himself face to snout with none other than the willowpig! It is every bit as vicious and ugly as Kym had fearfully imagined, and is staring at the frightened traveller with small red eyes that glow with sheer meanness.

Keeping his eyes on the ugly little animal, Kym takes a tentative step to the left. Without hesitation, the willowpig follows. Since it makes no move to charge, Kym tries again, hoping to get close enough to Watkin for the larger man to save him. Once again the pig follows, only this time, it also takes a step closer to Kym. Judging by how far apart he and Watkin were when the hunting dance started, and allowing for the shrinking of the circle's circumference as they move closer to the trunk of the tree, Kym concludes that at the rate he is going he will reach Watkin in about ten steps. Unfortunately, the willowpig will reach him in seven. Unable to think of anything else to do, Kym fills his lungs and yells for Watkin.

The willowpig charges just as Watkin bursts through the hanging fronds. As he aims his pike, a voice yells, "Wait!"

To wait, see #28. To throw the pike, see page 70.

Watkin doesn't hesitate. He hurls the pike as hard as he can, then catches Kym, who is collapsing out of fear, tension, and hysterical relief. Both men turn as Hey, followed by the rest of the hunting party, makes his way noisily through the vines.

Hey surveys the scene, taking in the breathless Watkin, who is supporting a completely boneless Kym, and the dead willowpig, speared neatly through the chest. "You didn't wait! You're not supposed to finish the beast until I blow the Pig Dirge!" Hey says, standing with arms akimbo and looking as though he's about to stomp his foot.

Watkin props Kym back on his feet. "If I'd waited, you would have had to blow two dirges—one for Kym!"

Hey considers this for a moment, then smiles. "You're right. A Spell for Tonedeafing on the dirge. Let's go feast!" So saying, Hey sets off for the camp, shortly followed by the others, with the unfortunate willowpig strung neatly between two poles for easy carrying.

The feast is every bit as good as the hunt was boring, proving that some things are indeed worth waiting for. After dinner, feeling more secure with their host, Kym and Watkin reveal the reason for their quest, and ask if Hey, or any of his people, has any information of use to them.

Hey pauses in the act of lighting a long, carefully carved pipe. "No, I'm afraid the only thing I have to say is watch out for Pri—you know who," he says, taking a quick, worried look around. "And on that score," Hey continues, "we could use a few good men around here. If you'd like to join us . . ."

If you want to settle down, see #29. If not, see page 71.

Kym and Watkin consult for a moment, and then Watkin smiles at Hey. "We are truly honored by your generous offer, sir, but I fear we must continue on our Quest," he says in his most courteous manner.

Hey bows and gets to his feet, then bows again as if aware that that's the order in which the thing should have been done in the first place, and indicates the nearest tree. Its branches have been strung with hammock-like slings, some suspended underneath a single branch, some hung between two. There are also specially built slings for the children that can be laced shut so that the child can't roll out. "It would be my honor, then, to offer you a branch for the night," Hey says. "We always keep extra sleepslings on hand in case someone else wants to join us."

Catching Kym's alarmed look at the height of the branch Hey is indicating, Watkin remains seated. "We would much prefer it if you would allow us the honor of taking the first watch," Watkin improvises. The leader agrees, and with much bowing and exchanging of Good Nights, the camp settles down to sleep, leaving Kym and Watkin to sit by the fire and watch.

Kym sits staring into the flames, thinking back on the hunt, and especially his meeting with the willowpig. He is deeply embarrassed by the fact that he panicked and had to call for help. He feels that he is a coward, and the realization shames him. He broods on this miserably, knees drawn up, staring into the fire, and wishing harder and harder that he was anyone else but himself. Before he realizes that he was intending to speak, he hears his voice.

"I'm not very brave, am I, Watkin?"

Watkin looks at his friend for several long moments before speaking. "There are many kinds of bravery, my friend. Some men are brave simply for the sport of it, while others are brave only for their king or their love.

I think maybe that your kind of bravery has not yet been put to the test, and so you think that it is not there. I think that it is."

Kym smiles gratefully at Watkin. He doesn't believe this line of reasoning for a second, but he appreciates the gentleness in Watkin that would make him offer it as comfort. Embarrassed by the sudden rush of warm feelings this causes, Kym is more relieved than startled when a sudden rustling in the bushes nearby breaks the mood. "What was that?" he whispers.

Watkin shakes his head and gestures for silence as he reaches for a heavy piece of firewood and gets to his feet. The rustling sounds again, from a large jellyberry bush to Watkin's right. The large man moves with surprising grace as he slowly stalks the bush.

Kym sits huddled by the fire, watching with terror as Watkin sneaks up on the intruder. Or, he thinks, what if it isn't an intruder? What if it's another willowpig? Kym uncurls suddenly as the thought sinks in. What if Watkin freezes for a second like he himself did? With no one to back Watkin up but his own cowardly self, Watkin would be killed! Kym leaps to his feet and grabs one of the pikes left from the hunt. Without a second thought he rushes past Watkin toward the jellyberry bush. The rustling increases as though whoever or whatever is inside the bush is getting ready to spring. Kym raises the pike and points it at the center of the bush, then pulls back his arm, preparing to strike.

To attack, see #30. If you'd rather think about it, see page 73.

Something about the way the bush is moving indicates to Kym that the being within is probably very small. Laying aside his pike, he slowly leans forward and parts the thin branches.

"Kym, no! It might be a wild—"

"—kitten?" Kym says, holding up a forlorn little feline covered with squashed jellyberries.

Watkin laughs. "That's right. Those creatures can be very ferocious!"

Kym laughs, too, and takes the kitten over to the fire to clean it off. He deduces that the little animal was attracted by the smell of the fruit, but once she was inside the bush, her every movement caused the overripe berries to squash into her fur. Kittens are fastidious beings, and the poor thing must have been frantic trying to clean herself when every time she turned to lick one spot clean, two more got sticky! Kym chuckles at the thought as the tiny cat settles into his lap, purring as she tries to nest.

Watkin assumes an air of great seriousness. "How can you laugh? You saved my life!" he says.

Kym shakes his head. "It was only a kitten!"

Watkin drops his pose and becomes serious for real. "But you didn't know that when you rushed past me. It could have been anything!" He smiles proudly at his friend. "You were very brave."

Kym ducks his head and murmurs a few confused denials, but inside he is filled with pride. He *was* brave!

As the fire dies down, two men come to take over the watch. Kym and Watkin settle down gratefully near the fire and sleep.

★Fierce sunlight awakens the travellers, and they stretch mightily trying to work out the kinks that sleeping on the ground always causes. The smell of something wonderful fills the air, and Watkin's discerning nose identi-

fies it as fresh spice bread and coffee. In another moment,
the smell of frying willowpig bacon joins in, making
their mouths water. After a visit to the privy tree and a
quick wash in the basin provided—very quick, as the
basin leaks—Kym and Watkin join the others for
breakfast.

The conversation is light and cheerful, last night's
hunt having been good. The leader and his pregnant
young wife preside over a happy group. Kym and Watkin
are reluctant to leave. Breakfast stretches on with joke
telling and tall-taleing, and soon someone brings out
the ale.

An hour later, a small musical band has assembled,
and Watkin dances with every woman in the camp
while Kym keeps unsteady time on two wooden goblets
with a pair of flat-bladed knives.

All too soon they realize that if they are to ever leave,
they must do it now. Watkin bids all of the women
goodbye, receiving from each a kiss or a blush, depend-
ing on their age and experience. Kym bids farewell to
the kitten he had befriended the night before, and with
an escort of half the men in the camp, they set off to
continue their Quest.

The journey to the forest's edge does not take long,
even though they try to prolong it by stopping twice for
lunch and three times to rest. Eventually they come to
the place where Kym and Watkin must travel on alone.

The tax renegades offer many good wishes and warn-
ings regarding the Princess Elvina, then set off for
camp. Kym and Watkin watch them go.

When the renegades are finally out of sight, the
travellers hitch up their belts, shoulder their packs, and
start off once again on their Quest.

The lovely forest begins to thin out after a while, and
is replaced by what can truly be called a desolate land.
The ground is cracked and dry, and there are no trees

at all save for some withered husks that may once have sported leaves. Ramshackle huts are scattered about, most of them looking too precarious to occupy. Old men and women stare silently as the two pass by, and Watkin immediately notes the absence of anyone under seven trines. After being rudely rebuffed several times, Kym and Watkin decide not to ask for any help from these obviously terrorized folk.

As they reach the bottom of a cracked, dry hill and settle in the dust to rest, both Kym and Watkin become aware of a ghastly, pervasive chill. After a few bewildered moments, they realize that they are seated in the shadow of a twisted tower. Turning to look, they see that the tower is but the smallest part of an enormous misshapen castle. Meeting each other's eyes, they both try to hide their fear, for there is only one person this castle could belong to—the Princess Elvina.

Watkin slowly gets to his feet. "We could go around it."

Kym shakes his head. "There is no way." He points.

Watkin looks, and sees that Kym is right. To either side of the twisted edifice is a long, high, sheer wall. It extends to the east until it joins with the impassable cliffs of a mountain range, and to the west far out to sea. There are no choices but to go back—or go ahead.

To go back, see #31. Foolhardy types, turn the page.

IV: The Kingdom of Ruin

Kym gets slowly to his feet, never taking his eyes from the castle. "If forward is our only choice, then forward we must go," he says. He swallows audibly with the effort that making such a brave statement has cost him.

Watkin gets to his feet and claps a hand on his friend's shoulder, making Kym jump. "You're right lad, although I wouldn't have had the courage to make the decision." He squeezes Kym's shoulder in hearty punctuation of this endorsement.

Kym nods solemnly and takes the first step deeper into the shadows of the castle. Not letting go of him, Watkin follows.

Slowly they make their way closer to the hideous sprawl of buildings that make up the castle grounds. There are no peasant shacks in the shadows of the walls, as are usually found in such places. Kym and Watkin can understand why. The chill that had first struck them has deepened, becoming a damp, almost oily presence all around them. Although the castle does not entirely block the sun, very little light filters down from the sky. and the closer the men get to the castle, the deeper the gloom becomes.

Kym looks around uneasily, becoming increasingly suspicious of being watched. Goosebumps spring out on his arms and legs, and a sly chill dances up and down his spine.

Passing under a decaying, mold-ridden archway, Kym and Watkin find themselves standing in front of the castle doors. Above the doors are the reason Kym feels watched—a pair of stone demons stand guard on the lintel. The door is open. Kym hesitates. "Should we knock, or just go in?"

To knock first, see #32. To enter, see #33.

Watkin peers into the doorway, not liking the look of the shadowy hallway that stretches off into darkness. "I think we should knock first," he says. "I don't think the folks who live here are the casual sort." He raises one large fist and knocks lightly on the heavy, rotting door.

Nothing happens.

Watkin shrugs and knocks again, a little louder this time.

Again, nothing.

He shrugs. "No one is at home," he says, ready to turn back. Kym steps closer to the half-opened door.

"Maybe they cannot hear you," he suggests. "Try using the doorknocker."

Watkin studies the door, unable to tell if there *is* a doorknocker. On closer inspection, however, he sees a small one set into the center of the door. It is apparently made of silver, but its sheen has long since been dulled by mold and neglect. In fact, its slightly furry appearance makes Watkin loath to touch it. But a sudden chill breeze stirs the hairs at the back of his neck, and Watkin realizes that he's more afraid of spending the night *outside* the castle than inside it. He lifts the knocker, stifling a disgusted noise at its cold and slimy feel, and lets it fall.

The knocker strikes its tarnished plate with a resounding boom. The men clutch at each other, startled, until they recognize the Spell for Making Loud Things Louder, a popular device among the owners of large castles.

After a few moments the echoes die down, and Kym and Watkin hear footsteps approaching the door. They seem to be coming from very far away, and Watkin realizes for the first time just how large the castle actually is.

Kym jiggles Watkin's elbow, suddenly not so sure

that he wants to go through with this. "I think we should go back," he says.

The footsteps get closer.

"Watkin, I really think we should turn back!"

Watkin shakes Kym loose of his arm, annoyed. The footsteps sound definitely feminine to Watkin, and the urge to find out what kind of a female could live in such a foul place is overwhelming. He knows that in all probability he won't be happy with the answer he gets, but he feels a need to find out anyway.

Kym sighs, exasperated and more than a little afraid, and takes up a slightly less conspicuous position behind his larger friend. He hears the footsteps stop.

The door is flung open so suddenly that Kym and Watkin both stagger backwards, grabbing at each other for support. A spill of light illuminates the stone porch on which they stand, throwing the person in the doorway into sharp silhouette.

It *is* a woman.

She lowers the glowbubble, illuminating her face, and both Kym and Watkin gasp. She is beautiful, maybe the most beautiful woman that either of them has ever dreamed of. Her hair is the color of morning sunshine, her skin a blushing rose. She is tall and slender, with pale sensitive hands. Her eyes are the blue of a twilit sky, and her long lashes have the soft glow of fine copper wire. A tear rolls slowly down one soft cheek as she raises her head to gaze sadly at the travellers.

"What do you want of me?" she says, her voice the softest silken sigh. Another tear chases the first down the delicate curve of her cheek.

If it's lodging you want, see #34. To offer assistance, see #35. To ask for directions, see #36.

Watkin is captivated. He sweeps off his battered hat and bends low in a courtly bow. "Madame, you are obviously in distress. Name your problem, and my brave companion and I will risk our very souls to set it right!"

Kym stares at his friend in disbelief. "Watkin . . ." he begins.

"Shush!" Watkin, still bent over in his courtly bow, waves his hat at Kym. "My lady, just ask and our services are yours." He straightens and looks soulfully into her eyes. "What is it that is troubling you?"

The woman sighs again, a breathy sound of despair. Her soft lower lip pouts prettily as another tear traces its path down her cheek. "I am ruined!" she exclaims. "Completely and forever ruined." She lowers her head, her golden hair a silken curtain to hide her shame.

"Show me the man who has dishonored you, and his life is mine!" Watkin proclaims.

She smiles sadly. "No man has touched me. It is not my virtue that has been stolen, but my magic."

"Then we will find it and bring it back to you!" Watkin says, bowing again.

All shyness forgotten at this preposterous boast, Kym grabs Watkin's arm and pulls the other man upright to face him. "How are we going to find her magic? And anyway—" He lowers his voice. "—we've been warned about the lady who owns this castle, remember? If this is the Princess Elvina, then we are very likely being set up for something horrible!"

Watkin turns red with anger. "This beautiful creature cannot possibly have an evil bone in her body. She's probably a guest or a prisoner or something. That's it! I'll wager she's one of Princess Elvina's captives!" He turns back to the lady in question and smiles. The expression, however, falters at her next words.

"But come! I am the Princess Elvina, and I am not in

the habit of letting guests freeze on my doorstep. Accept my hospitality, such as it is." She steps back into the shadows and indicates the long, dark hallway with a sweep of her slender arm.

Watkin strides across the threshold without a second thought, but Kym, eyeing the crumbling stonework and shredding tapestries dimly lit by the glowbubble, hesitates. Elvina smiles at Kym, and he notes that this is not the same soft smile she has been favoring Watkin with. This smile is cold and knowing, and her eyes are mocking. She beckons to Kym, an exaggeration of the gentle invitation given to his friend. Determined not to let Watkin be alone with this woman for even a moment, Kym enters the castle. He can feel her burning stare on his back as he follows Watkin down the rotting corridor.

After several moments of silent travel through the dark, twisting passageways, Elvina stops in front of a door. The wood is warped and peeling, and the iron bands and latch covered with rust. The princess pushes open the door with one slender hand, her long, tapering nails scraping unpleasantly on the wood. Kym notes with surprise that the door opens with suspicious ease, and that the rusted hinges do not squeak.

Elvina gestures at the dimly lit room beyond the door and smiles.

"Won't you come into my parlor?"

If you wish to enter, see page 83. If you'd rather back out, forget it—you had your chance.

Kym hesitates, becoming surer with every moment that he and Watkin would do well to run from this place as fast as they can and never look back. A firm push from Watkin sends him stumbling into the room, nonetheless. Squinting in the sudden light, Kym is surprised by the glittering opulence of the room. Opening his eyes fully, however, he finds that Elvina's parlor is a match for the rest of her castle.

The walls are lined with crudely sketched portraits, some of which are warped, as though they have gotten wet. In the center of the room, fraying silken chairs are set in a semicircle around a cracked ebony table. The fireplace, which apparently hasn't been cleaned since it was first built, boasts a small, sputtering fire which gives off far more smoke than heat.

In front of the fire, nearly hidden in a decrepit armchair, sits an old man. Bearded and gray, he huddles in front of the cheerless fire, hands wrapped around a chipped teacup. He glares as they approach.

"This is my father, King Wopar," Elvina says, gliding silently to his side. "He is the ruler of this land. Aren't you, Father?"

Kym notices uneasily that as Elvina leans down to kiss the top of her father's head, the old man shrinks from her touch, almost as though he's afraid. Before he can decide what to do with this intuition, Watkin steps up to the old king and bows.

"Your lovely daughter has told us of her plight," he says in his most respectful tone of voice. "We would like to offer our meager talents in her service."

The king hunches deeper into his chair. "No, you wouldn't," he replies. Elvina tightens the delicate hand resting on her father's shoulder until her knuckles are white with the pressure of her grip. The old king tries unobtrusively to squirm out of her grasp.

Kym speaks up, sickened by Elvina's undaughterly

display. "Tell us how to help you, madame. The sooner we get started, the sooner we'll be done."

King Wopar snorts. "You mean done *for*."

Startled, Kym glances at Elvina for her reaction. Oddly, she shows none. Clapping her hands sharply, she announces that it is time for some wine, and the telling of her tale. She settles into one of the old armchairs, and indicates that Kym and Watkin should also be seated. They are, Watkin never taking his gaze from the princess's face. Kym tries to sit without actually touching the chair.

Assuming an air of wounded innocence, Elvina begins her story. "A long time ago, I was a very powerful wizard," she says.

"Not so long, and not so powerful," mumbles the king. Again, Elvina ignores him.

"Some wizards draw their power from the everywhere, but others—and I was one such as this—have their magic focused in a single object, which they keep always with them." She looks up, annoyed, as the door opens. A homely young serving girl enters, bearing a dented bronze tray. On the tray is a large decanter and four cloudy glass goblets. The girl sets the tray silently on the table and leaves.

Kym, growing more suspicious by the moment, takes note of the fact that the girl is careful to stay well out of Elvina's reach.

Elvina picks up a goblet, fills it with thick purple wine, and sets it in front of Watkin, continuing her narrative as she does so. "The talisman in which my power rests is a crystal statue in the shape of a wizard. Some time ago it was stolen from me." Her voice breaks. To cover her apparently painful emotion, Elvina pours wine into a second goblet and places it in front of Kym. "Through careful searching, I have discovered that the thieves have hidden it at the bottom of a lake on the edge of my—I mean, my father's domain." A third goblet is filled and set in front of King Wopar, who glares at it. "It is protected by spells which make it impossible for me to rescue the statue myself." Filling the last goblet, Elvina does not drink, but sets it on the table in front of her. "I need your help." She directs this last remark to Watkin, who is seated on her right. She leans close to him, staring deeply into his eyes.

As she does so, King Wopar switches his goblet with hers.

Watkin tuns to Kym and grabs his wrist. "Kym, we've got to help her! This is what a Quest is all about!" As Watkin continues his impassioned plea, a quick movement catches Kym's attention. Out of the corner of his eye, he can see that it is Elvina who is moving.

She is switching her goblet with his.

Watkin is still enthusiastically trying to talk Kym into agreeing to help the princess. Kym leans back in his chair, trying to think, and as he sits back, King Wopar catches his eye. The old man smiles evilly, and turns to Watkin.

"My lad, your impassioned commitment to solving my daughter's dilemma has impressed me. If you carry out your task with as much devotion, then there can only be one reward. You may have my daughter's hand in marriage!"

Watkin's jaw drops. He is so delighted he cannot move or speak, but just stares at the king with an expression of astonished joy.

Elvina's reaction is just as astonished, but hardly as joyful. After her initial explosive "*What?!*", she regains some control and speaks in a quiet, intense tone of voice, all of her attention on her father.

Kym takes the opportunity to switch his goblet with hers, giving her the wine originally intended for her father.

King Wopar abruptly raises his voice. "It is all settled, then. Let us drink to a most favorable outcome to this adventure."

"And to the restoration of my full powers," adds Elvina, glaring ominously at her father. They all raise their goblets, and Kym is not at all surprised to see that the Princess Elvina only pretends to drink.

As soon as the toast has been drunk, Elvina rises to her feet. "If you are to be fresh and alert for your task tomorrow, then you must rest tonight. Come, I will take you to your rooms, where a servant will bring you your dinner." She turns and walks toward the door, her delicate grace in sharp contrast to the dismal room.

Watkin immediately follows, with Kym a step or two behind. As Kym passes the old king's chair, Wopar reaches up and grabs his wrist. "You'll be sorry!" he cackles.

As he pulls loose and catches up with Watkin, Kym is less disturbed by the warning than by the gleeful tone in which it was delivered.

Elvina shows them to a pair of rooms, side by side but without a connecting door. Kym thanks her politely, but as soon as she has disappeared down the mouldering corridor, he slips out of his room and into Watkin's, barring the door behind him.

Watkin is sitting on the bed staring at some glittery thing he holds in one hand, a moony, lovesick look on his face. He looks up as Kym approaches, but his expression does not change. "This is it, Kym, my old friend. This is the end of my Quest!"

Kym sits on the edge of the bed, hating at once its slightly damp feel. "Watkin, this worries me," he begins.

Watkin turns and clasps his friend by the shoulders. "I know, my friend, but it needn't. Once Elvina and I are married and she has her powers back, we'll use her magic to find you the perfect wife, and we'll all live here together!" He spreads his arms wide, indicating the castle.

Kym surveys the room, taking note of the ancient, ruined furniture, the rotting tapestries and moldy carpets, the windows so filthy that no light gets through. He is growing more depressed each moment. "What makes you think she will have you?"

Watkin hesitates, unsure as to how much he should tell Kym about his second visit with the wizard, back in their village. He decides to reveal a little and see how Kym reacts. "I'll shower her with gifts!" Watkin declares. He holds out the locket for Kym to see. "She can't help but be charmed by such as this, don't you think?"

A knock at the door saves Kym from having to answer. On inquiring as to whom it is that's knocking, and finding out that it is the serving girl, Kym unbolts the door.

She enters, carrying a tray of what has to be the least edible food that Kym has ever seen in his life, and pushes the door closed behind her. Setting the tray down on the bed, she bolts the door and turns to Kym, beckoning him closer.

Tentatively, Kym approaches, but the girl doesn't speak until he is nearly standing on top of her. In the barest whisper, she says, "You mustn't stay here! I can show you a way out!"

Watkin gets to his feet. "Here now, what's all of this whispering?" Kym grabs his sleeve and pulls him closer.

"I think that we should leave this place, Watkin! Now, tonight!"

Watkin is shocked. "I can't! I have found my One True Love. How can I leave her before I have even declared myself! Besides, we'd never find our way."

"Watkin, this girl can show us a way out! Isn't there a chance that you are mistaken about the princess?"

"Certainly not!" Watkin says, looking offended at the mere idea. "I should report you to your mistress!" he threatens.

The girl turns absolutely white and crumples to the floor at Watkin's feet. Clutching his boots, her terror is so great that she can hardly speak as she begs him not to go to Elvina.

Seeing her fear makes Watkin stop and think. Does his idea of what his True Love will be include the idea that she will inspire this kind of terror in her serving girls? He thinks it does not. Still, serving girls are notoriously flighty; she may be the kind to react hysterically to everything. He considers, unsure of what to do.

If you want to leave, see #37. If not, see next page.

Kym, for the first time in his life feeling strong and brave in the actual physical presence of a woman, raises the girl to her feet and wipes her tear-stained face with a corner of her apron.

Watkin's indecision is written clearly on his face, which is something that Kym can read. He knows that if they leave now, Watkin will never know if Elvina was his True Love or not, no matter what Kym may feel about her. He makes the decision for them both. "Don't be afraid. My friend won't tell, I promise you. It will be all right." With his hands on her shoulders, he can feel her trembling. He decides then that tomorrow he will find a way to use the truth stone on Elvina—in Watkin's presence—if only to find some way to avenge the terrible hurting the princess has put this poor serving girl through.

Sniffling a little, she smiles up at him, and the gratitude and naked *trust* on her face, along with his own righteous anger, give him such a sudden, overwhelming sense of his own heretofore unsuspected strength and goodness that he nearly staggers. He squeezes her shoulders and smiles gently. "My foolish friend has promised to help your queen, and right or wrong, we never break a promise." Kym brushes a stray hair from the girl's face. "Go now, and rest assured that everything will be all right." He smiles. "I *promise*." With a shy sound of gratitude, the girl slips out from under his hands and is gone.

Watkin, caught up in his own conflicting feelings, says nothing. The two friends eat what they can of the dinner provided and, for the first time since the start of their Quest, go to bed without speaking to each other at all.

A gentle knocking at the door awakens Kym the next morning. Sitting up groggily, he sees that Watkin is already awake and dressed. Watkin unbars the door.

Kym is surprised, and somewhat dismayed, to see Elvina herself carrying their breakfast tray. She smiles brightly at Watkin.

"Good morning—" Her smile freezes as she catches sight of Kym sitting in the bed, the torn coverlet clutched to his chest. "—to you both!" she finishes, one eyebrow raised questioningly at Kym, who returns the gesture.

"My friend is afraid of shadows," Watkin states, explaining Kym's presence in his bed while letting Kym know that their quarrel still stands.

Elvina smiles coldly. "Some shadows are worth fearing," she says to Kym, setting the breakfast tray on the warped wooden table.

Suddenly weary of the cat-and-mouse game, Kym sighs. "Just tell us what you require us to do and we'll be on our way." Watkin glares. "My lady," Kym adds, with ill-disguised sarcasm.

Princess Elvina ignores him, turning all of her attention on Watkin. "My talisman is hidden in a small lake not far from here. It is a journey of but a few hours. The crystal wizard is in a bronze chest at the bottom of the lake." She leans close to Watkin and rests a delicate hand on his chest. "It should be a simple matter for one built so strongly." She smiles up at Watkin, who almost literally melts.

Kym, who is by now dressed, makes a disgusted noise. He is becoming accustomed to the thought of himself being the clearheaded and sensible one. "Just tell us how to get there!" he snaps.

"I'll do better than that," Elvina says. "I'll send an escort."

To accept the escort, see #38. To refuse, see #39.

Kym is about to refuse when Watkin speaks up. "Thank you, my lady, we would be honored to have your soldiers escort us." For the dozenth time since they entered the ruined castle, Watkin sweeps his hat before him in a courtly bow.

Kym shakes his head in exasperation. He has always known that Watkin possesses a soft heart, but never realized before that the condition encompasses his head as well. "Call your soldiers and we will get this over with," Kym orders Elvina.

She smiles the same mocking smile that first aroused Kym's suspicions. "I'll have them meet you at the front door."

Too impatient to argue, Kym nods and, dragging the besotted Watkin behind him, heads for the front door.

In a few moments Elvina joins them, saying that her soldiers are on their way. As she makes small talk with Watkin, playing him along with shameless ease, Kym tries desperately to think of a way to get the truth stone into her hand. He is sure that if he can force her to answer a few questions honestly, Watkin would see what a mistake he has made and give this silliness up.

He decides to go ahead with it, and hope that inspiration strikes. "My lady, a gift for you!" He holds out the truth stone.

Elvina turns to Kym, surprised. "A rock? How—novel!" She makes no move to take it.

Watkin looks at Kym suspiciously. "What are you about?"

Kym does his best to look innocent. "It's no ordinary rock, I assure you!" he improvises. "It's—"

"—no fit present for a princess!" Watkin says, glaring at Kym.

If you wish to persist, see #40. If not, see next page.

They are interrupted by the arrival of two ill-equipped soldiers whose faces Kym recognizes from two sketches on the parlor wall. Introductions are made, and in the ensuing confusion, Watkin orders Kym to put the stone away. He seems to think that Kym was about to play a joke on the lady, and threatens bodily harm should he try it again. Kym sighs, puts the stone away, and resolves to try again after they retrieve the princess's talisman. After an embarrassing farewell speech by Watkin, they set off.

The journey is, as Elvina promised, a short one. Kym is glad that he let Watkin accept the escort, because the path is difficult to follow, and lined on either side with partially hidden catchswamps. Rather than feeling terror at the thought that he almost refused to let the guides accompany them, Kym feels a bit of pride at having made the right decision. In fact, he is proud of having made any decision at all. Unfortunately, there is no one with whom he can share this new feeling. Watkin, still angry at Kym's antipathy toward his intended bride, is remote and uncommunicative, reacting to Kym's one attempt at camaraderie with a scowl.

Feeling a little lonesome, Kym tries several times to draw the escort into conversation, but the two soldiers, intent on keeping to the badly marked trail, are silent.

When they reach the lake, the older of the soldiers opens the hamper strapped to his companion's back and pulls out two odd-looking suits made of some sort of glittery material. They are each all of one piece, as though someone had taken breeches, a tunic, stockings, and mittens and sewn them all together. On closer inspection, Kym sees that there are no visible seams, and that there is a sort of hood attached at each of the garment, necks.

The younger soldier takes one of the suits, shakes it out, and holds it out to Watkin.

"Here," he says, speaking for the first time. "Put this on."

Watkin reaches for the suit, but Kym stops him. "Why?"

The soldier looks at Kym, startled. "Because I said so," he replies. "The Princess Elvina ordered me to. It's magic."

Kym smiles, a little nervous, but suspicious enough of anything having to do with Elvina to stand firm.

"I'm afraid that my friend and I require a little more in the way of an explanation . . ." Kym begins, only to be cut off by Watkin.

"I am no longer your friend," Watkin declares. "And if my Lady Elvina requests me to wear this, then wear it I will."

"Ordered," the young soldier adds helpfully. "She ordered it."

Kym tries to pull Watkin to one side, but the larger man refuses to be pulled. Kym settles for lowering his voice to a near whisper, not wanting to share their quarrel with the openly eavesdropping soldiers. "Watkin, I am sorry, but I find it difficult to trust your lady."

Watkin holds his anger in check with great effort. After having doubts about Elvina because of the serving girl, Watkin is even more determined to trust Elvina, because love demands trust. Therefore, in his mind, if he can trust her, he must truly love her. But he is no happier about their quarrel than Kym, and although he is unsure how to end it, he tries. "Then trust *me*!" he states, holding the glittering suit out to Kym.

To take the suit, see #41. To refuse, turn the page.

Kym hesitates, realizing that Watkin is offering him a chance to redeem himself. He reaches for the suit, then stops, some instinct warning him against putting it on. While Kym is casting about desperately for some way to save his friendship without losing his life, inspiration strikes.

"It's all right, Watkin. I understand what you are trying to do, and I appreciate it, but it really is not necessary."

Watkin looks puzzled, as do the two soldiers. "It is?" and "You do?" and "It's not?" they say in unison.

Nervous, Kym has to bite his tongue to keep from laughing. "Yes, I do," he manages to say. "It is obvious that the princess recognized what a terrible swimmer I must be."

"She did?" asks Watkin, suspiciously.

"Of course!" Kym says, becoming more sure that his line of reasoning is going to work. "Look at the difference between my chest and yours! I have no place to keep a deep breath; obviously, I'd drown if I tried to swim to the bottom of the lake with no help!"

"Obviously!" agrees the older member of the escort.

"So she provided me with a magic suit to help me!" Kym explains, waiting for Watkin to ask the next, crucial question.

He doesn't.

Fortunately, the younger soldier does. "You are right that the suits are to help you swim, but why are there two?"

"Princess Elvina did not want to cause me embarrassment, so she provided Watkin with a suit, too!" Kym explains.

The soldiers nod in agreement, as impressed with Kym's reasoning as their sovereign's generosity. "What a woman!" one exclaims.

Kym smiles shyly at Watkin. "Of course, since I

know what she was trying to do, there's no need for you to spare my feelings. I know that you have no need of magic to aid you—your love for the lady will see you safely through." Looking at his friend, Kym realizes suddenly that what he says is much truer than he would like to believe. He may not approve of Watkin's love, but it is honest nonetheless, as are Kym's next words. "And if you can be strong and brave for your true love, then I, as your true friend, can do no less." He throws the magic suit back in the hamper and strides into the lake, relieved at being able to end his manipulation of Watkin with a bit of honesty.

Watkin laughs with affectionate delight and bounds into the water after his friend.

On the shore, the two soldiers realize with grudging admiration that they have been hornswaggled. Unable to do anything about it, they settle comfortably on the shore to wait.

The lake is cold and clear, and both men are immediately sorry that they refused the protection of the magic suits. On the other hand, Kym reflects, it is better to be cold and wet and alive than warm and dry and dead.

They wade out as far as they can before the bottom drops abruptly, and sure enough, they can see a small bronze chest nestled in the silt at the bottom of the lake. It is surrounded by porous-looking rocks, all tumbled together to form a network of caverns. Taking a huge deep breath each, Kym and Watkin dive under the surface of the chilly water.

No sooner has Kym reached for the chest than he hears Watkin release his breath in an explosion of bubbles. Holding onto a nearby rock to keep from floating back to the surface, Kym turns. To his horror, he sees that Watkin's ankle is encircled by a thick tentacle, and he is being dragged into a cavern between two rocks!

Surfacing quickly, Kym calls to the two soldiers seated on the shore. "Help! Something has Watkin!"

The soldiers exchange an uncomfortable look. "Well, we can't really do that," says the older one.

"What!" Kym explodes.

"Princess Elvina wouldn't like it!" the younger one explains.

A sharp pull at his leg keeps Kym from answering. Diving back under the water he finds that it isn't a tentacle, but Watkin's hand—the other man is beginning to turn blue from lack of air. Not knowing what else to do, Kym grabs Watkin's head and, pulling his friend closer, blows his own breath into Watkin's mouth. Watkin releases his hold on Kym and goes back to wrestling with the tentacle wrapped around his leg, while Kym surfaces again.

"He's going to drown!" Kym yells. "Give me your sword!"

The soldiers exchange another look. "We can't!" one says.

"He'll *die!*" shouts Kym, unable to believe that the men on shore could allow this.

"So will *we* if we help you! Didn't you see our portraits on the wall? She can kill us—or worse—if we cross her, no matter where we run!" the younger one replies, a note of pleading in his voice.

Kym delays answering so that he can give Watkin another breath. Beginning to tire, Watkin has been pulled farther into the cavern. Kym surfaces again, looking desperately around for something with which to help his friend.

"Give him a hollow reed to breathe through!" suggests the older soldier.

Kym stares in disbelief. "There are no reeds here!" he cries, ducking back under with more air for Watkin.

The soldier turns defensively to his friend. "That's how they always show it done in the tapestries."

Under the water Watkin is weakening. The mouthsful of air Kym has been providing are barely enough to keep him alive—he is staying conscious by a sheer effort of will. He pulls desperately at the tentacle wound around his rapidly swelling leg, praying to every god and goddess he can think of.

Kym appears with more air, and to Watkin's surprise grabs his hands and tugs them away from the coils pulling him farther into the cave. Instead, Kym grasps the tentacle below Watkin's foot and, bracing his legs on the rocks, begins to pull.

Watkin does the same, understanding Kym's intention: if they can't make the creature let go, they'll at least make it give ground, allowing Watkin to get his head above water. After two more trips for air, this is exactly what happens. Watkin's head barely breaks the surface of the lake, but it's enough.

Clinging to a rock to keep from being pulled back under, Watkin breathes huge gasping draughts of air, knowing that the tentacle—and whatever is at the other end—is too strong for him to resist for long.

Kym surfaces again and begins to swim toward shore, a look of murderous fury on his face.

The soldiers step back nervously. "What are you doing?" one calls.

"I'm going to save my friend if I have to feed both of you to that thing to do it!" Kym says, realizing with a shock that he is actually capable of doing so to save Watkin.

"Wait!" yells the older man. "Maybe we *can* help you!" He turns to his companion and they begin to confer.

"Kym!" Watkin gasps.

Turning, Kym sees that his friend is being pulled

under again. Grabbing the tentacle, Kym yanks with desperate, angry strength, allowing Watkin to climb higher on the rock.

"Kym, my leg is going numb," Watkin pants.

Kym starts toward shore again.

Seeing him, the soldiers hastily end their conference. "We'll help you! We've figured out a way!" the younger one says.

"Give me your sword!" says Kym, waist deep in the water.

"You see," the older guardsman explains, "Princess Elvina said to get the crystal wizard, and then take care of you."

Watkin's head jerks up in disbelief.

"Give me the sword!" Kym repeats, a warning in his voice.

"But she didn't say how!" the soldier continues, backing away. "So if we give you the sword, and you cut yourselves free, then we've taken care of you, in a way! So get the chest and we'll give you a sword!"

To get the chest, see next page. If you think you're about to be hornswoggled, see #42.

Without hesitation, Kym dives back into the deepest part of the lake. He suspects that Princess Elvina has been less than truthful about this whole affair, but more importantly, something tells him that giving her this statue may be the worst mistake he'll ever make.

As he lifts the bronze chest, it tangles in a bunch of lakelilies. Pulling it free, it opens, giving Kym an idea.

Swimming around to the far side of the rocks, out of view of the soldiers watching anxiously from the shore, Kym surfaces silently. Opening the bronze chest, he carefully lifts the statue out.

It is, as Elvina said, carven in the likeness of a wizard, and the craftsmanship is exquisitely unlike anything Kym has ever seen. The figure wears long glass robes so fluid in execution that when a sudden breeze comes up, Kym can almost see them stir. The long pointed hat ends in a faceted globe, and every beardhair and wrinkle is evident, although the statue feels absolutely smooth to the touch. Mesmerized, Kym stares at the play of rainbow light haloing the figure, until he hears the voices of the men arguing as to whether or not he has drowned.

Closing the empty chest, Kym ducks under the water. He swims to the lair of the tentacle's owner (which seems to be tiring; its pull is a bit weaker than at first, though still deadly) and pitches the talisman inside. Then he rewraps the chest in lakelilies—counting on the fact that Elvina's soldiers will be afraid to disturb it—and surfaces near his still-struggling friend.

"Here!" Kym yells, carrying the chest to the soldiers. He stops a few feet from shore, and holds out one hand. "Give me a sword."

The young soldier obeys, holding the sword just out of Kym's reach until he holds out the chest. They carry out the exchange and Kym wades back to Watkin, who is clinging wearily to his rock, making token efforts to shake the tentacle loose.

Holding the sword, Kym dives below the surface of the lake for what he hopes will be the last time. Regarding the tentacle with resigned frustration, Kym stabs it once, hoping it will just give up and go away. It does.

He swims back to Watkin and helps the larger man to shore, stumbling as Watkin tries to make his numb leg function. Kym collapses, too tired to be surprised when Elvina's soldiers begin to fuss over him and Watkin, supplying their tattered coats for warmth, and supporting Watkin as he tries to start the blood circulating in his leg.

As darkness falls, the guardsmen make a fire and bring out provisions to be shared—enough for two, Kym notices wryly—and settle in to wait for morning. They apparently feel that they have done their duty, and are ready to be friendly. They chat a while, and then the older one makes a startling proposal.

"Why don't you stick around, join us?" he says.

Kym looks at him, for the second time that day, in total disbelief. "Because your mistress would kill us."

"My mistress? No, she's a goodhearted bit of—oh, you mean the princess! Nah, once she did your portrait, got some of your fluids, she'd feel safe enough. You two are a good lot, and we could use a few extra hands. The kid here and me, we're all the army she has. What say?"

Kym turns to Watkin. "What say?" he asks gently.

If you wish to stay, see #43. If not, go to the next page.

Watkin raises his head slowly and gazes bleakly at Kym. "No," he says quietly. "I couldn't stay here—near *her*."

Kym reaches toward his friend, but Watkin has already turned away and is staring moodily into the flames.

"What brought you here in the first place?" asks the younger soldier, breaking the uncomfortable silence. "Weren't you, uh, warned about, well, anything?"

Kym explains their Quest in a matter-of-fact voice, feeling some astonishment at himself for how commonplace the whole situation is beginning to seem. When he is finished, the two soldiers hold a quick conference, and then the older one speaks.

"If you're looking for the Dream Palace, you're going in the right direction." The younger one pokes him, looking around fearfully.

"We are forbidden to speak of this place!" he whispers.

The older one doesn't seem worried. "We're out of her range. As I was saying, you are going the right way. There's a place not far from here that's supposed to be magic. It's in the hills. I've heard there's a colony of Fair Folk. They can maybe help you. Just follow the path and keep heading east—and for the sake of all that's living, watch out for the Nightspiders! All they have to do is get near you, and you'll feel a despair that's enough to make you do away with yourself!"

Kym thanks the men, and after a while they settle down to sleep.

Just before he falls asleep, Kym hears the soldiers laughing, and he hears something about the joke being on him and Watkin. Too sleepy to be alarmed, he turns to the fire and closes his eyes.

V: The Hills of Faerie

As the days go by and they continue their Quest, Watkin is uncharacteristically silent. Mourning his lost chance at love, he kicks aimlessly along the path, glaring at the various flora and fauna, and every once in a while startling Kym with vast, heartfelt sighs.

Kym is also quiet, concentrating on following the path, and keeping alert for any signs of the faeries that are supposed to live here. He is relieved that Watkin decided to keep going; he is intensely excited at the prospect of meeting real faeries. Since he was a boy, he has had a fascination with everything pertaining to the Fair Folk, but like most people, he didn't dare believe that they really exist. But why shouldn't they? The whole Quest has been filled with one impossible thing after the next, are faeries too much to ask?

Wating for Watkin to catch up to him, Kym stops and looks around, smiling. They are certainly in the right place, Kym thinks. If faeries live anywhere, it has to be here. Following the sketchy directions they were given, Kym and Watkin travelled for two days and two nights through a despressingly desolate landscape.

On the evening of the second day, they reached a wide meadow filled with every kind of wildflower that they could think of, and a few they'd never seen. Passing through it had taken another day and night, and as they walked the land began to rise, until they found themselves looking across a range of gentle hills covered by lush forest.

There are flowers here, too, covering the ground, and winding long tendrils among the branches of the trees. The smell is heavenly—delicate instead of overpowering—and in a few minutes Kym is dizzy from trying to breathe it all in at once. The early morning sunlight has called up a gentle mist from the dewy blossoms all around, obscuring vision and adding to the dreamy quality of the forest.

It is because of this that Kym stumbles and falls when a tiny figure suddenly darts across the path in front of him. Tripping so suddenly that Watkin stumbles over him, Kym is at first too spellbound by what he has seen to speak or move.

It had wings.

The tiny creature had two legs, two arms, one head and two *wings*!

Without a word Kym leaps to his feet and races off the path in pursuit of the little winged thing.

Watkin looks around for a second in extreme puzzlement, then follows. "Kym? What are we after?"

"A faerie!" Kym breathes. He is running in a dream state, unable to believe how wonderful the world has suddenly turned out to be.

Watkin stops short. "There are no faeries." The words are barely out of his mouth when he sees a blur of movement through the trees ahead. All heartbreak forgotten, Watkin gazes through the mist at a small winged person standing not ten feet away, absolutely still in a spill of hazy sunshine filtering down through the trees.

With a high-pitched giggle, the vision melts into the sunlight and is gone.

Kym, madly in pursuit, crashes through the underbrush and into Watkin. "Hurry! We've got to catch it!" He races off.

Watkin stares after his friend in amazement.

If you wish to chase the faerie, turn the page. If not, see #44.

Not really believing what he saw, but not knowing what else to do, Watkin follows. He soon loses Kym in the mist, and stops to try and get his bearings. A quick footstep makes him turn, and before he can react, a small figure crashes through the underbrush just inches away. Automatically, Watkin reaches out and catches one thin arm in his huge hand. With a squeal, the faerie tries to free itself just as Kym arrives, out of breath and glowing with excitement.

"Be careful! Don't let it get away! Don't hurt it!" Kym orders.

Watkin struggles to hold on to the delicate creature, yelling in shock when it kicks him in the shin. He tightens his grip while trying to keep himself out of harm's way, and suddenly, as the faerie tries to wriggle out of his grasp, there is a terrible ripping sound, and Watkin finds himself holding a gossamer wing in his hand.

Horrified, he lets go of the squirming faerie, barely registering Kym's cries of dismay. He stands holding the wing, struggling to comprehend the magnitude of what he has just done, until slowly Kym's voice begins to penetrate.

"Watkin, it's all right. It's all right!"

Watkin looks up slowly, barely able to speak. "How can you say that?"

Kym shakes his head, disappointment struggling with amusement in his face. "It's not a faerie," he says.

Watkin holds up the torn wing. "Well, it isn't *now!*"

Kym laughs, and Watkin finally notices that the faerie—or whatever it is—is peeking out from behind a nearby tree. Kym turns to it and beckons. "You'll have to come out, or you won't get your wing back."

"Are you trolls?" it asks, not moving from behind the tree.

"No," Watkin answers, puzzled, "We are travellers."

"All right, then." Shyly, the little being, lone wing flapping behind it, steps out from behind the tree, and Watkin has to laugh.

It's a little girl.

She is no more than five or six years old, and the top of her head barely comes to Watkin's belt buckle. She marches up to him and holds out her small hands. Careful not to do any more damage, Watkin hands her the torn wing, noticing for the first time the careful stitching where it was attached to her dress. In fact, her whole outfit is very well done, and Watkin realizes that even without the benefit of their misty surroundings, the child would still appear authentically fey. "How come you to be so far from home, little one?" he asks, squatting down to her level.

"It's not so far," she replies with the hint of a lisp.

"Why are you dressed like a faerie? Is there a masquerade?"

The child looks at Watkin as though he has suddenly lost his mind. "I *am* a Faerie!" she insists.

Watkin is taken aback. "No, you're not, you're a little girl."

"A little girl *Faerie*."

Kym and Watkin exchange amused glances over her head, but are interrupted from further discussion by a male voice calling nearby.

"Tympani!"

The child looks up, pleased. "That's my father. Now you'll see!" She takes a few steps closer to where the voice is calling from. "I'm here, Daddy! Here I am!"

With impressively little noise or disturbance, a very beautiful young man appears in the clearing where they stand. He is tall and slender, and dressed as fantastically as Tympani, in a satiny dark-blue tunic, soft leather boots dyed to match, pale shimmering tights, and a long, gossamer cape cut to fit around his iridescent wings.

He smiles at first, but when he notices his child's missing wing, his face goes dark with rage. "Trolls!" he shouts, sweeping the child into his arms. "She's only a baby! How could you?"

Kym and Watkin react as one, attempting to explain. "It was an accident! I didn't mean it, she ran into me! We didn't know she was a child! We aren't trolls!"

After a few moments of heated babbling from Kym and Watkin, the man nods, understanding, and they quiet down.

"I am sorry to have accused you of so vile a crime." Still holding the child, he extends a hand in greeting. "Welcome to the Hills of Faerie," he says solemnly. "I am Elaric, and this is Tympani, my firstborn."

Kym and Watkin introduce themselves, Watkin hesitating to state his name, at first, and pleasantries are exchanged all around.

"Travelling is hungry work, and we have plenty of food. Will you join us at table?"

The travellers accept and follow Elaric, still carrying his daughter, as he steps off the path.

Lagging a few feet behind to discreetly discuss their host's delusions of faeriehood, Kym and Watkin are startled by a sudden yell from just ahead of them.

Turning to see where his guests have gotten to, Elaric has missed seeing a crude rope loop set on the ground and badly camouflaged. As soon as he steps in it, the trap is sprung, and Elaric is suddenly dangling upside down, trying not to drop his squealing daughter!

As Kym and Watkin hurry to the rescue, they become aware of voices in the near distance, rapidly getting closer.

Elaric looks up, terror on his face. "Hurry! A party of Trolls is coming!" Handing Tympani to Kym, Elaric attempts to pull himself upright to slip his foot out of the noose. Watkin searches for something with which to cut the rope; finding nothing, he boosts Elaric on his shoulder, taking his weight off of the rope and allowing him to free his foot. To Watkin's surprise, Elaric reaches for the branch above his head and climbs into the tree.

"Where are you going?" Watkin calls.

"Ssh! Be quiet! Hand Tympani to me, then get into trees yourselves! The trolls will be here any second!"

"Shouldn't we run or something?" Kym asks.

"No! They can't look in the trees. Trolls are stupid. Just hide in the tree, and if anything happens, let me take care of it!"

Mystified, Kym and Watkin do what their winged host suggests, and wait.

The sounds of a small party moving through the forest are much louder now, and a second or two after everyone is settled the underbrush parts, and with much stamping and cursing, the party of trolls surrounds the tree in which Elaric and Tympani are hiding.

At least, Kym and Watkin assume these are the trolls Elaric mentioned. In truth, they are trolls the same way Elaric and Tympani are faeries—in costume only.

There are four of them, three men and one woman, all of them relatively normal-looking, except for their clothing. The men wear rough leather breeches, and dented armor made of metal kitchen implements and trimmed with fur. The woman, a rather boyishly built young lady, wears a leather loincloth and a halter whose main feature seems to be two egg cups held in place with ornate leather braid. All four wear helmets made of soup tureens pounded into vaguely helmet-like shapes, and each carries a dangerous-looking, if inelegant, weapon.

"Looks like the Faerie got away!" says the largest of the Trolls, indicating the empty rope.

"Yup." The other Trolls nod in agreement.

"Maybe it'll be back," suggests the only one with red hair.

"Nah." The rest shake their heads.

The Trolls look around, study their fingernails, and whistle off-key for a few minutes, then the smallest one makes a suggestion. "Say, do you suppose the Faerie is hiding around here somewhere?"

Kym and Watkin hold their breaths while the Trolls consider this. Unfortunately, on drawing in his breath, Kym has also drawn in a small insect, which he now expels with a cough.

All four Trolls react, looking around in every direction except up. "What was that?" one asks.

Kym looks at Watkin, who mouths a suggestion to ambush the Trolls while they have the chance.

To ambush, see #45. To stay put, see #46.

Kym shakes his head, causing him to cough again.

"I heard it, too," says the woman. "What was it?"

"A bird," Elaric answers. Kym and Watkin exchange startled glances. Their astonishment increases as the woman answers him.

"I don't think birds cough," she says, looking around suspiciously.

"It has a sore throat from singing," Elaric explains.

"Oh. That makes sense." She turns to her companion. "Let's go."

As Kym and Watkin watch incredulously, the Trolls clatter off into the underbrush, not looking back.

As soon as they are out of sight, Elaric climbs out of the tree, carefully helping Tympani down after him. Increasingly confused, Kym and Watkin also abandon their hiding places.

"That was close," Watkin ventures, hoping to elicit some sort of information.

"Yes, very," Elaric agrees. He smiles reassuringly and starts off, with Tympani trotting along beside him.

Kym starts to follow, but Watkin holds him back. "Lad, I don't know if I'm up to this," he says.

"What do you mean?"

"I mean, I—we—have had a full time of it; meeting new people, doing new things, getting our hearts broken—"

"My heart isn't broken," Kym interrupts.

"It isn't *yet*. I think we should set our sights on finding this palace we are looking for, and not get sidetracked."

As Kym considers Watkin's idea, Elaric notices that he is no longer being followed, and turns back. "Are you coming with me, my friends?"

To go with Elaric, see next page. To bypass the Faeries. see #47.

Kym looks at Watkin. "A Quest is supposed to be difficult, and if we don't take the chance to investigate everything, we may miss something important—like our true loves!"

Watkin sighs and lays an arm across Kym's shoulders. "All right, my boy, but this is *weird*!"

They follow Elaric through the forest, amazed that his wings and cape never seem to catch on anything. Both Kym and Watkin suspect at first that he wears that new spell-woven fabric "Ripless Wonder," but it doesn't make sense for Elaric to have heard of it, and anyway, magic always gives itself away by a unique tingle in the air, and there is none near Elaric.

Watching him more closely, they realize that Elaric has simply become accustoned to travelling through the forest dressed in this manner, and what they thought was magic is skill.

They walk for a while, and then Elaric stops before a large, steep hill. "Here we are," he says.

"Where?" asks Watkin, for once being the nervous one.

"Home!" Elaric says, holding out his arms. As he does so, the hillside opens to reveal a door. Again, Kym and Watkin feel for magic in the air and are mystified to find none.

They peer into the opening, and are astounded to see a long, smoothly polished hallway leading deep into the hillside.

Tympani runs past them, starting to call for her mother, but Elaric grabs her and sweeps her off her feet. "Wait, kidlet! If your mother sees the shape you're in—" he indicates her missing wing "—she'll faint away before we can explain. I think we should all go in together, calmly, all right?"

If you want to go in together, calmly, see #48. If you don't, see #47.

Holding tightly to his daughter's hand, Elaric steps into the opening. As soon as Kym and Watkin step inside, he claps his hands and the doorway swings silently closed, revealing a complicated pulley system, with an adolescent boy seated to one side. He is dressed as elegantly as Elaric, but in deep greens, instead of blue. The boy smiles a greeting, then goes back to embroidering what looks to be a belt.

Looking at each other doubtfully, Kym and Watkin follow their host through the hallway, and into a large room filled with light and music.

The travellers stop, overwhelmed by the splendor. In the center of the room is a fountain spraying scented water into the air. To one side sits a small, informal group playing exotic instruments. They are not too skilled, but their playing is soft and melodic, and they seem to be enjoying themselves a great deal.

Flowering vines and brightly colored ribbons dangle from the high, vaulted ceiling, and the very rocks that make up the walls sparkle, giving the room a dreamy, indistinct quality. It is unquestionably the most beautiful place Kym and Watkin have ever seen.

There is one jarring note, however.

Not all of the Faeries are as beautiful as Elaric and Tympani. In fact, the latter seem to be the exception. A great number of the beautifully dressed and bewinged people drifting about the room are amazingly unattractive, and they are certainly not ageless.

Kym and Watkin exchange yet another puzzled glance, too fascinated to speak. As they stare, a plain young woman sets down her flute and hurries over to where they stand, her lovely wings floating behind her.

"Mommy!" Tympani calls. "Look what happened!" Before Elaric can stop her, she holds up her detached wing.

The young woman stops dead in her tracks, a look of

despair on her face. Quickly, Elaric explains how it happened, and she nods her understanding. Turning Tympani around, she inspects the child's dress, shaking her head and tsking.

When she has finished, Elaric introduces her to his guests.

"Kym, Watkin, this is my wife, Larila."

They exchange "How do you dos," and Larila offers them a place to freshen up. Grateful to have a moment alone to sort things out, Kym and Watkin follow the lady down a bright corridor and into a small bed and bath chamber, where she leaves them to freshen up, which they do.

Once they are clean, the two men discover that clothing has been laid out for them in the adjoining bedroom. Each has been given a lovely outfit of tunic, tights, and boots, and both men are relieved to see that complimentary wings were not included.

Once dressed, and with their talismans hidden in their pockets, they make their way out into the great hall, looking for Elaric. He is nowhere to be found, nor are Tympani and Larila.

Wandering through the brightly dressed crowd, Kym and Watkin can see greater differences in the styles of clothing being worn, and especially in the level of workmanship.

Some of the outfits are as well done as Elaric's, but other's are downright crude, with large ungainly stitching, mismatched fabrics, and crooked wings.

The Faeries themselves also vary. There are fat ones, ones with bad complexions and physical handicaps, and just plain unattractive persons, as well as people too skinny, and nearsighted, and just shy-looking. Apart from Elaric and Tympani, not one other person in the room fits the popular notion of how the Fair Folk look.

Wandering over to a small group of people involved

in various handicrafts, Kym and Watkin draw them into conversation. They discover that one of them, a girl named Liramar, was the first baby born in the hill.

"Then your people have lived here for some time," Kym observes. He is no longer tongue-tied in the presence of women, but he still has a bit to learn about tact.

Liramar smiles, putting down the flute on which she is carving pretty designs. "Yes. Before I was born, my parents and their friends used to come here once a seven-part to meet. They wore wings only then, to distract them from their ordinary lives." Liramar settles her wings with a pretty, practiced flick of her shoulders, and continues. "The Fair Folk used to be scattered all over the land, and only got together in small enclaves, except for the one Grand Convocation each seventh. There was dancing, and discussions and contests, and some of the Faeries even gathered all their wares in one room and sold them. It was great fun, I'm told." She picks up her carving tool and resumes decorating her instrument.

"A whole gathering of nothing but Faeries?" Watkin asks, trying to imagine people coming from all over just to dress up.

"Oh no," another Faerie answers, this one a boy named Aran. He is repotting a miniature starflower bush and the rich fragrance fills the room. "There were many other kinds of folk, too. Elves and Sprites—even people claiming to be from other worlds!" He pauses, shaking his head at such silliness.

"What about the Trolls?" asks Kym.

A third Faerie answers, a very regal-looking woman whose dark-blue eyes hold calm and gentle wisdom. She is snapping podbeans, opening the crisp blue pods and dumping the little beans into a gorgeous ceramic bowl. "They used to come, too, and they were the only group as numerous as we were. There was a great rivalry between them and the Faeries, but it was all in fun. They used to have mock wars in the forest." She pauses to empty the bowl of beans into a large cooking pot a few feet away, and another Faerie picks up the tale.

"Near the end of the fourteenth Convocation, one of the Faeries stumbled across a warren of caves in a hillside," says the narrator, a blind boy who is fashioning an exquisite goblet out of soft clay. "They explored it, and for several years at Convocations, they used to camp out in there, and little by little, they turned the caves into a livable place."

"This is that place!" Kym guesses.

"That's right," agrees the older woman, back from the cooking pot. As she returns to snapping pods, she hands Kym and Watkin each a handful of the succulent little beans. Her voice saddens as she continues. "Then, one seventh, one of the Faeries, a very popular one, was lost in the caves. They searched for her until the time the Convocation was to end, but they couldn't find her." She pauses, and the blind boy, Mirin, reaches for her hand and squeezes it.

Kym and Watkin are shocked by the story. "What happened?"

"No one knows. Maybe she fell and was too hurt to cry for help, or maybe she just got lost. Whatever happened, her lover refused to leave when the Convocation ended. He said that she gave her life to be a Faerie, and that he could do no less. He vowed to live here in the Hill and never to remove his wings or return to the outside world."

"And did he?" Kym and Watkin ask together.

"Return? No. He stayed here, and eventually, one by one, the others joined him. After each Convocation a few more Faeries would stay, until we were all here, and they stopped having Convocations. There was no need anymore."

"And the Trolls?" Kym asks, completely charmed by the story.

A voice from behind Kym answers his question. Turning, he sees Elaric. "They joined us, and the war goes on. We have very specific rules—"

"Like the Trolls being stupid!" Kym interrupts, glad to have unraveled the mystifying scene in the forest.

"Just so." Elaric laughs. "When they catch us, they tear off our wings, which doesn't hurt, but the time it takes to sew them back on costs dearly."

"And when you catch a Troll?" asks Watkin, getting into the spirit of the thing.

"We make them watch while we turn their weapons back into kitchen implements. It's a terrible insult, and the time it takes the Trolls to hammer them back out of shape is equal to our having to resew our wings."

"And that's how war is waged?"

"Those are the worst things we do. In skirmishes we'll occasionally grab a Troll and bathe him, or they'll catch one of us and roll us around in the dirt. The children love it."

Kym and Watkin laugh, thoroughly charmed by the idea of these people living out their fantasies. One thing disturbs Watkin, however. He doesn't bring it up until much later in the evening, though, after a modest but delicious feast.

The grand room is softly lit by candles, and everyone is scattered about on richly embroidered cushions; couples snuggle together, and children cuddle like kittens, not caring on whose lap they are cradled, as long as it is warm and soft.

"I have seen no evidence of magic here. Why do you not purchase spells? Would it not be more realistic?"

The blue-eyed older woman, called Sira, shakes her

head. Tympani is curled on one side of her, and on the other is an unkempt little boy of about Tympani's age, dressed in leather and fur. "Faeries do not have magic, they *are* magic. We couldn't afford to buy spells strong enough to generate magic one by one, so none of us have them."

"Why do you not learn to be wizards?" asks Kym.

"We would have to leave here, and we have all sworn not to."

Kym and Watkin nod, satisfied but for one thing. Watkin points at the little boy lying on Sira's lap. "Isn't he a Troll?"

The adults laugh. "Yes," Sira answers, tousling the boy's hair. "This is Torn. We encourage the children to play together so that no one grows up with the mistaken idea that the rivalry is for real. Children are also exempt from wing-ripping and weapon-beating because their feelings are too easily hurt."

Kym and Watkin smile and wriggle deeper into the soft cushions, with identical sighs of contentment. They barely react at the first few yells from the far side of the room, until they can decipher what is being said.

"Troll raid! Troll raid!"

The adults leap to their feet and scatter, while the children, suddenly wide awake, laugh and dance around in excited delight.

Kym and Watkin get to their feet, immediately caught up in the merry confusion. The adults are all wearing expressions of mock seriousness, and the children are obviously having the time of their lives.

As the travellers watch, a horde of yelling Trolls spills out of the hallway at the far end of the room. They wear the same good-naturedly ferocious expressions as the Faeries, and neither Kym nor Watkin are surprised to see that the "war party" contains a large number of children.

A long, loud, good-natured skirmish ensues, with some half-hearted wing-ripping and weapon-beating, but mostly lots of laughing and chasing and wrestling. After the first frantic minutes, Kym and Watkin are pulled into the tussle, running about like they were kids.

Surprised at himself, Kym laughs until he can hardly catch his breath as he wrestles with Tympani and Torn. Once they have him helpless on the ground, the two youngsters chase each other, squealing and giggling, down a side hallway whose opening is partly covered by a torn tapestry. Too exhausted to give chase he chuckles—for the first time he can remember—as they disappear around a corner.

Eventually, everyone tires and the Faeries bring out food and drink. Watkin lends a hand rolling out the barrels of ale, and runs into a disheveled—but intact— Elaric.

"Does this happen often?" Watkin asks, tapping the barrel and drawing the first tankard. He passes it to Elaric, who accepts it gratefully.

"No," he answers, wiping foam from his mouth in an unfaerielike gesture. "The Trolls can't remember how to get in here too often!"

This strikes Watkin as funny, and he laughs heartily, joined by Elaric. The appearance of Larila, his wife, cuts their humor short, as she is in tears.

"What is it, my darling?" Elaric asks, drawing her into a hug. He notices that her wings are gone. "Oh, sweetling, you can sew them back on. I'll help you."

She shakes her head, and pulls away as a female Troll rushes in, also crying. They clutch at each other, fear in their eyes, trying not to talk at once.

"Rend, did you find them?" Larila asks.

The Troll shakes her head. Looking at Larila, she knows the answer she's going to get, but she has to ask anyway. "Did you?"

Before the question is out, Larila answers in the negative, and the women embrace. Watkin steps forward as Elaric asks what's going on.

Both women answer at once: "Tympani and Torn are missing!"

Watkin calls for Kym while Elaric confers with several of the other Faeries and Trolls. When Kym appears in the doorway, he reacts with startling calmness when Watkin tells him what's happened.

"It's all right," Kym says. "I saw which corridor they went down."

"We have looked in all of the corridors, and in all of the rooms," says a large man whom Elaric identifies as Rip, the little boy's father. "Which corridor do you mean?"

"The one near where I was sitting," Kym answers, feeling good that he can help. "It had part of a tapestry hanging on the opening." He is totally unprepared for the reaction this causes. Everyone looks at Kym in shock, and Rip grabs him by the shoulders.

"Why didn't you stop them?" the Troll demands.

Larila and Rend pull him away from Kym. "How could he know? He's a guest here!" Turning to Kym, she explains. "That tunnel collapsed not too long ago. It's still unstable. The children know that they aren't supposed to play there, but Torn and Tympani have been fascinated with it lately."

Kym is speechless. "I'm so sorry! I'll search for them at once!"

Watkin grabs his arm as he strides toward the doorway. "The tunnel is unstable! It could collapse on you!"

Kym takes a deep breath. Unaccustomed to standing up to anyone, he is getting used to it on this Quest. "It is my fault that they are in danger. I'm not very big; my passing through the tunnel shouldn't disturb it." He turns to leave, and Watkin grabs him.

"Kym, wait, please! You could get lost!"

Elaric agrees. "The corridor isn't lighted past the first few feet."

Kym nods. "Then the children most probably haven't wandered too far. They aren't likely to go exploring in the dark." As one who is familiar with night fears, Kym speaks with confidence. "I will find them."

Watkin grabs him. "Kym, wait!"

If you are determined, see #49. To be talked out of this, see #50.

Kym turns, fixing Watkin with a determined glare.

"I'll come with you," Watkin says, and together they set off.

"I will also come," says Elaric. "I do not believe that our mere passing through the tunnel will cause it to collapse, but we must be careful—and *quiet!*"

"In that case, we will join you," Rend states, squaring her shoulders as though expecting to be contradicted. Rip takes her hand and squeezes it.

"You are very brave," he says. At Elaric's quizzical look, Rip smiles. "My wife has a fear of enclosed places," he explains.

"A claustrophobic Troll?" Kym says, amazed.

Rend smiles and shrugs, and with a deep breath, steps into the tunnel with the others close—but not too close—behind her.

The corridor is fairly well-lit by the candlelight spilling in from the gathering room, and Kym can see the piles of rock and rubble lining the sides.

"We tried to clear the tunnel when it first collapsed, but every time we moved one rock, two more fell," Elaric whispers.

The search party carefully makes its way to the curve where Kym last caught sight of Tympani and Torn, and stops. The tunnel branches into three smaller corridors here. The right tunnel is dark and quiet. The middle one is dusty and piled high with rubble, but fairly well-lit. The left tunnel is brighter than the others, and strewn with dustlace.

"Which way did they go?" Watkin whispers.

"I don't know," Kym says. "We will have to guess."

To take the right tunnel, see #51. For the middle tunnel, see #52, and for the left tunnel, see #53.

"We should be able to outguess two little children," Rip says.

"We can if we consider this in a logical manner," his wife replies, making Kym wonder why they decided to become Trolls, and pretend to be stupid. Probably for the challenge, he decides.

"I imagine they would have taken the brightest fork," Larila suggests.

Kym shakes his head. "It is covered with dustlace."

Rip starts toward the right tunnel. "Dustlace is no danger," he says quietly.

Kym remembers his childhood days in his parents' house. His mother was an indifferent housekeeper, and the corners of his tiny bedroom were strewn with dustlace. He used to lie in bed at night, convinced that the collections of dust in the spaces between cobbled walls and thatched roof were moving closer and growing. He shakes his head. "Not to adults," he answers Rip. "I do not think that they would go that way."

Larila points to the dark tunnel. "If they were daring each other, maybe they decided to brave this corridor. It is the cleanest, and there is no rubble."

Kym shakes his head again. "It is too dark. A little darkness is scary in a fun way, but this is *too* scary. I think that they took the middle tunnel."

Rend disagrees. "It is nearly impassable, and look how filthy it is. They would have had to climb over all of those rocks covered in dust!" Her voice trails off and she smiles. "I think you are right, That is the way they went." Overcome with worry, her voice breaks on the last word.

Kym takes her hand reassuringly. "We will find them. Let's go."

Kym steps up to the pile of rubble partially blocking

the middle tunnel and begins—carefully—to remove the topmost rocks. There is plenty of space for two energetic little kids to have clambered over the rockfall, but not even the smallest of the adults could squeeze through.

It is hot and dirty work, and after a few moments Elaric returns to the gathering room to tell the other Trolls and Faeries what is happening, and to get water for the searchers. By the time he re-enters the corridor, Kym, Watkin, and the others have cleared an opening large enough to climb through.

After a quick drink of water and a cursory swipe at the dust on his face, Kym climbs through the opening and starts carefully down the corridor. The others follow, Watkin bringing up the rear.

As he emerges on the far side of the rockfall, Watkin starts to say something, and is immediately "shushed" by Kym. "Be quiet, I hear something," Kym orders.

After a moment, the others hear it, too—a child crying.

"That's Tympani!" cries Larila, rushing past Kym. As soon as the words are out there is a threatening rumble from the ceiling, and the searchers are showered with dust and small pebbles.

"Stay quiet," Elaric warns, moving slowly toward the child's voice. "Tympani," he calls softly. "Can you hear me?"

"Daddy, help!" she answers, bringing down another fall of stones and dust.

"Sh! Hush baby, you'll make the rocks fall. Are you hurt? Talk to me so I can find you," Larila says, walking forward slowly and with extreme care.

"We aren't hurt at all, Mommy, but we can't get out! The rocks fell on the stairs!" Tympani says, her voice an exaggerated whisper that brings smiles to all of the searchers.

"Torn, can you tell me where you are?" asks Rip.

"Under a lot of rocks!" comes the answer.

The searchers exchange grins of adult amusement. If the kids are not hurt, then the situation is not too serious, they all think.

Until they see just where the children are trapped.

Walking a few feet ahead of the others, Larila finds the children, and stifles a sudden rush of tears. She points silently, trying not to cry, and the others surround her, unable at first to take in the significance of what they are seeing.

There is a spiralling stone staircase that leads from the level they are on to a planned lower level, and it has partially collapsed and been covered with huge blocks from the fallen ceiling. The children are trapped under the blocks at the bottom of the stairwell.

Because of the size of the blocks, and the way they fell, the children were not crushed. There is enough room for the two of them to walk around a little bit, but there is no way that they can climb out. The staircase was never finished, so they are in a dead-end tunnel.

Watkin suggests lowering a rope, but there is no space between the fallen blocks that would allow straight passage of a rope, and even if they did get one to the children, there are no spaces large enough to pull them out through. They can breathe and be heard, but they will starve unless, of course, the ceiling collapses and crushes them.

Behind them, Rip paces nervously, running his big square hands through his unruly hair. "There's *got* to be a way to get them out!"

"Maybe we can move the blocks," Watkin suggests. "We could rig up a pulley system, and if everyone helped . . ."

It takes a few hours to get together everything that is needed. While this is being done Rend and Larila manage to get a waterskin down to Torn and Tympani, after several frustrating tries, but their several attempts to lower food are unsuccessful.

It is a long and difficult struggle to get a strong rope wrapped around the topmost block of stone. There is nothing to which a pulley system can be anchored, so the combined strength of the Trolls and Faeries is all they have to try and move the stone. It is not enough. Someone suggests breaking the block into pieces small enough to be moved, but as soon as they start to chisel at the stone, the roof rains dust and rocks on them.

Rip throws the chisel down in disgust. "If I were truly a Troll I could save them!"

Kym catches his breath. He could use the Spell of Being!

The idea frightens him, yet he can think of no other way to save the children. But who to use it on? Turning Rip into a Troll would allow him to dig out the rocks with the preternatural skill for tunneling that Trolls supposedly possess, but it would take too long. He'd have to go in through the back, or risk collapsing the rocks further, and that could take weeks. What if there were another rockfall?

Looking down through the spaces between the rocks, his eyes fall on the two little kids, huddled together, and he realizes what he must do. Taking the velvet bag from his pocket, he opens it slowly—and hesitates.

If he uses the powder now, he will have nothing to offer his One True Love but himself, as he is. If he doesn't use it, the children will die.

If you wish to use the Spell, see #54. If not, see #55.

"I can save them," Kym says.

Everyone looks at him.

He holds up the velvet pouch. "I can save them, but they'll be changed."

There is an ominous rumbling from the ceiling, and they are once again covered with dust. This time a few larger rocks fall. Rend grabs Kym's arm. "Do it, whatever it is. Please save them!"

Stepping up to the edge of the stairwell, Kym closes his eyes and thinks carefully about what he is wishing. Certain he has remembered everything, he upends the little pouch into a gap in the blocks, where it falls on Tympani and Torn.

Nothing happens at first.

Then Torn sneezes.

And Tympani giggles.

And everything happens at once.

From the stairwell comes a sound like a thousand windchimes, and a softly diffusing rainbow light, and then the sound of digging and the soft whickering of wings. It takes a seeming eternity, during which everyone holds their breath, and then comes a final burst of sound as the topmost stone is delicately chipped away from the underside and the children appear.

And they *are* changed. Tympani's wings, once a fanciful decoration, are now real. They are much more beautiful than any of the handmade ones, and they work perfectly to lift her and Torn out through the spaces the little Troll—now a Troll for real—has made.

Tympani sets down lightly, and Torn lets go of her and runs to his parents, waving the child's toy that has suddenly become a precision tool. There is much embracing and many tears, and Kym is thanked again and again.

As the Trolls and Faeries take their transformed children out of the tunnel, Kym pulls Watkin aside. "Let's go now," Kym says.

Watkin understanding as only a true friend can, nods and places a strong arm about Kym's shoulders.

"You did the right thing, my boy," he says. "It was clever, and it was brave, and these folk will honor your memory forever."

Kym nods, but he doesn't share the general elation. He is glad that the children are safe, and he is proud of the most important part of the wish he made for them; they and their descendants will breed true—from this day on, the fantasy has become real.

Slipping silently through the celebrating crowd, Kym and Watkin make their way back to where they left their clothing. They change and pick up their packs, and then make their way to the door in the hill. The young girl operating the mechanism smiles as she lets them out.

It helps.

VI: *The Forest of Souls*

．

The forest stretches on and on, seeming to have no end. Kym and Watkin travel silently, beginning to tire of the relentless greenery all around them. Kym feels that if he hears one more bird singing, or sees one more magnificent sunlit clearing, he will go mad. Watkin heartily agrees.

In a short while, it begins to seem that their sanity will remain intact for, little by little, the birdsong fades out. As they travel on they hear fewer birds, until eventually there are none. Then the insect sounds stop, and after that even the sunlight seems to weaken.

They hike along in total silence, and as the forest becomes darker, somehow the silence feels ominous. They begin to feel watched. Twigs snap for no apparent reason, and once Watkin swears that he felt something touch him. The underbrush seems to grab at the travellers as though trying to halt their progress.

Kym reaches out for Watkin's arm, needing to be reassured that he is not alone here. Watkin clutches Kym just as tightly, his normal good-natured bravado forgotten.

"This place is very creepy," Watkin whispers. "I need a bit of something to bring up my courage!"

Kym nods, looking around fearfully. He jumps as something rustles right by his ear. "If only it wasn't so dark and quiet!"

"I can't do anything about the dark," Watkin says, mourning his glowbubble. He brushes at his ear as something tickles it, and continues trying to force his way through the underbrush.

Kym grabs the back of Watkin's tunic and stumbles along behind the larger man. All of the courage he has discovered during the Quest deserts him as he is faced with a danger he can neither see nor hear, but only sense. How can you fight something when you not only don't know where it is, you are not even sure *if* it is?

This has always been Kym's greatest horror—this sly, creeping fear of *everything*. He had thought that he was changing, that there really was bravery in him, and that he had something to offer that a good woman would recognize. He knows now that he was wrong, that the whole Quest was a mistake. He should have stayed back in his unimportant village, living his unimportant life until his equally unimportant death.

Watkin is also struggling with his fears. Feeling Kym clutching at his tunic, he feels a responsibility to protect his smaller, weaker friend. But how do you protect someone from a menace that you cannot see? People have always depended on Watkin for his strength and size, to the extent that they have all overlooked the fine and gentle intellect underneath. All except for Kym.

Since they were small children, as far back as either of them can remember, they have been friends. They have never failed each other, and Watkin knows in his heart that he is going to fail Kym now. He can't bear to think of the look of betrayal he will see on Kym's face when his friend realizes that Watkin is neither as strong nor as brave as Kym thinks. Rather than see that look, Watkin would die.

Overcome by despair, the travellers stop. At once, they are surrounded by eight-legged shapes dropping silently from the trees.

Neither man has any particular fear of crawling things, so their first reactions are a mixture of apathy and mild disgust at the sheer numbers of fat, eight-legged bodies littering the ground in front of them. But, the more spiders that appear, the greater their apathy grows. Sunk in black depression, Kym suddenly realizes what they are. "Nightspiders!"

"What are nightspiders?" Watkin asks, horrified in spite of his ignorance.

"Don't you remember? We were warned about them! This despair we feel is their doing!"

The thought cheers Watkin up a little. "But what do we do about them?" he asks, edging closer to his friend. The thought of trying to cope with so many of the creatures is too much for Watkin, and he sighs, ready to sit down on the ground and let them have him. It's just all a little too much.

Kym watches Watkin's mood degenerate once again into gloom, and his own follows suit. How can the two of them cope with so many of the disgusting things after all they've been through? He watches disinterestedly as a spider crawls toward his foot, but as soon as it touches him, he recoils in disgust. "No!" he shouts, startling Watkin out of his gloomy reverie. "We have to fight them!" He feels a surge of hope as he says this, and is further cheered to see the crawling horrors retreat a little.

Watkin looks up, not sure what Kym is going on about, and not sure he cares. He sighs.

Kym grabs his larger friend and shakes him, too filled with the need to get through to Watkin to notice that he is having no trouble at all in shaking the larger man so hard his teeth rattle. "Watkin, snap out of it! We *can* fight them!"

The fact that Kym is shaking him so hard his teeth are rattling is not lost on Watkin. Angry, he pulls away from him, roughly breaking Kym's grip on his shoulders. "Take your hands off me, lad, if you want to keep them on your wrists!"

Kym is delighted to see the spiders retreat from the vehement emotions being brought into play. "That's it, Watkin! Get mad at me!"

Watkin stops, aware that he was about to hit his best friend. "I couldn't hit you, lad. You're the best friend I have in the world!"

Before Kym can explain further, Watkin is once again overcome with despair. Silently he curses himself for even thinking to do harm to Kym. He is soon lost in a tide of self-pity, wishing that he had not been born so big and strong or, better yet, that he had not been born at all.

Kym watches as Watkin allows himself to be taken over by his deepest fears and insecurities. Trying to keep himself from being caught, he thinks of the happiest moments in his life.

Unfortunately, Kym hasn't had a very happy life up until now, and the more he tries to think of some happy moment, the more he realizes that there haven't been any. In a matter of seconds he is every bit as depressed as Watkin.

The two men watch with a total lack of feeling as the nightspiders creep closer, venturing so far as to scuttle across Watkin's boot. Getting no reaction from the man, the spider crawls up Watkin's leg, making its way to his neck and the soft flesh that will be so easy to bite.

Kym watches, and the sight is enough to snap him out of the deepest layers of his depression. He notices that the first nightspider is being followed by others, climbing freely on his friend! Kym thinks, desperately trying to get past his fears. What do you do when you are too scared to think? Unthinking, he pulls out his whistle.

If you want to use the whistle, see #56. If not, see #57.

Seeing that Kym is not going to give up easily, Watkin takes his fears in hand, and everything that Kym has been trying to tell him suddenly sinks in. He realizes that it is the nightspiders that are causing his uncharacteristic sense of defeat, and he begins to get angry. As soon as he does, the fog around his emotions lifts, and he is somewhat more in control of himself. He steps in front of Kym, willing to take as many of the terrible stings as are needed for Kym to escape.

With a proud—and very relieved—smile for Watkin, Kym puts the whistle to his mouth. He doesn't really believe that this will do any good, but if he must die here, then he will die defiant, not cowering in terror. Taking a deep breath, he blows into the little silver whistle.

A high-pitched blast of sound cuts through the forest, clean and sharp as a new sword. The nightspiders retreat at once, scrambling over each other in their haste to get away from the terrible piercing whistle. Kym continues to blow, and the slower spiders are literally shriveled by his joyful noise.

Watkin begins to dance to the tuneless blasts, stomping on the nearest nightspiders, crushing them with macabre abandon. Kym joins in, looking oddly graceful as he dances and blows the whistle with more coordination than he thought he possessed.

In no time at all, the nightspiders are no longer a threat. The ones that didn't retreat from the whistle were heartily crushed, so after wiping the spider goo off their boots, the travellers travel on.

The forest seems to lighten a bit, although both men know that this is an illusion; it is still evening. Kym puts the whistle away, but both men purse their lips and whistle, just in case. As they journey deeper into the forest, it even seems as though the underbrush has drawn back, making their passage almost effortless.

Neither man speaks of the fears he has experienced. They never will, for in standing up to them, the fears have been conquered. Kym is still not sure that he can win a woman on his own, but he knows that his courage can never be questioned. And Watkin knows that, while the time may come that he may fail Kym, it won't happen for lack of trying on his part, and so what if he is big and strong? There are worse things to be.

Keeping a sharp eye out for further signs of night-spiders, they forge ahead. Both are tired, but after what they have just been through, neither wants to stop and sleep. Just the thought of lying down on the ground, unprotected, gives them goosebumps.

Before they know it the moon has risen, filling the forest with an eerie white glow. Trees are suddenly backlit, and everything is shaded in twilight blues and purples. Kym and Watkin see each other as shadows moving through a dreamscape, and the total silence, coupled with their exhaustion, reinforces the illusion.

Kym stumbles along, one hand still clutching Watkin's sleeve. He is dreaming of his One True Love, so clearly that he can see her. After a minute he realizes that his eyes are open—and she is still there!

Standing right in front of him he sees a woman, tall and sleek and proud, and he knows that she's the one, but there's something wrong—he can see right through her, and then she's gone.

Kym stops short, pulling Watkin to a halt. He searches the shadowed trees, not quite convinced that it was a dream. And he is right, for there she is again, a few feet ahead of where she was. There is no doubt at all in Kym's mind that he has seen his One True Love. He starts to run after her, but he is still holding on to Watkin, who is asleep on his feet. Kym jerks him awake.

"Wha'? Wha's wrong?" Watkin mumbles, for some

reason trying sleepily to draw a sword—something he neither possesses nor knows how to use. "Kym? Wha're you doing?"

"Come on, we have to hurry!" Kym says, shaking Watkin's arm.

Watkin is immediately awake. "Nightspiders?"

"No!" Kym is quick to reassure his friend. How to explain what he has seen is another matter, however. Deciding to say nothing about the woman for the moment, Kym shrugs. "I just want to be out of here."

Watkin nods. He can certainly understand that! Looking at Kym, however, he realizes that his friend is not telling him the whole truth. When two people have been friends for their whole lives there is little they can hide from each other. Watkin folds his arms across his chest, prepared not to be moved until he finds out what this is all about.

Kym is staring over Watkin's shoulder, for his One True Love has reappeared.

And then Watkin sees her, too, and sees that he can see right through her. "Oh, no," he says, turning to run the other way.

If you wish to run, see #58. If not, see page 137.

Kym grabs the back of his tunic. "I have to follow her," he says, gasping in almost physical pain as she disappears again.

"Well, I don't," replies Watkin, freeing his tunic.

"I need you with me," Kym whispers, not meeting his friend's eyes.

Unable to refuse, Watkin throws an arm around his smaller friend, and they wait to see if the apparition will show herself again. A few seconds go by, and then suddenly they can see her. She doesn't beckon, or in any way gesture that she wants them to follow; she simply fades out, and reappears a few feet farther on.

She leads them deeper into the forest, off of the doubtful security of the faint trail they had been following. They follow her through the weirdly lit landscape, and as they go on they are surrounded by ghostlights. The whole forest seems filled with them. They look like fireflies, but there is nothing at their center, just an empty glow.

Watkin can see that his friend is being somehow called, and it scares him. He feels something sad about this apparition, a sorrow so intense it is frightening. But Kym is all he has, and if Kym follows, then so must he.

Kym, intent on seeing where his vision will lead him, is not unaware of Watkin's fear. Wishing to lend him some comfort in this eerie place, Kym turns to tell Watkin that everything is all right, and as he does so, the ghost rushes at them.

Mouth open in a terrible banshee wail, she swoops straight at them, hands outstretched like ghostly claws.

Watkin turns to run, but Kym stands firm. "Kym, hurry!"

If you want to run, see #58. If not, see #59.

Seeing that Kym isn't running, Watkin stops. To the astonishment of both men, the ghost rushes past them, leaving a frigid wind in her wake. In the strange light they can barely make out what she is attacking until her prey begins to retreat, and it looks as though the very ground and the trunks of the trees are crawling, and then they understand. It was a nest of nightspiders, and she frightened them away from Kym and Watkin.

Afraid to breathe for fear she will disappear, Kym attempts a courtly bow. "Thank you," he says, his voice rather strangled from holding his breath.

To his surprise, the apparition returns his bow, but with somewhat more grace. "You are welcome," she says, and her voice is rich and hollow and sad.

"Who are you?" Watkin asks, staying close behind Kym. He is shivering from the freezing air that surrounds the apparition.

She doesn't take her cold gaze from Kym as she answers him. "My name was Alyssa. I am a ghost."

Kym stares back, totally captivated. "Why?" he asks.

She laughs, a sound unlike any they have ever heard, and for just a moment the air loses some of its chill. "Because I died before I was ready," she says, in answer to Kym's question.

Kym is too overcome with pain for her to answer, so Watkin does. "How did it happen?" he asks, hoping that this is not a breach of some sort of spiritual etiquette.

"I know a place where you can be comfortable," she says, by way of an answer. "Come, and I will take you there."

Kym starts to follow, and Watkin stops him. "Should we?"

If you want to follow Alyssa, see #60. If not, see #61.

The look on Kym's face answers Watkin's question. He is staring past Watkin, eyes fixed on Alyssa. His expression is one of longing and joyful completion all at once. Watkin smiles. "I guess we should," he says, more to himself than to Kym.

Not hearing, Kym moves silently past Watkin. Instead of appearing and disappearing as she has before, Alyssa glides next to Kym, as though she were walking beside him. To Watkin the scene is as beautiful as it is eerie—a pair of young lovers strolling in the moonlight, heads bent together in soft conversation. The only upsetting detail is that he can see through the female half of the pair.

Alyssa leads them through the densest part of the forest, where they occasionally have to skirt thick knots of underbrush and rejoin her on the other side. Accustomed to walking through things, she has forgotten how to deal with obstacles.

The moonlight makes it easy to see as she leads them on a winding path past clumps of deathberry bushes, small but deadly catchswamps, tanglevines, and the ever-present nightspider webs.

Just as Watkin is getting ready to suggest a small rest stop, Alyssa leads them into a moonlit clearing ringed by elder trees, their white trunks glowing faintly in the light. Climbing the trunks and entwined in their branches are exotic night blooms, adding a touch of color with their deep red and rich blue and purple blossoms. In the center of the clearing are several fallen elders and some polished white boulders that have been arranged to form makeshift eating, cooking, and sitting places. Off to one side, a tiny waterfall splashes into a clear stream glistening silver and filling the night with the soothing sound peculiar to running water. It is extremely beautiful, and very inviting.

Kym stands transfixed as Alyssa glides into the clearing and hovers near one of the stone chairs. She indicates the seat with one slender, ghostly hand, and Kym steps into the clearing and sits down, moving like one in a trance.

Alyssa beckons to Watkin. "There are good berries to eat, and in the stream there is wine. It has been here a long time, but I do not think that it has turned." Her voice is unnerving; it is not unlike any woman's voice, but it has a hollow sound, as though she were speaking from the bottom of a well.

Seeing that he is going to get no help from Kym, Watkin bows slightly and walks to the stream. He picks his way carefully, as though afraid that a sudden noise will break whatever spell they are under.

In the stream, he finds two wine bottles wedged in among the rocks. They are covered with moss and mud, but the seals are intact, and when Watkin holds them up the moonlight shining through the bottles shows that the wine is still a fine, clear red.

Kym and Alyssa are at the other side of the clearing, picking berries. At least, Kym is picking berries. Being insubstantial, Alyssa can only point them out. As Watkin looks on, Alyssa bends close to Kym and whispers something in his ear. Kym laughs, and Watkin suddenly wants to cry.

Kym's soft chuckle speaks volumes as to what he is feeling, and Watkin already hurts in sympathy for his friend, for the heartbreak he knows is coming. Everyone knows that ghosts may only walk from sunset to sunrise—when dawn breaks, Alyssa will be gone.

Hearing Watkin's approach, Kym looks up and smiles. His whole face has changed—he is relaxed, for once not guarded, and he looks younger and almost handsome. Watkin forces a smile and holds up the wine bottles, but inside he is desperately trying to think of a way to save his friend from what he knows must come.

They seat themselves on the white stone seats, and Watkin opens the wine. Having no glasses, he carefully cleans the mouths of the bottles, and passes one to Kym. "I propose a toast," Watkin says. "To the success of our Quest."

Kym smiles and raises his bottle. "To true love," he says softly, looking at Alyssa. It is impossible to really see her face, but the freezing air surrounding her gets suddenly warmer, and Watkin thinks that he can see her more clearly, just for a moment.

Kym passes the berries—gathered in an old woven basket—to Watkin, and takes some for himself. Alyssa settles herself a little closer to Kym, radiating concern.

"Will berries be enough for you?" she asks.

"They will have to be," Kym answers, in a tone of voice that Watkin hadn't known his friend was capable of. "It is too dark to hunt."

"I could scare a rabbit to death," Alyssa offers, causing Watkin to choke on his wine.

Alyssa manages somehow to look demure. "When one is dead, one tends to forget how the idea of death affects those who aren't."

Kym is quick to reassure her, starting to change the subject, but Watkin is quicker with his question, taking advantage of the fact that Alyssa introduced the topic. "How exactly did you, eh, come to be in the state in which you are, er, in?"

This time she does not avoid the question. "My friends and I used to gather here, once every seventh. I was lost in a maze of underground caverns in the hills nearby. I fell, and the next thing I knew, I was here."

Kym and Watkin exchange startled glances. "You used to come here?" Watkin asks. "You were a Faerie?"

"Yes!" Alyssa says, her hollow voice sounding surprised and pleased. For a few seconds, Kym and Watkin can see the faintest hint of wings fluttering gracefully behind her.

"We have met some of your friends, or, rather, their descendants," Kym says.

Alyssa looks past them, her demeanor appearing sad. "It is strange to think of my friends having descendants. We were all so young." She sighs, a sound like wind blowing through the branches of a bare tree.

Everyone is silent for a moment, not knowing what to say.

Possibly aware that she has made her guests uncomfortable, Alyssa speaks. "But how do you come to be here?"

"I came to find you," Kym says.

Alyssa becomes a little more solid for a second, and the air grows a bit warmer. "To find *me*?"

About to correct her, Watkin hesitates. Remembering how terrifying she was when she caused the nightspiders away, and her offer to scare up a rabbit for their dinner, he isn't sure that he is ready to deal with the wrath of a jealous ghost.

To tell Alyssa of the Quest, see page 143. To not, see #62.

Watching Alyssa with Kym, he decides that discretion is called for. "We are on a Quest to find my true love," Watkin says. "We have been told of a place called the Dream Palace. Do you know of it?"

Alyssa fades a bit, and the air in the clearing is suddenly winter cold. "Yes, I have heard from travellers passing through that a terrible thing happened there. A spell of some kind went awry, and all that were at the palace are forever asleep. It was done for love, but no one seems to know by who."

"Whom," Kym corrects, proving that not even true love can stand in the way of good grammar.

Watkin shivers slightly. "If true love caused the spell to go awry, then maybe true love can put it right."

Kym gazes at Alyssa, wishing that he could touch her just once. "True love can do anything," he states, desperately wanting to believe it.

Alyssa shakes her head. "Even true love cannot bring back the dead." She and Kym sit motionless, not able to look away from each other.

Watkin stirs uncomfortably, not wanting to interrupt, but not willing to see his friend suffer. "It is chilly here," he says softly. "I will make a fire." He clears his throat, and Alyssa and Kym both shake themselves slightly, as though awakening. "I am going to make a fire," Watkin says a little more loudly. "Is that all right?"

Kym nods, but the moment that Watkin has called up a spark, Alyssa cries out, "No! The shadowbats!"

To put out the fire, see #63. To wait for an explanation, see #64.

The flames are already too big to be extinguished quickly, and Watkin scorches his fingers as he tries. Alyssa vanishes, leaving Kym and Watkin to stare at the sky in fear.

After a moment, Watkin realizes that he doesn't know what it is he is afraid of. "Alyssa!" he calls. "What are shadowbats?"

Her voice comes from directly in front of Watkin, startling him. "They are a creation of the Princess Elvina. They are attracted to warmth and light, and if they can fasten on you, they will suck out your soul." The voice retreats, becoming so faint that Watkin and Kym have to strain to hear her.

"I cannot help you fight them, for all I am is a soul. Good luck!" Although he can't say for sure how, Watkin feels that Alyssa is gone. A glance at Kym confirms this; his friend looks as though all of the light has gone out of him.

The slowly building sound of wings calls their full attention to the sky. They can see nothing but the elder trees throwing shadows on each other, but the sound is coming closer. Suddenly the shadows take shape, and Kym and Watkin realize that they are looking at the shadowbats!

Watkin pushes Kym down behind one of the larger boulders just as the first shadowbat makes its run. It swoops low, nearly brushing the top of Watkin's head as he ducks behind the rock next to Kym.

"How do we fight them?" Kym asks, sounding not nearly as frightened as he would have at the start of the Quest.

"I don't know," Watkin answers, trying to make himself smaller. His hand comes into contact with a sharp rock, and he hefts it, testing its weight.

To throw the rock, see #65. If you don't think that's a good idea, see #66.

Watkins takes aim as best he can, and throws the rock in the general direction from which the shadowbats seem to be coming.

This serves to awaken several shadowbats that had been asleep in the treetops. Kym and Watkin watch in horror as they join their fellows in attacking them.

Kym pats Watkin on the shoulder. "It was a nice idea," he says reassuringly.

Watkin grins briefly. "I think, lad, that what we need is a *good* idea."

"The fire!" Kym exclaims.

"No, the fire wasn't a good idea," Watkin reminds him. "That's what brought—"

"No!" Kym interrupts. "We can use the fire against them!"

"How?"

Kym thinks for a moment. "If we build it up to bonfire size, then maybe the shadowbats will be attracted enough to fly too close!"

Watkin shakes his head. "These are *bats*, Kym, not moths."

"Have you a better idea?" Kym demands. Taken aback by the vehemence in Kym's voice, Watkin merely shakes his head.

They wait until the latest attack passes. Watkin wonders why the shadowbats haven't been able to fasten on him and Kym so far, and concludes that they are too chilled to be overly attractive, especially in comparison to the fire. This sparks an idea, but before Watkin can bring it into focus, Kym pushes him out from behind the rocks.

"Gather sticks to feed the fire!" he orders.

If you'd rather not, see #67. To obey Kym, see next page.

Having no choice, now that he's no longer in the shelter of the rock, Watkin scrambles to the circle of elder trees and begins picking up twigs and small branches that have fallen. Looking back to check the whereabouts of the shadowbats, he sees that Kym is also gathering firewood.

Arms full, they meet in the center of the clearing and throw the wood into the fire. The flames leap a little higher, but the fire can by no stretch of the imagination be called a bonfire.

Racing back to the edges of the clearing, Kym and Watkin work frantically to gather enough kindling to make their plan work.

They dodge the attacks of the shadowbats by weaving, crouching behind rocks, and other maneuvers, but the shadowbats seem to be recovering much more quickly now, and are able to zero in on Kym and Watkin no matter which way they turn.

It is only a matter of time before the men will get too tired to be able to dodge the bats effectively. The plan isn't working.

The reason why hits Watkin suddenly as he watches Kym wipe sweat from his eyes before foraging for more firewood. "Kym," he calls, "this isn't going to work!" Watkin executes a nimble tuck and roll as an alarmingly big shadowbat dives at his head. He bumps to a stop against one of the fallen elder branches which is balanced on two rocks to form a table. Calling for Kym to join him, he slides under the log.

Kym slides in a second later, out of breath and sweaty. "Why isn't this going to work?" Kym pants.

"Because we are making ourselves warmer and easier for the blasted creatures to find! Call Alyssa. Her coldness can save us!"

Kym considers this, afraid to endanger her.

To call Alyssa, see page 147. To try another idea, see page 148.

"Alyssa *is* cold, maybe she can frighten the shadowbats away. I do not want to endanger her, though."

Watkin looks at him incredulously. "Kym, she is already dead. A person cannot possibly be more endangered than *that!*"

Kym can think of no reasonable way to refute this, so he calls to Alyssa. "Help, Alyssa! We need you. We cannot hold out any longer!"

Alyssa does not appear.

For a terrible moment, Watkin entertains the thought that maybe Alyssa will let the shadowbats get them so that she can be with Kym. But if they suck out Kym's soul, then he will not be a ghost, and they will not be together. The thought makes Watkin feel a little better, and he adds his pleas to Kym's. "Alyssa! If the shadowbats were going to get you, they would have by now. You are too cold to attract them!" Watkin looks helplessly at Kym.

Kym sticks his head out of their hiding place to better assess the situation, and before he can duck back in, a shadowbat fastens on his neck! He finds himself suddenly experiencing a profound hopelessness, a draining emptiness that pulls at him, tugging him away from his world and his love and everything that he knows.

Just as suddenly it is gone, and instead, Kym feels a soul-chilling cold. Opening his eyes, he sees Alyssa. She has wrapped herself around him, and her cold has driven the bats away.

Kym beams at her, and at Watkin, who is close enough to be protected. "You came," he says to Alyssa, overwhelmed with love.

As she beams back at him, she begins to warm. The shadowbats attack, and Alyssa—taken by surprise—disappears.

To rely on Alyssa once more, see #68. To rely on yourself, see #69.

Watkin grabs Kym and pulls him toward the stream. "We have to make ourselves cold enough for the bats to lose their appetite!" he yells, dragging the recalcitrant Kym behind him.

Kym fights Watkin, trying to dodge the attacks of the eager shadowbats at the same time. "We will make ourselves sick!" he protests.

"If you don't stop fighting me, you are going to make ourselves *dead*!" He yanks Kym off his feet and pushes him into the stream. With a large splash, Watkin follows.

The shadowbats hover around the stream, feinting and weaving, but as Kym and Watkin begin splashing them with the ice-cold water, they get discouraged and go away.

Cautiously, the two cold and very wet men climb out of the stream, poised to leap back in at the first flap of leathery wings. Both are too miserable to react when Alyssa appears in front of them.

"Oh! You are all wet! You will catch your death!" She glides back and forth between them, fussing first at one, then the other. "You must build up the fire!"

"*No!*" Kym and Watkin shout at the same time. The last thing that they want to do is call attention to themselves.

"It's all right, the shadowbats will not be back." She points to the sky. "It is almost dawn."

"No," Kym says softly. "Not so soon."

Watkin places an arm about his friend and guides him to the dying fire. Heedless of his own condition, he gathers what kindling is left and stokes the flames. After carefully warming them, Watkin hands a wine bottle to Kym and takes the other for himself.

Alyssa settles next to Kym—close enough for him to touch, if it were possible. For a long time neither of them speaks, as in the east the sky begins to lighten.

Watkin watches, wishing that he had somewhere to

go, to give Kym and Alyssa their privacy. But he is too warm, now, and too sleepy to move. He closes his eyes and tries not to listen, that being all he can do.

Kym sits huddled against the white stones, forehead resting on his knees. He cannot get the thought of the Spell of Being out of his mind. If he had it, he could bring Alyssa back to life, and they could live out their lives together, happily ever after.

As it is, they are more than worlds apart, and he cannot even touch her.

Alyssa sits beside him, watching with concern. Being a ghost for as long as she has, she is accustomed to coming to terms with all of the things that she will never have. Knowing that her time with Kym is short, she tries to draw him out, so that they may at least spend the time they have *together*. "Tell me of your Quest."

Kym raises his head and studies Alyssa's face. Although she appears only vaguely to Watkin, Kym can see every detail about her as clearly as he can see his own hand held before him on a bright day—and to him, she is that familiar.

Lined with fatigue, Kym's own face looks older, but it is more than just the strain of their harrowing night. Something has left him, some enthusiasm, or maybe it was even a kind of innocence. Taking a deep breath, Kym grants Alyssa's request, his voice bitter. "Our Quest? On our Quest we travel through lands either remarkably hostile, or completely unremarkable. We meet people who are worse off than we are, but do not seem to know it, and people who are much better off than we, and they know it even less. We have been threatened and taken prisoner and attacked by all manner of creatures, each one worse than the last." He sighs and looks at Alyssa, his face so sorrowful that she wishes she had tears to shed for him.

"We were on a Quest to find our true loves," Kym continues, "and now I have found you, and I cannot have you, and my Quest is over. As is my life."

Alyssa searches helplessly for something to say, and faintly, from far away, they hear the first notes of a dawnsparrow's song.

"Listen to me." Alyssa leans forward, already beginning to fade. "Your life is not yet half over. You will find your true love, and when your life is done, I will be here, and we will be together forever."

The sky is lightening too rapidly now, the sun rising as it always has and always will.

Kym reaches out and tries to touch Alyssa's face, heart breaking as she fades. "We had no time!" he cries.

Alyssa smiles, and touches a hand to his cheek. "We'll have forever!" And she is gone.

When Watkin awakens he finds Kym huddled by the ashes of the fire, an empty wine bottle in his hand. Without speaking, Watkin rebuilds the fire and gathers the best breakfast he can. They eat silently, and attend to all of the other mundane rituals that are habit, and they once again set off.

✿Neither speaks until the clearing is far behind them, and then it is Watkin who breaks the silence. "You will find her again," he says.

Kym stops walking and turns to his friend, his expression desolate. "When I first saw her I was in despair, beset by all of my worst fears. I looked at her once and they were gone. And now she is gone." He sighs, as though unable to muster the strength to go on. "This Quest, for me, is over. I think that you had better go on without me." Kym sits down on a gnarled stump, looking for all the world as though he is never going to move again.

Watkin gazes down at his friend, unsure of what he

should say or do. Always bluff and hearty, he is at home with his own emotions, but has never really been comfortable with the deeper emotions of those around him. Rather than lose his best friend, however, he will try.

Setting down his pack, he sits down next to Kym, sharing his friend's sad silence for a few minutes before speaking. "I do not want to go on without you, my friend."

Kym doesn't even look up. "I cannot go on, *my* friend," Kym says. His voice sounds deeper and sadder and *older* than Watkin has ever heard it.

Watkin sighs, wanting so badly to comfort Kym, and not knowing how. He realizes that his motives are not purely altruistic—a Quest is much more fun with a partner. But there is more to it than that. What will happen to Kym if Watkin leaves him here? Will he just sit here until he dies? Watkin has a sudden shocking feeling that this is exactly what Kym is intending—to sit in this place until he can die and be with Alyssa.

Watkin believes in True Love as much as anyone else, but he is not willing to see his friend give his life for a dead lover, when he could live out his life with live one, then die and have the dead one, too! Watkin thinks that there may be a flaw in his reasoning, but that has never bothered him before, and it doesn't now. He is determined to snap Kym out of this somehow.

Unable to think of anything else, Watkin falls back on his old standby—jolliness. "Oh, come now, lad, there are plenty of other women about—live ones, too—who'd be glad to have your company. You can't pine away for what you can't have!" He watches Kym, unsure as to how this is going to be received. To Watkin's great surprise, Kym smiles.

"You are wrong about that. There will never be anyone else for me. But this is your Quest, too, and you'll find it hard enough to convince some woman to marry you without my haunted face scaring her away!"

Watkin pretends great offense at this, then slaps Kym lightly on the back—noticing that, for the very first time, this doesn't cause Kym to stumble—and laughs heartily. "Let us take your haunted face onto the next stage of our journey, my friend, and we'll just see how much convincing the women will need!"

Kym doesn't laugh—it will be some time before he can—but he smiles and looks about, deciding which way to go. To the northeast the forest gives way to a barren plain, while in the southeast it comes up against cliffs. To the east is more forest.

To go northeast, see #70. To go southeast, see #71. To go east, see #72.

Kym decides that he has had just about enough of the forest, and turns toward the northeast. What better place than a barren plain to make him forget the sorrow he's encountered in the lush woods? "Let's go this way," he suggests.

Watkin agrees and they set off, trying to pretend that they are ready for whatever is coming next.

VII: *The Endless Desert*

The desert seems endless, nothing but sand in every direction. Kym and Watkin stumble along, feeling more exhausted than is physically probable because of the unrelenting landscape. They can see the vague outline of rocky cliffs on the horizon, and the faint blue-green haze of the forest behind them, but there is nothing nearby to break the monotony of their travel.

Almost nothing.

Looking up to measure how far it is to the cliffs, Watkin is stunned to see a brightly colored tent about ten feet in front of them. He stops, shaking his head until he is dizzy—which only confuses him more, as there now appears to be two tents—and reaches out for Kym.

Kym barely falters at the tug on his sleeve. Head down, he is wearily counting his steps, hoping to get through this part of the journey as quickly as possible. Watkin's tugs are becoming more urgent, however, and Kym finally raises his head to see what is the matter. He, too, is somewhat nonplussed by what he sees.

There is a tent standing in front of them, gaily striped

silk walls flapping merrily in a nonexistent breeze. A pair of large guards stand to either side of the tent's opening, and from somewhere inside the tent, Kym and Watkin can hear the sound of running water. As they cautiously approach, a familiar voice bids them welcome and invites them to enter.

Watkin and Kym stop at the opening, peering through the opaque gauze curtain hanging there. "I don't like the look of this," Watkin says. "What do you think?"

To bypass the tent, see #73. To enter, see next page.

Kym shakes his head at Watkin's caution. "Don't you know who this is? It isn't possible, but I would swear that was the voice of the young man who started all of this!" Kym pushes aside the gauze and steps inside the tent, with Watkin a step behind.

They are greeted warmly by what turns out to be the very same young traveller who first encouraged their Quest. He is dressed as before, but his ramshackle wagon has been replaced by this bright tent. "Welcome, adventurers!" he says, his voice as soft and rich as the velvet cushions on which he sits. "Care for some ale?"

Watkin accepts with enthusiasm, settling his dusty body carefully on the soft pillows. He takes a large draught of the cold ale and sighs, perfectly contented.

Kym accepts also, but remains standing, looking inconspicuously about for the source of the running water sounds he had heard.

The brightly dressed young man smiles up at Kym and indicates a cluster of shiny curtains in the corner of the tent. "What you are seeking may be found there, and you are welcome to it."

"Our true loves?" Watkins gasps, choking on his ale.

"No" the young man laughs. A bath, of sorts." He reaches out and pulls a tassel hanging near the shiny curtains, and they part to reveal a small waterfall, cascading out of thin air and disappearing into a silk handkerchief placed on the ground.

Kym steps behind the curtains—modestly closing them—disrobes, and steps under the little waterfall. It is an interesting feeling, but he cannot see where the water is coming from, so he asks.

"It is very simple," the young man replies. "A Water-Out-of-Air spell, combined with a special Handkerchief-for-Mothers-with-More-Than-Three-Children spell. Works every time."

"Every time?" Watkin asks, not trusting magic as much as most people do.

"Well, no," the young man replies, his face suddenly sad. "Sometimes spells get out of hand, especially if the person casting them chooses one too complicated for his ability."

Watkin nods, vowing never to mess with magic that's too complicated—which lets out just about *all* magic, as far as he's concerned. He and the young man share a simple meal of bread and cheese, and chat about various things until Kym returns from his shower-bath, all clean and ready to tackle the rest of the Quest.

He sits down across from the young man and gratefully accepts a full plate and a second tankard as Watkin disappears behind the curtains to wash his dusty body in the magical waterfall

When Watkin reappears, his homely face scrubbed pink, the young man presents them with a small sack containing provisions, and a fascinating proposition.

"I have a spell here that might be of interest to you," he begins in a serious voice. "You have come far, and seen and done a lot, and I wonder if there aren't things that you would change, had you the chance."

Kym and Watkin both nod.

"I have a spell that would let you go back and face a situation afresh, as though it had not happened before. I have no use for it. If you want it, it is yours."

If you want the spell, see #74. If not, see #75.

Watkin and Kym exchange glances, and are surprised to find themselves in agreement. At Kym's nod, Watkin speaks for them both. "There are many things that we would each change, but such is the nature of life. We have no wish to do any of the things we have done over again. The choices were made, let them stand."

The young man smiles at the travellers, making them feel as though they have just passed a test. "In that case, you must be on your way—there are many more choices ahead of you."

Kym and Watkin stand and make their way out of the tent, noticing as they pass by that the guards flanking the entrance are not real, but painted wood. As they once again begin the long hike toward the cliffs, the young man calls to them a last bit of encouragement. "What you seek is not far away," he calls.

"We have already had a bath!" Watkin yells back, laughing.

The man laughs also. "I meant your true loves!" he answers, his laugh fading into the sandy silence of the desert.

Kym and Watkin hike on.

VIII: The Warrior's Tale

When they finally reach the forbidding cliffs, Kym and Watkin at first despair of finding a way to climb them. They travel along the rocky foothills, skirting huge tumbled boulders and sliding in patches of talus caused by uncounted years of rockfalls from the cliffs. When they do find a path leading over the rocks, they are extremely surprised to find a guard standing at its foot.

They duck behind a nearby boulder before the guard notices them, so that they may decide what to do.

"I suppose we could simply overpower him and go on through," suggests Watkin.

"Why not just talk to him, and find out what he's guarding?" Kym asks.

Watkin frowns. "Because he might shoot us on sight."

Kym peers around the rock for a better look at the sentry. "I don't think that he can shoot us with a rusted lance, and that is the only weapon he appears to have." Kym looks again. "In fact, I doubt that he can even lift that lance."

Watkin looks for himself, and has to agree with Kym.

The sentry is a very old man, thin and frail, and he doesn't seem much of a threat to anyone. His lance is rusted, and his mismatched armor is tarnished and dented. As they watch, he shifts wearily from foot to foot, looking tired and hot and very bored.

"Well, let's go," Kym says, standing up and starting out from behind the boulder.

To approach the guard openly, see next page. Sneaky types, See #76.

Kym's footsteps crunch loudly on the gravel as he approaches the guard, who doesn't seem to hear him. Looking back at Watkin and shrugging, Kym clears his throat loudly. There is no reaction from the sentry.

Thinking that the situation calls for more direct action, Watkin steps in front of Kym and raps sharply on the old man's helmet.

The sentry jumps and screams, inadvertently throwing his lance aside, where it strikes the ground an inch from Kym's left foot.

Kym leaps backward and catches his heel on a small rock. Pinwheeling his arms for balance, he hits Watkin in the eye, causing his larger friend to stagger backwards with a loud yell, which scares the old sentry, making him scream again. Watkin puts out a hand to reassure the poor man, but with one eye squeezed tightly shut his depth perception is off, and he strikes the old man's helmet instead, causing the visor to slam shut with a bang.

In the ensuing silence a voice not belonging to any of them calls out, "What in the seven trines is going on here?"

Kym, sprawled on his back in the dirt; Watkin, hunched over with both hands pressed to his eye; and the old man, walking around in small circles as he tries to reopen his visor, all react straight from the heart of their childhoods. Becoming perfectly still, each one answers, as sincerely as possible, "Nothing!"

The owner of the voice marches into sight, fussing at them one by one and collectively. He is an old man, even older than the easily startled sentry, and much smaller. "Well, I never, not in all my born days. What *is* this world coming to?" he asks, grabbing the sentry and pulling him over to a nearby boulder. The little man steps up onto the boulder and begins to tug at the stubbornly closed visor. "Now how did this—stand still—I declare, this is just too much, turn around and—*there* we go!"

He pops the visor open with a well-aimed knock on the top of the helmet, making the sentry sit down abruptly, shaking his head as though he had water in his ears.

Kym and Watkin watch this performance in silence, hoping to escape the fussy old man's notice, but they are not that lucky. Hopping down from his rock, he rushes over to Watkin and demands to inspect his injured eye. When Watkin refuses to bend down, the old man grabs his beard and tugs hard, bringing Watkin to his knees.

"There now, let's have a look! This won't hurt a bit, nothing to be afraid of, well, I never!" Satisfied that he has identified the problem, the old man pulls a handkerchief out of his pocket and ties it around Watkin's head, covering his injured eye, and a good part of his uninjured one.

Before Watkin can say so much as a thank-you, the old man has discovered the stunned Kym, and is busily helping him up and brushing him off, filling the air with expressions of sympathy alternating with exclamations over Kym's skinniness. Ending his running commentary with a promise to Kym to "fatten you up a bit, you sorry critter," the old man brushes off his hands and folds his arms across his chest with the air of someone who has just managed to straighten up the entire world singlehandedly, and a better world it is for it. "Now suppose you tell me just who you are and what you're doing here!" he demands.

Kym looks at Watkin and shrugs.

If you wish to tell him the whole story, see #77.
If you wish to tell him part of the story, see next page.
If you don't want to tell him anything, see #78.

Watkin considers for a moment, and then decides to share part of their story in the event that the two strange old men possess some information that might be of help on their Quest. "My friend and I are on a Quest," he begins, wary of stating his name to strangers.

"What are your names, you ill-mannered creature? Well, I never! Do you think we want to hear the life stories of a pair of perfect strangers, hmm?" He turns to the sentry, still seated as before. "Have you ever? I most certainly haven't, I must say." He looks at Watkin. "Well, go on, I dare say, standing there gaping. We could all be dead of heat frustration before you're through!"

Not sure whether to be intimidated or amused, Watkin introduces himself and Kym. The fussy little man reveals that his name is Ilex, and that he is a powerful wizard and companion to Tarran, a great and fearless knight. Kym and Watkin both ask where the knight is, and suffer some embarrassment when Ilex points to the old sentry.

As they attempt to apologize without making things any worse, Tarran gets slowly to his feet and removes his helmet. Seen close up his face is very pleasant— plain but good-natured. It is obvious that he must have been a handsome young man, in an earnest sort of way. He is tall and still very straight—it is the ruined armor that gives the impression of feebleness. His voice is soft and slow as he reassures the travellers, and Kym and Watkin find themselves liking him immediately, as he invites, them inside for a cool drink.

If you wish to go inside, see #79. To decline, see #80.

Kym and Watkin look at each other in confusion. They are standing at the base of a rocky cliff, at one end of a flat desert, and there doesn't seem to be any "inside" that they can see.

Noticing their bewildered looks, Tarran smiles. "Forgive me, gentlemen, I should have been more specific. What I meant, I suppose, was more along the lines of *up* and inside." He points to a spot in the cliff face about ten feet above their heads. Looking closely, Kym and Watkin can see that a small piece of the rock is not rock at all, but rock-colored cloth hanging over an opening set far back on a shadowed ledge.

There doesn't seem to be any way to reach it, however.

Ilex frowns at their confusion and begins waving his arms wildly, a running commentary beginning as though set in motion by the movement. "Well, of all the—I never! Stand here all day, die of thirst. One would think you whippers could do a little thing like this yourselves. I declare!" His arm-waving increases, accompanied by much foot-shuffling and a creditable bump and grind.

The end result is a wild tornado of dust, rocks, and sand, (mixed with a good bit of water when the stopper in Tarran's dented canteen comes loose) which lifts the four men and carries them safely onto the rock ledge in front of the camouflaged opening.

"Is that the only way up and down from here?" Kym asks when the dust settles.

Tarran smiles his slow, sweet smile, and shakes the sand out of his helmet. "How do you think my armor got this way?"

Kym and Watkin laugh, and are glared at goodnaturedly by Ilex, who seems much happier now that he is out of the hot sun.

The knight and his companion show the travellers

through the opening behind the curtain and into a large, comfortably furnished cave.

There are heavy carved chairs and inlaid tables; thick rugs woven in plain but comfortable patterns; and, surprisingly, growing plants of various kinds set about the room in colorful pots. The roof of the cave is cut out in an open lattice pattern which lets in plenty of sunlight and fresh air, but very little of the desert heat. There is the familiar tingle of magic present, but neither Kym nor Watkin can identify the numerous spells woven together to such perfect effect.

They are rather impolitely stunned when Tarran credits the work to Ilex. After his performance in airlifting them, the travellers had surmised that he was a wizard of very little power. Neither is rude enough to mention this, but they are curious enough to be pleased when Ilex brings it up himself.

"See the power I had? And to think, gone for the sake of that—what can you do? Damn brat!" He bustles out of the room, his voice trailing off as he goes.

Tarran smiles and winks at Kym and Watkin. "Don't mind my friend. His power was all but ruined trying to help someone who'd gotten in over his head. He hasn't been the same since." He gestures Kym and Watkin to two cozy-looking chairs, and excuses himself to slip into something more comfortable. Kym remarks that *anything* should prove more comfortable than that armor, but Tarran smiles and says that he's grown used to it over the years.

Alone in the sunny room, Kym and Watkin have a moment to take stock of their situation and confer.

"What do you think of all of this?" Watkin asks.

Kym thinks a moment. They have seen some strange things, so far on their Quest, but few things more intriguing than this. "I think that we should tell these men of our Quest and see if they can help us. They may have information of value to us. And we may be able to help them."

Watkin laughs, recognizing at once the look in Kym's eyes. "And maybe if we tell them our story, they will tell us theirs." He has to laugh again at Kym's guilty look.

Although his friend was always too shy to pursue it, Watkin has long been aware of the fact that Kym possesses enough curiosity to kill ten cats, nine times each. The Quest is very noticeably building Kym's self-confidence, however, and the added willingness to explore is nearly as exhilarating for Watkin to watch as he is sure it is for Kym to experience.

In perfect agreement, they sit companionably and watch the sunset through the latticed roof. Two moons have risen by the time Tarran returns. It takes a long time to remove armor, especially when half of the closures are rusted and all of it is dented out of shape.

Delicate glasses of equally delicate wine are passed around and Ilex asks again what Kym and Watkin are doing so far from nowhere.

Watkin tells the whole story, stopping often to wet his throat with the exquisite wine.

When the story is told and the wine is done, Ilex suggests that they get some sleep and prepares to show them to the guest quarters.

"But aren't you going to tell us the tale of how you and Tarran came to be here?" Kym asks.

"Tale? Well, I never; there's no tale, impertinent whipper, ask *me* about a tale! I could tell you a few things about tales, I'll wager. Honestly!"

Unable to make sense of this latest string of mixed indignation and insult, Kym and Watkin allow themselves to be led off to the guest quarters.

These turn out to be cleverly constructed beds, one above the other, hidden away in a wall cabinet in a rear corner of the cave. The mattresses are stuffed with soft down, and there are fat pillows and thick comforters. The stars shining through the openwork roof light the room with a soft, friendly glow, and the rhythmic snoring from Ilex's room sounds more and more like waves breaking on a warm, rocky beach, as Kym and Watkin settle happily into sleep.

Kym is still dreaming of that beach when Watkin awakens him the next morning by rudely pulling Kym's comforter off his sleeping body and onto the floor. Forgetting that he is sleeping on the higher of the two beds, Kym, too, ends up on the floor when he rolls over to retrieve the blanket. Making the best of a bad situation, he rolls himself up in the comforter and, despite Watkin's insistence that he wake up, attempts to go back to sleep.

If you really don't want to be awakened, see #81.

Watkin is determined, however, and Kym eventually gives up and raises himself on an elbow so that Watkin can see him glaring. "What is it?" he asks, sounding much grumpier than he really feels.

"I think that we should get up. Listen!"

Straining his ears, Kym can hear the sound of an argument coming from Tarran's room—or rather, half of an argument.

Ilex's voice is louder than it seems usual for it to be—which is very loud—and, if possible, he sounds even more agitated. Tarran's voice is still the same soft rumble it was last night, but there is a slight edge to it.

Although Kym and Watkin cannot make out what is being said much of the time, they do recognize their own names, and several references to some sort of helmet. Both men begin to get excited when they clearly hear the words "Dream Palace."

Kym clutches the comforter to his chest. "What do you think this means?" he asks Watkin.

"Well, obviously they know something about the place we are seeking!" He reaches for his clothing, thrown over the back of a nearby chair. "Let's see if we can find out what!" He begins to dress.

Kym sits up, the warm comforter forgotten. "You mean eavesdrop? That isn't polite." He stands and reaches for his shirt, which is folded neatly with the rest of his clothing, on a small table.

Watkin stops in the middle of buckling his belt. "So what?"

If you want to eavesdrop, see #82. If not, see page 171.

"So it isn't polite!" Kym says, sitting firmly down on the nearest chair. "If our hosts wish to tell us something, then they will." He crosses his arms, then, for good measure, crosses his legs, too.

Watkin scowls. While Kym's newfound confidence is gratifying to see when turned on other people, Watkin doesn't care too much to see it used on himself. Unable to think of a good argument for spying on people who have offered them hospitality, he drops disconsolately down onto his bed and endeavors to sulk for a while.

Seeing this, Kym knows he's won. Watkin is too jovial to sustain a really good sulk, and sure enough, before Kym can count to ten, Watkin is back on his feet suggesting heartily that there is at least no harm in spying out some breakfast.

After remaking their beds—Kym's idea—they head toward what looks at first to be a kitchen. On closer inspection, they realize that it is a laboratory of the kind used by alchemists and midwives and physicians. There are all sorts of interestingly shaped bottles and jars; stacks of books—some dusty, some well-worn, and clean; utensils, from the sinister to the silly-looking; and pots full of dark blue flowers all lined up on a shelf near the ceiling under very bright glowsticks.

Standing on tiptoe underneath the pots, Kym can see a sloppily lettered sign saying "Sleepshade." This means nothing to him, of course, as he cannot read, but the flowers look a lot like wine poppies—flowers that give off a pleasant wine flavor when chewed, but have no other effect. He reaches for one, and hesitates.

If you wish to chew on a blossom, see #83.

Deciding that tasting things with labels one cannot read is not a good idea, Kym wanders over to a different part of the laboratory. He is examining what looks like a crystal ball, with the image of a lady's face somehow embedded inside, when he and Watkin hear footsteps approaching. They glance at each other guiltily, and turn to face whatever is coming.

It is, of course, Ilex and Tarran, and to the travellers' relieved surprise, they are not angry to find Kym and Watkin in the laboratory. On the contrary, when they compliment Ilex on the fascinating array of objects, he offers them a tour.

Kym points first to the dark blue flowers. "What are these?" he asks. "They look like wine poppies."

Watkin looks up at Kym's words. He hadn't noticed the little flowers before, but seeing them now, he is surprised by recognition. "My old granny makes tea out of those! They only bloom at the trine!"

Kym is taken aback. "Seven years is a long time to wait for tea!" he says. "Why does it take so long for them to flower?"

Ilex answers, his normal hysterical rambling toned down considerably. "Sleepshade has inner magic, don't you know. And the trine, well, that is the most important magical influence in this world, I must say. Any spell performed at the time when all three moons are full is magic that will last forever!"

"Forever?" Kym asks, awed by the concept.

"Well, no, not really forever. You think anything lasts forever? *Nothing* lasts *forever!* A spell cast at the trine will last very *close* to forever, I have to tell you— unless the person who cast it undoes it at the next trine, that is. You see?"

Kym and Watkin see. "What kind of magic does sleepshade have?" Watkin asks, picking up the crystal ball that Kym had noticed earlier.

"What does it sound like? Honestly, I never!" Ilex answers, snatching the crystal ball from Watkin's huge hand. "Sleepshade puts you to sleep, and if you take too much of it, you don't ever wake up, do you?"

At this point, Kym becomes aware of an uncomfortable emptiness in his stomach, and asks shyly about breakfast. Ilex herds them all out of the room and into a large, bright kitchen opening off the south side of the cave.

He bustles around the firepit and the warming ovens, fixing wonderful cinnamon-scented coffee, a delicious hot bread baked with honey—the recipe for which comes from his sister, he says, amusing Kym and Watkin with thoughts of what his sister is probably like—hot fried tuberoots, and fresh eggs.

As they eat, Kym continues his line of questioning, stopping every once in a while to pass the bread or freshen his coffee. "Lots of plants make one sleep. What is magical about sleepshade?"

Ilex scowls, but Kym gets the impression that the scowl is not for him. "*Some* people have discovered that sleepshade doesn't have to be given to a person for the magic to work, if you can credit that! I mean to say, if you sprinkle it on their image, it works just as well. And I daresay, it doesn't even have to be a real image, either! Imagine! Any more questions, you whippers?"

Whippers with questions, see #84. Whippers without, see #85.

Kym looks at Watkin, who nods, his face serious. Travelling together for as long as they have, under such trying conditions, has intensified their rapport to a remarkable extent. In times like this they need only a look to convey their thoughts. So it is with the full confidence of Watkin's unspoken support that Kym confesses that he and Watkin overheard the argument between their hosts.

Watkin adds that they are not interested in anything other than the clearly heard reference to the place called the Dream Palace.

The effect of his words is startling. Ilex stands up so quickly that his chair topples over with a crash. "Well, I never!" he exclaims, and runs from the room.

Looking to Tarran for some explanation, Kym and Watkin find that he is paying no attention to them. He has a faraway look in his eyes, and his face is very sad.

Kym touches his arm, moved. "Is there anything that we can do?"

Tarran comes back to himself slowly. "I don't think that there is anything anyone can do. But if you will join me, I think I have a tale worth telling, and one that can use the comfort of a little ale and a soft chair."

He stands and beckons for them to follow. Once back in the comfortable room where they spoke the night before, Tarran gestures the men to chairs and pours three tankards of ale. He does not sit, preferring to pace as he speaks. "Ilex doesn't like to talk about the Dream Palace. You see, one of his relatives caused the, uh, problems." Tarran's voice fades a little as he paces the length of the cave, then becomes louder as he approaches.

Kym and Watkin exchange glances, then make a noncommittal noise. So far, Tarran has told them nothing they do not already know.

Tarran watches the travellers and smiles. "Well, I

guess you know all of this already. He paces for a while, sipping his ale and thinking.

"The problem at the Dream Palace," Watkin prompts.

"Yes," Tarran agrees, apparently ready to continue his narrative. "Ilex tried to fix it, but the spell was too large even for him. Most of his powers were burned out in the attempt."

"I didn't know magic worked that way," Kym says. He, like most people, had never given the mechanics of magic much thought. Learning that it has some internal laws pleases him for some reason.

"A person can't use more of a thing than that person has. That's true for anything. Ilex tried to use a kind of power that he just didn't have enough of, and in the end, he was left with almost no powers at all."

"But I'm regaining them, I should say!" Ilex shouts, hurrying into the room. "There are spells and there are *spells*, and I daresay I know which are which!" He stops in front of Kym and Watkin, glaring. "You want a Quest, well, let me tell you, I can give you a Quest! Talk to *me* about Quests, will you, hmph!"

"We already have a Quest," Kym remarks, anxious to learn more about the Dream Palace. "Who put the people to sleep, and how, and why?" He is intensely curious.

If you are as curious as Kym, see #86.

"Never mind about that! What kind of a Quest?" Watkin asks. He is beginning to wonder if there might be a variety of Quest more interesting than the one in which he is engaged. Catching Kym's eye, he is amused to see that his friend is thinking much the same thing.

"An important Quest, you can count on it! A Quest which, if completed with success, will bring you all that you desire—" He pauses for effect, and it seems to be the first time that he has so much as paused for a breath in two days. "—and more!" he finishes. Without another word, he runs to the nearest cabinet and removes a rope, some pitons, and two dented canteens. "Well, then, let's go! Just sitting there, I declare! You've got things to do, places to go!"

"Ilex, old friend, you haven't told these gentlemen just what it is they're supposed to be doing," Tarran says. Since Ilex entered the room, Tarran has been sitting in a corner chair, just watching. He unfolds himself from the low chair and walks slowly across to where Ilex waits impatiently, arms full of the mysterious supplies. Smiling down at his agitated friend, Tarran gently takes the supplies from Ilex and guides him to a chair. "Now suppose you let me tell the story, all right?"

Ilex nods.

"Well, you see, gentlemen, there is this helmet. It's in an eagle's nest in this very cliff," Tarran begins in his slow, soft voice. "It's called the Rose-Gold Helmet, because of its color, I guess, and it contains all of the knowledge in all of the world. Whoever wears it knows everything there is to know."

"If it's so special, what is it doing in an eagle'e nest?" Watkin asks.

"That is where it is being hidden," Tarran explains. "There are certain people who should *never* get their hands on this helmet. We were put here to guard it until someone worthy of its power came along."

Kym looks at Watkin, beginning to get excited. If he had the helmet, he would know how to finally be with his One True Love! He could solve all of the problems of all of the people he and Watkin have met in their travels!

The ideas chase each other through his mind, the beginning of a new and more exciting thought barely giving the preceding ones time to sink in. They could travel together, he and his Love, and Watkin and *his* True Love, and they could solve all of the problems they came across! His face shines with excitement.

Watkin is feeling much the same way. All of the knowledge in the world! If he had this helmet, no one would ever again think that he was all muscle! People would respect him for what he *knew* and he would use that knowledge to help them. After he used it to help himself and Kym on their Quest, of course, but that wouldn't take long, not with the Rose-Gold Helmet.

His elation fades as the helmet's potential sinks in. Kym voices the thought for both of them, before Watkin has completely formed it.

"Why are you telling us about this?" Kym asks.

Tarran and Ilex exchange glances, deferring to each other as though each were too embarrassed or overcome to speak.

"We are old men," Tarran says, clearing his throat. "Even if we had all of the knowledge in the world, what use is it to us in the face of the one piece of knowledge of which we are always aware—our own mortality?"

Kym looks at Watkin. Tarran's words are pretty, and their meaning compelling, but Kym is not quite reassured. It is true that Tarran and Ilex are old, but Kym has heard of youthening spells. If the helmet possesses all of the world's knowledge, then surely Ilex could find out how to get his powers restored to full potency. Once he did that, he could rejuvenate himself and Tarran. This seems to be an incredible treasure. Why give it away?

Ilex speaks up, his ranting tone breaking Kym's line of thought.

"All of this gawking—I beg your pardon. Has the obvious not occurred to you whippers?"

Watkin looks at Kym. Without speaking, they agree to wait and see before making any further decision on the matter. They look at Ilex and indicate that it has not.

Ilex sighs, as though really vexed that he has to say this out loud.

"Honestly! The blasted helmet is in a damn eagle's nest! I must say, us two old codgers are too feeble to get up there and get it back, don't you know? Are you going to get it for yourselves or not?"

"Why can't you use your magic whirlwind to get it down?" Kym asks, ever sensible.

Ilex snorts. "Because it's all I can do to get as high as this cave. Now, are you going to get this helmet, or not?"

If you are, see #87. If not, see #88.

Watkin stands up. "All right, let's go," he says, marveling at himself. It amazes him how easily he has adapted to this life.

Kym also rises, also surprised at himself. His feelings, unlike Watkin's, reflect a certain amount of pride in himself. Where Watkin has always known he has courage, Kym is realizing his own bravery a little more fully each day.

With a wild waving of his arms and a bit of foot stomping thrown in for emphasis, Ilex whirlwinds the little party down to the ground. He points out the eagle's nest, set high in the sheer wall of the cliff.

Watkin and Kym study the featureless rock. "Is there a way up there?" Watkin asks.

"There are two ways, both difficult and dangerous."

Watkin grins at Kym. "There hasn't been much on this Quest that wasn't one or the other."

"Or both," Kym adds, grinning back at his friend. "Tell us about the two ways."

Tarran does. "The first way is a path up through the rocks, over that way." He points to a faint trail winding up the face of the cliff, invisible unless one knows where to look. "The other way is to scale the wall using ropes and pitons. One way is just as dangerous as the other, but they are your only two choices."

Kym studies the cliff, not overly pleased with his options. "Are you certain Ilex couldn't just . . ." Kym waves his arms in imitation of the old wizard's method of airlifting.

Tarran laughs, averting a breathless tirade from Ilex. "Don't you think that if he could, we would have retrieved the helmet ourselves? No, these are your only choices."

To scale the wall, see #89. To take the path, see #90. To do neither, see #91.

Watkin and Kym both tend to feel that their chances for success will be better if they use the rope and pitons. Neither has ever done any climbing, but they are both intimidated by the narrow, twisting trail that is their only other alternative.

They waste a good bit of time trying to figure out exactly how the pitons are used, and finally Kym suggests that they simply have Ilex whirlwind the rope up to the nest and attach it to the ledge with a Spell for Sticking Things to Other Things.

Ilex acknowledges that such a feat is well within his capacities, don't you know, and with a remarkably small amount of arm-waving and other esoteric body language, the thing is accomplished.

It is decided that Kym should go first. Being lighter, if he should for some reason slip, Watkin has a better chance of saving them both than if their positions were reversed.

Using a nearby boulder, Watkin's strong hands, a boost from Tarran, and plenty of shouted run-on instructions from Ilex, Kym climbs precariously onto Watkin's shoulders and grasps the rope.

There is some debate as to whether he should attempt to retrieve the helmet on his own, but Watkin refuses to stay behind and let his friend face the danger alone.

Touched at his friend's loyalty, Kym resolves to do him proud. Wrapping one ankle in the rope, he reaches up as high as he can, grabs the rope firmly in both hands and leaps off of Watkin's shoulders.

The Spell for Sticking Things to Other Things comes unstuck and Kym falls to the ground in a heap, unhurt, and spectacularly unimpressed with Ilex's powers of cohesion.

★After a quick conference, Kym and Watkin decide to

take the precarious-looking path up to the nest of the eagle.

It takes some delicate maneuvering to get Watkin as far as the start of the path, which is really no more than a narrow ledge cut into the sheer face of the cliff.

In some parts there are a series of ledges, and the ascent must be made by climbing from one to the other. Some are wide enough to be relatively comfortable, but others are so narrow and short as to be no more than hand- and footholds. For the first time in his life, Kym is thankful for his small appendages and light-weight body.

Halfway up the cliff the men become aware of a pitiful noise. Clinging to the narrow ledge on which he is perched, Watkin carefully leans back his head to peer at the eagle's nest.

There are baby eagles in it.

Both Kym and Watkin had assumed that the nest in question was long deserted. The presence of baby eagles can only mean one thing—a mama eagle.

Watkin and Kym pause in their harrowing ascent to reflect upon what will most probably happen to them when the mother eagle finds them poking around her babies. The thought is not a pretty one.

By now, however, they are almost there. Both men can see the glint of gold in the nest, a helmet the rose-gold of a sunset. Sitting in the nest, it appears to be a giant, shiny egg. Both men hope fervently that the mother eagle does not see it that way.

Kym is just preparing to climb onto the ledge holding the nest, when one of the baby eagles suddenly either swoops or falls—Kym cannot tell which—out of the nest and straight at him.

To bat at it, see #92. To catch it, see #93. To do nothing, see #94.

Kym ducks in against the cliff wall and covers his face. As softhearted as he is, he hopes sincerely that the baby eagle is flying and not falling. On the other hand, he is not willing to risk the wrath of the mother eagle should she come back in time to find him clutching her baby in his sweaty fist.

With a tiny screech, the baby eagle flies in a circle around his head and glides back into the nest. Kym has just enough time to exchange a relieved glance with Watkin, who had also decided to duck and cover, and grab the helmet before the mother eagle swoops majestically down on him, talons extended.

Once again, both men duck, and the eagle flies past them and into the nest. She doesn't appear overly upset that her great golden egg is gone, causing Kym and Watkin to consider the fact that birds may be somewhat smarter than they had always assumed.

The climb down is every bit as precarious as the climb up; more so for Watkin, who carries the helmet in a large drawstring sack tied to his belt.

Feeling the helmet bumping against his leg, he stops his descent to consider what they should do with it, causing Kym to mistake his head for a foothold and try to stand on it.

"Ouch! Kym, do you really think this helmet is what those two old men say it is?" he asks, wishing he could let go of the ledge and rub his head where Kym stepped on it.

Kym looks down at his friend. Seeing the pained look on Watkin's face, Kym rubs the man's injured head with his foot while he thinks. "I think that we should try it out when we get down there."

If you want to try out the helmet, see #95. If not, see #96.

Their arrival back on horizontal ground is accomplished in a combination slide and fall that leaves both men dusty and bruised but otherwise unhurt.

Ilex has conjured up ice cold ale in frosted mugs, thick sandwiches, and fruit. The four men find a moderately shady spot near a pile of boulders and have a picnic.

Swallowing a mouthful of the cool ale, Watkin asks jovially if Tarran will fill them in on the details concerning the rose-gold helmet.

"Well, now, I don't know if I should do that," Tarran answers.

Kym and Watkin exchange startled glances. "Why not?" Kym asks.

"Because you may as well try it on and find out all you want to know yourselves. That way you'll be sure before you leave that it really works the way we said it would."

Watkin shakes his head. "I don't think so."

Tarran looks surprised, but he calmly holds out a hand to stifle the inevitable outburst from Ilex. "You don't think so. What does that mean?"

"It means," Watkin says, "that we were willing to trust you enough to risk our lives to get it, so we trust you enough to believe you. We'll try it on later, when we are more rested."

Tarran and Ilex insist, however, and Watkin, aware that he is beginning to feel a little fuzzy, decides that he'd better do this before he fades out altogether. Taking the helmet from where it is tied to his belt, Watkin places the powerful device on his head.

At first nothing happens, but when he says so, Kym encourages him to try to open his mind and let the helmet do the work.

Watkin does so. Taking a deep breath, he imagines his mind as a dry sponge, and the helmet a well of cool, deep water. Immediately his head is filled with a thousand bits of information, so much that he cannot sort it out, and it makes him dizzy. He pulls the helmet off and stands up to clear his head—and immediately falls over.

Kym stands up also, trying to reach his friend, and also falls. He realizes at once that he and Watkin have been drugged. But why? His thoughts are beginning to drift off in all directions, and he struggles to stay awake. Because he has not drunk as much of the drugged ale as his friend, Kym is still awake enough, a few minutes later, to see Tarran take the Rose-Gold Helmet gently from Watkin's outflung hand.

Tarran moves close to Watkin and arranges the large man into a somewhat more comfortable position. "They seemed like real nice fellows, don't you think?" he says softly.

"Well, I never! Of course I do, and that's why they're sleeping, not dead. They'll be all right in a few hours, I dare say. Hung over, and they won't remember much of this, but they'll live. Honestly."

As he fades into unconsciousness, Kym hears Tarran's sweet, slow voice instruct Ilex to "send them somewhere nice."

Ilex's answer is also soft, and there is a pleasant rustling sound, as though someone wearing heavy clothing were casting a spell with a lot of arm-waving.

Kym has enough consciousness left to realize that is exactly what is happening. There is a soft, cool breeze on his face, and a very nice sensation of floating, and then he is asleep.

IX: The Realm of the Wizard King

Kym becomes aware of a soft voice and an even softer touch, a long time before he realizes that the place in which he is awakening is not the same place in which he went to sleep. Or was it *put* to sleep? He vaguely remembers drinking cool ale, and things got fuzzier and fuzzier, and now he's—where?

Sitting up seems like the best idea, until he tries it and is assaulted by the worst headache he has ever had in his life. It is so bad that the name "headache" doesn't even apply. Trying to think up a better name for it increases the pain, however, so Kym decides that going back to sleep might be the wisest thing to do.

He awakens again sometime later. Even without opening his eyes, he can tell that it is now dark outside. There is an evening coolness in the air, a feeling different from the thin, crisp cool of morning by virtue of its depth and peacefulness.

A rustling on the other side of the room tells him that he is not alone. Sitting up—carefully—he peers into the darkness, just barely able to discern a lumpy shape huddled under the covers of a small wood-frame bed. A familiar snore reveals the lump to be Watkin, still suffering the effects of whatever it was that affected them. Kym is still unsure about that.

The door to the dark room opens, and a small shape is briefly silhouetted in the soft pink-yellow light peculiar to glowbubbles. The shape hesitates at the door, as though unsure whether or not to enter.

"I am awake but my friend is not, so come in quietly," Kym whispers.

The door closes, and Kym hears footsteps cross the room. There is a different sort of rustling, and then the room is flooded with moonlight. Kym sees that his guest—or should he say his host?—is a young girl. She moves to the side of his bed and places a cool hand on his forehead, and in the moonlight, he can see that his first impression was mistaken. The character lines bracketing her eyes and the confident set of her jaw tell him that she is not as young as he had first thought. But her light movements, straight back, and slim waist defy his efforts to estimate how old she is. Content to let this small mystery alone in favor of the larger one, Kym waits until the lady is looking directly at him, and whispers, "Where am I?"

She glances at Watkin and bends close to Kym, speaking softly so as not to waken his friend. "Are you well enough to walk?"

Kym nods, and with the lady's help, gets carefully out of the bed. They make their way out of the dark bedroom without disturbing Watkin.

Kym expects to be momentarily blinded upon leaving his darkened room for a well-lit one, but he is pleasantly surprised. The glowbubbles set about the kitchen in which he finds himself are softly shaded, so that the room is well-lighted without being bright.

It is an extraordinarily comfortable room—obviously functional, but at the same time inviting. There is a long wooden table, polished but not overly so. It is very pretty, but covered with scratches and nicks that attest to its usefulness. The chairs surrounding it—there are eight—are well-cushioned and deep, but easy to move around.

In one corner is a sparkling clean wash basin filled with sweet water, and a different basin for the washing of dishes. A table between the two holds all of the accoutrements needed for both—soft scented soaps and stiff brushes, coarse linen toweling and thick woven cloths, a nail brush and hand mirror, and an ingenious carved wooden rack to hold the bright pottery dishes and cups while they dry.

Potted plants are everywhere, set in standing pots and in clever knotted hangers suspended from the ceiling. In the far corner is an enormous wood-burning stove emitting the appetizing smell of baking bread.

Kym's hostess introduces herself as Liane. Instead of opening the way for the barrage of questions Kym wants to ask and had expected to answer, Liane takes a watering can and sets about tending to the plants, chatting amiably about household things.

Kym is impressed by her quick intelligence as she shares her knowledge of plant lore, showing a quick but gentle wit in the process. A door at the end of the kitchen opens suddenly, letting in a refreshing draught of cool night air, and with it four people.

Liane greets each newcomer with smiles and hugs, and Kym's still-aching head makes him grateful that they all seem to be the silent type. Three of the people pass him with friendly nods, not stopping to talk. They are all young men, the oldest about three trines— legally an adult—the youngest no more than two trines or so, and the other somewhere in between. This is as much of a first impression as he can manage, as the young men stride quickly—and quietly—out of the room.

Liane smiles at Kym's obviously befuddled expression. "Those are my sons, Sandor, Tolan, and Roen. You will get a chance to meet them tomorrow." She turns to the tall man standing beside her. "This is my husband, Rael."

Kym attempts to get to his feet to shake the man's hand properly, but his shaky legs will not support him. The man, Rael, reaches out a large hand and catches Kym's arm. Kym is amazed at the strength of the magic he feels in the man's hand. He has always been sensitive to the magic in things, but to feel power such as this in a person is new and strange. Before he can stop himself, he blurts out his discovery. "You are a wizard!"

Rael nods. "Yes, I am a wizard. And you were drugged. How are you feeling?"

Kym would never admit it, but how he is feeling is like a pampered child. Liane has taken such gentle care of him, and now Rael shows genuine concern—why, Kym could just weep!

Liane smiles at Kym. "Sleepshade plays on the emotions when too large a dose is given. You will be all right in the morning."

Kym is grateful that Watkin is still asleep. His friend is normally so unhesitant about showing his emotions, Kym would hate to think what Watkin would be like if those emotions were completely uncontrolled!

All that Kym can do is nod, however. His voice seems to have gotten away from him.

"I think that you had better go back to sleep for a while," Rael suggests. His voice is so compelling that Kym nearly collapses where he sits.

Rael helps Kym up and takes him back to the room

he shares with the still-sleeping Watkin. Easing himself under the covers, he is asleep almost instantly.

The next morning, Kym feels much better, which is very fortunate, since he is awakened by Watkin shaking his bed. The warm sunshine and fresh fragrant air pouring through the room's open window, coupled with the fact that his headache is gone, put Kym in a good mood. He kicks half-heartedly at Watkin, who dodges him, laughing.

"Get up, Kym-boy! We have a wonderful new place to explore!" Watkin grabs Kym's big toe and wiggles it enthusiastically.

"Go away!" Kym laughs. "I've been exploring, while *you* were snoring!" Both men fall into gales of laughter at the unintentional rhyme.

When they settle down, Kym tells Watkin of his visit to the kitchen, and of meeting Liane and Rael and their sons. He repeats what was said about their being drugged, and how the Sleepshade would affect them. The fact that the travellers remember nothing of the person or persons who drugged them strikes them as terribly funny, proving Liane's statement about the drug affecting emotions.

Worn out from laughing, they wander into the kitchen, where Liane is preparing breakfast.

"Go and get washed up for breakfast!" she says. "The stream is through that door and to your left." She points the way with a dripping wooden spoon, and Kym and Watkin step outside.

"Let's just wash our hands," Watkin says when they reach the stream.

To wash your hands, see #97. To really get clean, see #98.

"We could have done that in the washbasin inside," Kym says. "I think that after sleeping for however long we slept, we should have a proper bath." Without waiting for a reply, Kym marches off.

Grumbling good-naturedly, Watkin is right behind him.

They follow the stream as it twists and turns through the grassy yard. There are wildflowers growing everywhere, and Kym and Watkin can hear the different calls of several kinds of farm animals. They take their time, enjoying the peaceful domesticity that envelops the place.

The stream widens as they go on, becoming almost a small river. It rushes over varicolored rocks and stones, splashing Kym and Watkin from time to time. The water is very cold.

Kym stops when they reach a bend in the stream hidden from the house by a thatch of bushes. "This is a good place," he says, disrobing.

Watkin undresses also, and the friends wade out into the icy water. After the first shock the water doesn't feel quite so cold. Kym says that this is because all of his nerve endings have died of shock. Watkin maintains that their bodies have merely gotten used to the temperature, and he grabs Kym and holds him under the water for a while to prove his point.

Gasping and spluttering—and maybe laughing a little— Kym comes up for air. Watkin, watching him, thinks that Kym has put on a considerable amount of muscle since they started this Quest. His chest looks much broader. He puts out a hand to give Kym an experimental push, but Kym's attention is on something glittering coldly in between the rocks just upstream.

"Look at that!" he says. "It looks like crystal. What is it?"

If you want to explore, see #99. If not, see #100.

Watkin peers in the direction in which Kym is pointing. "Look at what?" he says, unable to discern anything but a glitter of sunlight. "It's just a shiny rock."

"I don't think so," Kym says. He begins to wade toward the source of the shine, fighting the waist-deep water. "It looks as though there is something caught in the rocks there."

Still unable to see what Kym is talking about, Watkin follows him upstream. Sure enough, Kym is right, there *does* seem to be something glittery caught in the rocks.

They approach it cautiously, as though afraid it might leap at them. All that they can see is what looks like glass, under the moving water. Kym clears away a few of the smaller rocks and log-jammed leaves that are hiding the thing, and he and Watkin bend down for a closer look.

The glitter that first caught Kym's attention is now revealed to be a sort of tiny crystal ball, wedged in between the rocks. Looking very closely, the travellers can see the image of a palace, overlaid with a clear representation of a young girl's face. Next to it is a tiny wand of the sort used by wizards.

They exchange puzzled glances. There is some sort of wrapping around the crystal ball that looks like dustlace. Of course it cannot be; dustlace all but dissolves in water.

"What should we do?" Watkin asks.

"Leave it here, I suppose."

"But what if someone lost this?" Watkin insists.

"Then they will have to find it," Kym says. "Let's go back to the kitchen."

If you want to move the crystal ball, see #101. If not, see #102.

On the way back to the kitchen, the pair try once more to unravel the mystery of why they were drugged, and by whom. The more they think about it, the vaguer it gets. Both Kym and Watkin feel somehow cheated, but that is as definite as their memories will get. The men resolve to put the mystery out of their minds for the time being and get on with the business at hand.

Which, judging by the wonderful smells wafting out of the open kitchen door, is definitely breakfast.

Upon entering the kitchen, Kym and Watkin are directed to two of the comfortable chairs set around the big table and handed mugs of hot spiced coffee by Liane. Her middle son, introduced as Tolan, provides them with thick sweet cream in a little glazed pitcher and a delicately painted bowl filled with powdered sweetroot. The travellers settle comfortably into the deeply cushioned chairs and soak in the warm sunshine and good smells.

Tolan, dismissed from helping his mother for the moment, plops himself down in a chair facing the travellers and smiles at them.

They smile back.

He reaches for the bowl of sweetroot and toys with it, every now and again smiling pleasantly at the amused travellers. Finally, he clears his throat to say something, but in his nervousness he upends the sweetroot bowl and spills the pinkish powder all over the table.

Kym and Watkin help the boy clean up the mess, exchanging smiles with Liane over his head. Kym, especially, feels sympathy for the boy—he can see a lot of his younger self in him. When the sweetroot is cleaned up and the bowl, as well as their coffee mugs, refilled, they take their places and resume gazing uncomfortably at one another.

Tolan obviously has something he'd like to say, but is too shy to come right out with it. He is a gawky, pleasant young man who would, in another world, wear eyeglasses and get top grades in science and math. Here, he wears his clothes slightly too big for him, and his thin wrists stick out of his sleeves. He gives the impression of being at odds with his body, as though it has a mind of its own and goes merrily on its way unconcerned as to whether he comes along or not.

He clears his throat and speaks, his voice an uncomfortable compromise between the soprano of his childhood and the pleasant tenor it will become. "Are you guys really on a Quest?"

Watkin answers. "That we are, lad. The most important Quest there is!" At Tolan's wide-eyed look, Watkin begins to launch into an enthusiastic retelling of their adventures to date, but midway through the third sentence he stops.

This place is too comfortable, too placid, to boast about adventures in. Instead of sounding glamorous and exciting, Watkin's narrative sounds hollow and bragging, even to him. Sipping the hot sweet coffee, Watkin realizes with a small shock that he is tired. He merely wishes to rest, and think of nothing more pressing than whether to have jam or honey on his bread.

"Well, Questing is hard work, and not always as rewarding as a man would like to believe," he finishes. Watkin smiles at Kym, whose thoughts are quite obviously running much the same course. They are spared further explanation as the kitchen door opens and Rael, followed by his other two sons, enters the kitchen.

Liane joins Kym and Watkin at the table, mug in hand, as Rael and his sons serve the wonderful breakfast she has prepared. Kym and Watkin are surprised and impressed by this example of fair division of labor, and vow to keep this system in mind should they ever have families.

The table is filled with laughter and warmth as the

hungry group sets to work on Liane's handiwork, which includes more spiced coffee, a puffy egg-and-cheese concoction which is surprisingly light, chopped tuberoots filled with bacon, and a delicious bread baked with honey that Tolan says is Liane's specialty, baked from a recipe she developed.

As the meal continues, Kym and Watkin have a chance to study the other members of the family. They very much like what they can see, and both men relax and enjoy the company of the widely disparate personalities.

Liane is as kind and giving with the rest of her family as she has been with her guests. She sits at the head of the table, with Watkin on her left, and her youngest son, Roen, on her right. Rael sits at the other end of the table, Kym at his right, his eldest son, Sandor, at his left. Tolan sits between his brothers.

The men of the family are very different from each other, Kym notices. Rael is an obviously powerful man, and he wears the power comfortably. He does not join in with the teasing wordplay going on about him, but he gives each person who addresses him his full attention, and the way he looks at his wife and sons reflects the love and respect he feels for them—feelings that the family very noticeably shares with him, and with each other.

Sandor and Tolan tease each other and their parents, and there is even some hair-ruffling, arm-pinching, and under-the-table kicking in evidence—but all of it carefully calculated not to hurt.

The only person apart from all of this is Roen, the youngest son. He sits to the right of his mother, eating very little and saying nothing at all. He doesn't appear to be sulking; on the contrary, there is nothing temporary about his mood. He seems beset by something too big for him, some sorrow that he can barely live with.

Kym wonders if Roen is ill, but this notion is contradicted by his incredible beauty. The rest of the family is attractive, and Rael is certainly striking, but Roen is simply and honestly the most beautiful being—male or female—that Kym has ever seen.

Roen is small, but in no way fragile. His arms and chest are smoothly muscled, like a dancer or a wrestler, or one of the master swordsmen that Kym once saw at a fair. His face is delicately shaped, with a sharp chin and straight, narrow nose. His skin is very fair and clear, his cheeks and lips touched with a faint blush that is in no way feminine or even androgynous—he is definitely masculine.

Kym is fascinated as he watches the boy play with a piece of warm bread. To his embarrassment, Roen sees him staring, and Kym hurriedly occupies himself putting cream in his coffee, rather than meet the boy's incredible gaze.

His eyes are large and so dark as to be almost black, although at times they seem to be blue. His face is framed perfectly by thick, black hair that falls in unruly curls just to the collar of his tunic. It looks at once perfectly arranged and as though it has never been touched by a comb.

Kym also notices that for all of the horseplay going on around Roen, no one—not even Liane—ever touches him.

After breakfast, Kym and Watkin are firmly guided back to their rooms for a nap. They do not resist very strongly. When they awaken, Liane fixes them a cold lunch, then leads Kym and Watkin out through a series of rooms as thoughtfully furnished as the kitchen and into a lovely garden. Explaining that she has an errand she must take care of, she leaves the men in the shade of a huge nut tree, where Tolan joins them.

The wizard's middle son is carrying a large empty

basket in one hand and a pottery bowl in the other. Greeting Kym and Watkin cheerfully, he asks them to move out from under the branches of the tree for a moment. They do so, and Tolan points to the tree and mutters an incantation (practicing it a few times under his breath first). Kym and Watkin recognize the Spell for Charming the Birds Out of the Trees, a very common spell in their village. They have never seen it used on nuts before, but it proves very successful.

The pair help Tolan gather the nuts into the woven basket, and all three settle comfortably in the shade to shell them.

Time passes pleasantly, and Kym and Watkin watch with mild interest when Liane, accompanied by Sandor, leaves the house and starts off down the lane. Tolan laughs at this, and Kym inquires as to why he finds it funny.

"It isn't really," Tolan explains. "Mother is taking Sandor to meet a girl." He giggles again. "Sandor was going to get married, but the bi— the lady changed her mind, and he's been moping around ever since."

"It seems to me that Roen is the one who mopes," Watkin remarks, thinking of the boy's silent presence at breakfast.

"Roen has reason to do a lot worse than mope," Tolan says thoughtfully. "But then, so does Sandor," he continues, shifting moods so subtly that Kym and Watkin almost miss the sadness that accompanied the reference to Roen.

"What reason is that?" Kym asks, referring to Roen.

"Well, being jilted," Tolan replies, referring to Sandor.

Kym gets the distinct impression that Tolan is deliberately misunderstanding him to avoid further questioning about Roen.

Watkin, who sees clearly what is happening, steps in to ensure that Kym's curiosity doesn't get them in any trouble. "Who jilted Sandor?" he asks, idly chewing on the nut he has just shelled.

"A princess named Elvina," is the answer.

Watkin begins to choke on his nut, and Tolan and Kym both pound him on the back, the Heimlich Maneuver being unknown to them. By the time Watkin can breathe again, the subject is forgotten, which is a good thing, because by this time, Sandor has returned. He joins the little group under the tree, and Tolan picks up the basket of nuts and heads toward the kitchen.

"Are you going to come back with me, or do you want to stay here?" Tolan asks.

To go with Tolan, see #103. To stay with Sandor, see #104.

"Oh, I think we'll stay here for the moment," Watkin says. Both he and Kym are anxious to see what they can learn from Sandor. Besides, though neither man is really willing to admit it, the sleepshade they were given has not completely worn off. The slightest effort is rewarded with thumping headaches and racing hearts. Staying put seems the wisest choice.

When Tolan is out of sight—and earshot—Sandor turns to the travellers. "So," he begins, "you are on a Quest."

Kym and Watkin exchange smiles. The young man is pretending nonchalance, but they can see that he is much more curious than he is willing to let on. They are hoping to use this curiosity to their advantage.

"Yes," Watkin answers. "We are Questing for our True Loves."

Sandor nods understandingly. "I thought I had a True Love, once." This is exactly the topic that Kym and Watkin were hoping to introduce.

"What happened?" Kym doesn't have to feign concern; the subject is obviously a painful one for Sandor.

"She broke the betrothal in favor of some fool who calls himself the "Scarlet Prince." There's a masculine name, hey?" Sandor pulls a few tufts of soft grass out of the ground and twists them into a pulpy mess. "What a fool."

"The Scarlet Prince?" Kym asks, feeling real sympathy for the young man. He had obviously loved his Princess Elvina, although according to what Kym knows about her, he cannot imagine how such a sincere-seeming man could fall in love with her.

And Sandor is nothing if not sincere. Tall, blonde, and good-looking in a very clean-cut way, he is about as opposite from his brooding youngest brother as two people can be. Sandor seems to be the kind of young man who becomes a hero in spite of himself. Courage, gentleness, and simplicity are quite clearly his foremost characteristics, and a man like this should be able to see right through a woman like her, yet he is unmistakably smitten.

"She is a wonderful girl," Sandor continues. "Sweet and gentle, kind, and honest. And she didn't at all deserve what the Scarlet Prince did to her after they were betrothed!"

"What did he do?" Watkin asks, unsure as to whether he will get an answer, and if he does, whether it will only confuse him more.

"He broke the engagement for someone else!" Sandor answers, outraged. "He should have found some other family to bother! He was first betrothed to my sister, then my beloved, and then he threw her over for my little brother's betrothed! Poor Elvina, how she suffered— Auriane wasn't even a proper woman, just a little girl. Poor, sweet Elvina!"

Kym begins to wonder if they are talking about the same princess. "She lives in a castle?" he asks, to clarify things.

"Yes. It's falling down because her father won't allow her to fix it up. Poor girl." Sandor shakes his head.

Becoming more confused by the moment, Kym changes the subject. "Why didn't you call this Scarlet Prince out in a duel?"

"At the time, I wasn't old enough," Sandor answers. "And by the time I was, it was too late."

"Too late, how?" Watkin asks, risking a pounding head to sit up and listen more closely.

"The Scarlet Prince was in the Dream Palace when— well, enough of this gloomy talk, hey?"

"Wait," Kym insists. "Which brother was betrothed to Elvina?" Kym is so confused by the story by now that he wouldn't be surprised to find that he himself was betrothed to the Scarlet Prince!

Now Sandor is also confused. "No brothers! At least, only me, hey? My little brother was betrothed to Auriane, before either of them was born, and before the Scarlet Prince talked Auriane's father into breaking her betrothal."

"I didn't know you had a sister," Watkin says, apropos of nothing. He smiles to himself, rather enjoying the confusion, and pleased with himself for adding to it.

"We don't talk about her," Sandor answers, not angry, just a little sad.

"You don't talk about much of anything, do you?" Kym says, forgetting his manners in his exasperation.

"And when you do, it doesn't make any sense," Watkin adds, only loud enough for Kym to hear. Kym realizes that their overdose of sleepshade is playing on them again, making Kym more confused and fueling Watkin's mischievous mood.

"No," is the frustrating answer. It looks as though Kym and Watkin are going to have to remain frustrated, for Sandor suddenly gets to his feet.

Turning around, the travellers find that Liane and Rael have appeared behind them.

"I am going to prepare dinner, and Rael is going for a walk; would either of you care to join either of us?" Liane asks.

To go with Liane, see #105. To go with Rael, see #106.

Kym and Watkin excuse themselves and head slowly toward the kitchen, both holding tightly to heads that ache at any movement.

The kitchen is filled, as it always seems to be, with heavenly smells. Tolan stands at the table, mixing the shelled nuts into a thick batter. "Took you long enough to get here!" he says by way of a greeting.

"Tolan, manners," Liane admonishes mildly. She has tied a clean white apron around her bright blue dress, and is stuffing a pair of wildfowl with some delectable mixture that neither Kym nor Watkin can identify, but are both sure that they will love.

Mindful of their own manners, Kym and Watkin offer to help fix dinner (which is the meal she least enjoys preparing, Liane tells them), and so they find themselves peeling and slicing tuberoots.

They are both trying to think of some way to bring up the Dream Palace, when Liane does it for them. "Tolan tells me that you two are searching for your True Loves," she says in a conversational tone.

"That's right," Kym answers, adding a thank-you as Tolan hands him and Watkin each a cold glass of pale green wine.

"I never cook without wine," Liane explains with a wink.

"I have always been under the impression that the term 'cooking with wine' means putting the wine into the food, not the cook," Kym remarks.

Liane blinks at him in mock confusion, then brightens and pours a little of her wine over each stuffed bird. Pausing to think, she brightens again and pours a little *more* wine into her mouth, then sighs, exaggeratedly self-satisfied.

There is laughter all around, and in the warm silence that follows, Kym feels comfortable enough to pursue the subject of the Dream Palace. He has learned, however, that straight questioning doesn't seem to work, and so he attempts to be circumspect. "We have heard that there is a place near here where a strange thing has happened, and we were told that if we go there, we will find our True Loves."

"Which place is that?" Liane doesn't look up from the cheese she is grating, filling the room with its sharp aroma, so she doesn't see the exasperated looks traded by Kym and Watkin.

Tolan *does* see, however, and decides to help the pair. "Kym and Watkin were telling me all about their Quest before, Mother." The boy takes a deep breath, then says the next sentence in a rush. "The place Kym means is the Dream Palace."

Liane's shoulders tighten for a moment, and Kym and Watkin can see her squeezing both the cheese and the grater so tightly that her knuckles are white. She relaxes slowly, and turns to face the men sitting uncomfortably at the table. "That place has caused nothing but trouble for my family. We do not speak of it."

Kym and Watkin are both disappointed, but they manage to be gracious. They still have no idea how they got here, or what occurred *before* they got here, so they are in agreement that it is probably wise not to press their luck by pursuing the matter.

Liane turns and walks to the table, where she gathers the peeled and sliced tuberoots into a bowl. She smiles at Kym and Watkin, signalling that as far as she is concerned, the matter is ended. "Dinner is about ready. Why don't you go and find Rael?" she suggests.

If you don't want to, see #107. If you do, see #108.

Rael is standing in the midst of a well-tended wild-flower garden by the time Kym and Watkin catch up to him. They are reluctant at first to disturb him.

Standing among the wildflowers with the sun setting behind him, Rael gives the appearance of a man completely at peace with his world and himself. Kym and Watkin would not have been surprised if they had been told that Rael was not a man at all, but some sort of changeling belonging to the very heart of the earth.

He turns as they approach, and smiles in welcome. The travellers have to suppress the urge to kneel, an impulse all the more puzzling in that they do not quite understand why it is there.

"I was waiting for you."

Kym finds himself suddenly at a loss for words, and is not surprised to see that Watkin is affected the same way.

Rael smiles as though used to this. "The effects of the sleepshade have not yet worn off completely," he says, his voice rich and deep.

Kym and Watkin nod.

"Come, there are things I would like to show you." Rael turns and begins to walk along a curving path which leads into shadow. He does not look back to see if Kym and Watkin are following; he knows that they will.

And they do. The path is covered in some sort of crushed stones or shells that glow slightly as the day begins to darken toward night. There are flowering hedges to either side of the path, and the blooms are also luminous.

A few feet ahead of them Rael has stopped, and is standing between two exotic flowers. They are unlike any that Kym and Watkin have ever seen, and they are the only ones of their kind in the garden.

Rael beckons. When Kym and Watkin are standing

with him between the strangely compelling blooms, Rael begins to speak. His voice is soft, but it carries a strange intensity.

"These are called nightshade," he begins, indicating the bizarre flowers. "They grow in pairs, and can only reproduce in those same pairings. For each plant there is only one other, and if one dies, they both die." He looks at Kym and Watkin, and his eyes glow a dark blue-black, holding them still and silent.

"No one may interfere with their growth. If they are transplanted, or are tampered with in any way, they shrivel and are lost."

Kym and Watkin begin to get the uneasy feeling that they are being warned, but against what? Both are too frightened to ask.

Rael smiles, and the eerie light fades from his eyes. He changes the subject with startling abruptness, and takes Kym and Watkin on a tour of the rest of the garden.

There is every variety of flower and vegetable that the travellers can name growing in the garden, and many that they cannot. Rael points all of them out, testing what knowledge the pair possesses, and adding to it when necessary. He seems like a completely different person from the man whose eyes glowed as he gave them a cryptic warning not an hour ago. He is just a man now, a husband and father, escorting his guests back to the house to join his family for dinner as the day begins to wane.

★Dinner proves to be another absolute delight. There is roast wildfowl stuffed with an interesting spicy dressing, tuberoots baked in cheese and cream, hot nutbread baked by Tolan, and a rich red wine.

The conversation is lively, ranging over a wide variety of topics, none of which are of any help to Watkin and Kym on their Quest.

Neither man cares.

They are tired, and still feeling the effects of the sleepshade, and the unsettling loss of memory it caused. Dinner ends with sweet, warming sherry in front of a crackling fire. Tolan reads aloud from an old, thick book of adventure stories, making Kym once again wish that he could read. Liane sits on a chair and plays a handlute, with Rael at her feet, and Sandor lies on his stomach in front of the fire dreaming of love and adventure.

Only Roen stays apart. He sits in a deeply carved chair in the shadows, not speaking or reading, just there.

The nights end, and the mornings come, and Kym and Watkin recover from all that has so far befallen them. Liane assigns them daily chores, and Sandor learns wrestling and bawdy songs from Watkin. They become used to Rael's moods and their fear and awe of him turn slowly to respect. Tolan begins to teach Kym how to read.

And apart from it all is Roen, who is mostly silent and always alone.

The warm summer turns to cool autumn, and Kym and Watkin begin to feel a strange restlessness. They begin to speak of leaving, but Liane always has one more project for them to complete, or Sandor has forgotten a favorite song, and anyway, Kym has so much more to learn.

Then one night, as they are sitting in front of the fire, Liane asks Rael how the garden is doing, and he tells her that the nightshade is dying, and Kym and Watkin realize that his answer is meant for them.

They know that it is time to leave, that they must continue their Quest. They say goodbye right then and there, and although Rael and his family are sad to see them go, they know that Kym and Watkin have to see this through to the end, or they might as well not have started out at all. And so they will leave in the morning.

As Kym is digging their knapsacks out of the back of the closet where they have lain forgotten all of this time, Liane enters with some water and food, including her special honey-baked bread. "We will all miss you," she says, and with a hug for each, she leaves.

Watkin, sitting on the edge of his little wood-frame bed, notices musingly that Kym not only didn't blush at Liane's embrace—he returned it. *We've come a long way*, Watkin thinks.

Kym, standing at the bedroom window, is thinking much the same thing. He barely remembers the shy, mysterious man he was when this Quest began. He tells himself that he doesn't feel that much different on the inside, but even as the thought completes itself in his mind, he knows that it isn't true. He is a much different man than he was, and he is pleased and very proud to add to that a *better* one.

Watkin joins Kym at the window, his train of thought following much the same path as Kym's. He is about to remark on this when a movement from outside catches his eye. "What's that?"

"What?" Kym searches the darkness for whatever has caught his friend's attention. "I don't see anything."

"There!" Watkin points to a spot one hundred or so yards away, near the stream that runs past the house. "I saw something moving there."

"It was probably the moonlight reflecting on the water," Kym reasons. "There are two full moons tonight."

Watkin shakes his head impatiently. "No—look!"

Kym looks, and this time he sees it, too. There seems to be someone walking along the stream. He remembers hearing everyone as they settled in for the night, however, so who could it be? He looks at Watkin, who has moved away from the window and is shrugging back into his shirt. "What are you doing?" Kym asks, already knowing the answer.

"We're on a Quest, are we not, my friend? And the purpose of a Quest is to find out things, is it not?" Watkin asks, his tone playful.

"So let's go find out who that is!" they finish in tandem, laughing.

Tiptoeing so as not to awaken anyone else, Kym and Watkin make their way out of the house and through the moonlit yard. The grass is already wet with dewfall, and the moonlight reflecting on the tiny wet droplets makes it seem as though they are wading through a field of diamonds.

The night is perfectly silent save for the sound of the stream, and the light is so bright that as they pause to listen their shadows appear solid, as if they had been cut out of heavy black cloth and laid at their feet.

Not speaking, Kym and Watkin make their way to the place where they thought they saw movement, but they find no one. They are startled nearly out of their skins when a soft voice comes suddenly from the shadows directly in front of them.

"My father is a king. Did you know that?"

Clutching his chest with one hand and Watkin with the other, Kym shakes his head. Standing so closely that they are casting only one shadow, Kym can feel that Watkin is doing the same.

"He probably did not tell you." A figure steps out of the shadows, and Kym and Watkin can see that it is Roen.

Both men feel vaguely silly for being frightened by a young boy, but their fear is not entirely misplaced. Roen has about him the same aura of power that his father carries so easily. There is no magic in him, though—not that Kym can feel.

"You are out very late," the boy remarks. His eyes

are so cold that, for a few long seconds, neither Kym nor Watkin can speak. There is no menace in the boy's presence—he does not appear dangerous—but his eyes are strangely empty. Looking into them is like looking into a dark well; they reflect back what faces them, but add nothing. This soulless gaze, coupled with his conversational tone, is terrifying.

Kym gathers his courage and answers, inordinately pleased when his voice doesn't squeak. "I could say the same for you, young man."

If Kym was expecting Roen to smile, or show some other sign of relaxing, he is disappointed. The strange boy shows no reaction at all, except to say simply, "Do not try to charm me."

Astonished, Kym falls silent. He is struck once again by Roen's incredible beauty, which seems intensified by the cold light of the full moons playing over the exquisite bone structure of his face. The shadows under his cheekbones seem a part of the boy, generated by him rather than cast by something outside of him. His dark curls blend perfectly with the inky shadows, making it impossible to tell where he ends and the night begins.

As uneasy as he has ever been in the presence of a living being, Watkin breaks the silence. "It may not be late for you, but it is for us. Good night." He tugs on Kym's arm, surprised that Kym does not seem to want to move.

Kym slowly comes back to himself, and allows Watkin to pull him toward the house.

Once inside, Kym looks out of the kitchen window and is not at all surprised to see Roen standing where they left him, watching the stream. He is standing in a shaft of moonlight so perfectly formed that it seems to have been cast just to illuminate him. This does not surprise Kym either.

At first light the travellers slip quietly out of their rooms and through the kitchen, where they find hand-written directions from Tolan propped against the sweetroot bowl on the heavy table. Kym's reading skills are not yet very advanced, so Tolan has also drawn a map on the back.

Excited to be on their way once again, the pair sets off down the path to the edge of the yard and heads into the woods.

★It is only a matter of hours before Kym and Watkin realize that the directions that they have been given are faulty. After passing the first two landmarks described to them they do not come across anything vaguely resembling the third one, which should have been no more than half an hour past the second one.

Tired, hungry, and footsore, they are about to sit down and rest when Kym suddenly points, his mouth open in astonishment.

Over the tops of the trees they can see spires, the spires of a palace.

X: *The Dream Palace*

No longer weary, the travellers make their way through the woods as quickly as possible, trying to keep the magnificent spires in sight. The woods thin out gradually, but due to the difficulty of maneuvering through the undiminished underbrush, Kym and Watkin don't see the place they are seeking until it seems as though they are almost upon it. When they finally look up and see, it stops them where they stand.

The palace—the Dream Palace, finally—is simply magnificent. Set in a wooded clearing, like a priceless jewel in a velvet box, it is everything they have been dreaming of, and more. It is bigger than Elvina's castle, grander than the castle of Queen Rayanne and all of the other castles they have ever imagined, all thrown together.

They are standing on the top of a long, steep hill, and though there are many more like it between them and their destination, they *feel* like they are almost there.

With a jubilant yell from Watkin and a bit of unexpectedly graceful dancing from Kym, the pair sets off down the road to whatever end their Quest is destined to have.

The long, twisting road is difficult to walk, as the wheels of many a heavy cart have left deeply embedded tracks which were frozen over in the first frost of autumn.

This bothers the travellers not at all. Watkin strides along, arms swinging, bellowing out snatches of bawdy old songs, some so shameless they turn Kym's lately unembarrassable ears a deep embarrassed crimson.

On noticing this, Watkin laughs heartily and throws out his arms, embracing the day. "It's good to be back on the road, Kym!"

And even though the frozen road is beginning to melt into mud, Kym has to agree. The air is cold and crisp, with that indefinable afternoon something that makes one think of home and hearth, fresh apples and dead leaves. The sun is bright and the air is filled with the sounds of the chilly wind and a nearby stream. Not far away someone has lit a fire, and the smell of burning leaves overlays it all, like the scent of a fresh-baked treat.

Kym nods in response to Watkin's words, and then stops.

Watkin, who has forgotten a particularly delightful set of lyrics and fallen behind while attempting to work them out, bumps into his smaller—but not as *much* smaller as when they started out—friend. "What is it?" He wonders if there will ever again be a time when he can ask that question and not be nervous about what answer he is likely to get. He peers around Kym, and then is also still.

They stand at a fork in the road. The left fork is paved with broken, weed-choked cobblestones; the right with smooth, well-travelled earth. Above the treetops they can still see the spires of the Dream Palace, but the roads of the fork are lost in trees at the bottom of the hill. They cannot see which fork is the correct one to take, and as close as they are to actually, finally *getting* there, they do not want to risk getting sidetracked by guessing.

Unfortunately, they have no other choice.

To take the left fork, see #109. To take the right fork, see #110.

Kym shrugs and sets off down the left fork, making his way carefully over the neglected cobblestones, which are tilted and disarranged, making it very difficult to walk.

Watkin laughs and follows. "You always were one for doing a thing the hard way!" he exclaims. Concentrating on keeping his footing, Watkin begins to hum. As he falls into a rhythm of stepping and sliding, he begins to sing under his breath to pass the time—an old sailor's chanty concerning a nubile young mermaid and a one-finned shark.

The road gets no harder, but certainly no easier, as it goes on. The trees overhead block out all but the strongest of the late afternoon sunshine, making strange patterns on the road ahead. Tiny pieces of quartz embedded in the cobbles catch the sunlight, causing bright flashes and sparks. The effect is hypnotic, and soon even Watkin falls silent, leaving the only sounds those of carefully placed boot heels, and occasional muttered curses as a loose cobblestone turns underfoot, or a supposedly controlled slide ends in a twisted ankle.

After stopping several times to rest, and several more times to see to scrapes and painfully throbbing muscles, Kym and Watkin eventually come to the end of the awful cobblestone road, and onto a path made of glittering stone.

Following it with their eyes, they see that they have arrived.

The path leads straight to the foot of the enormous stone stairway that leads up to the door of the Dream Palace.

They hesitate, overcome.

This is your very last chance to back out. If you want to give up now, see #111. If not, go on to the next page.

"This is it," Kym says.

"We're here," Watkin agrees.

Not being able to think of anything suitably grand to fit the occasion, the men trade smiles and then, simply, begin to climb the steps.

There are a great many steps, and both Kym and Watkin are out of breath by the time they reach the top. Watkin leans against the door and wipes his forehead, stopping in mid-mop at the strange look on Kym's face. Following Kym's gaze, Watkin takes his first good look at the door on which he is leaning.

It is *enormous*.

Watkin is a fairly tall man, but this door is easily two times his height. Its size is not the most remarkable thing about the door, however. The truly amazing thing is that it appears to have been hewn from a single piece of pale stone.

Above the door, so high up that they can barely make out what it is, there is a stained-glass fanlight. Kym, whose eyes are a little sharper than Watkin's, can just make out the fact that the colored glass is a tiny representation of the palace itself.

The lintels to either side of the door are made of intricately worked wood, carved to represent flowering vines twined about fluted columns.

In the center of the huge door itself is set an enormous iron doorknocker cast in the shape of a fettered griffin. To the right and left of the door hang a wooden key and a glass bell. There is no doorknob or keyhole.

To use the key, see #112. To ring the bell, see #113. To knock, see #114.

Kym and Watkin exchange nervous glances. No one has told them that the palace is guarded by spells, but then, no one has told them that it is not, either.

They have not come this far to give up now, however, so they flip a coin to see who will make this decision. Kym wins—Watkin gets to choose.

Watkin cracks his knuckles. Then, reaching out with one hand, he pulls the bell cord with a surprisingly delicate tug.

The bell rings out, clear and pure, and slowly, with a groan, the door swings open.

Watkin bows and graciously invites Kym to enter first.

Kym peers around the stone doorjamb, ready to pull his head back at the slightest hint of trouble. None seems forthcoming, so he steps gingerly inside, followed closely by the equally cautious Watkin.

They find themselves in an entranceway—a long narrow hallway carpeted with fine rugs. They suffer from neglect, telling Kym and Watkin that there is probably no one living here. On the other hand, if the palace were completely empty, there would be a lot of dust, and there isn't any. None at all.

The pattern of care gets odder as Kym and Watkin explore more bravely. As they had first discovered, there is no dust, but neither are things all clean. Portraits line the walls, their gilt edges flaking and canvasses drying out, but the exotic vases underneath are spotless and filled with fresh flowers.

Kym empties one of the vases of its bouquet and upends it. To his and Watkin's astonishment, the water spilling out is fresh and clean.

"I thought everyone here was asleep," Kym says, puzzled.

"Everybody but the florist," Watkin suggests.

Kym makes a face and continues his exploration,

turning up more strange facts. Such as: at the end of the hallway is a doorway framed by thick, red velvet curtains, except that a large piece of the left one has been cut away—not ripped, *cut*. Holding the curtain out, they can see that the missing piece was a perfect rectangle.

And: all along the hallway are small, ornamental tables holding a variety of objects, from additional flower-filled vases to sculptures and artifacts of all kinds. The strange part is that not all of them have been cared for. Some are cracked and chipped and dusty; others look as though they have been polished as recently as this morning.

Kym shakes his head and moves on, preparing to enter one of the side rooms.

A sudden rustle of cloth startles him and he jumps, bumping into Watkin as the larger man turns suddenly.

"What was that?" Too startled to whisper, Watkin's voice is loud.

Kym, finger to his lips, shakes his head. As they watch, the rustle comes again. "Look there!" Watkin points to the doorway framed by the oddly mismatched curtains, which seems to be the source of the sound.

Kym turns quickly, just in time to see a small figure dart out from behind the curtain and go through the doorway. He barely has time to catch the flash of a small bare foot, and the figure is gone.

"Quick, follow her!" Watkin commands.

To follow the bare foot, see #115. To ignore it, see #116.

Kym shakes his head at his friend's assumption. "How do you know it's a she?"

Watkin answers without turning, intent on pursuing the elusive barefoot vision. "I know, Kym! I don't know how, but deep in these old bones I know! Hurry!" He takes off down the hallway at a run, and skids to a stop before the doorway. Peering through it, he exclaims in surprise at what he sees.

Kym steps carefully behind his friend and looks over one huge shoulder—and is also surprised.

Beyond the doorway, the hallway branches—one side continuing on like a normal hallway, the other opening suddenly out into a garden. Caution forgotten, Watkin rushes into the garden, and Kym has no choice but to follow.

In stark contrast to what they have seen of the inside of the palace, the garden is completely neglected and overgrown. Vast white orchids peer out from between thick growths of ivy, lining a path with glazed flagstones that are still perfect, but for the small weeds and flowers growing in the spaces between them.

The path wanders between intricate trellises, dead-ending and doubling back on itself, revealing little secrets as it goes. Here there is a pair of wineglasses—one whole, the other tipped and broken; a spider spins its web in the cracked glass. Over there is a china doll, untouched by time, sitting as though in wait for its owner to return. All is completely silent.

At the far end of the garden is a wooden gate, just swinging shut, as though someone has recently passed through.

Without hesitation, Watkin runs for the gate, leaping over it in a wild bound. "Wait, please!" he calls to his unseen quarry. "I won't hurt you!" He sounds sincere, if a little breathless.

Kym follows at a more sedate pace, reflecting to

himself that if he were being chased by someone who took such obvious glee in the sport, he'd be likely to hide very carefully! It isn't like Watkin to act like this, but then they've never been in quite this situation before. Leaving Watkin to do what he must, Kym stops and looks around.

He is standing in a sort of statuary, consisting of fantastic stone beasts. There is a winged serpent, a cat with the tail of a fish, and a pair of bear cubs with horns and hoofs. They are all overgrown with moss, although otherwise in good condition. Kym turns to look for Watkin.

He is standing next to the statue of the winged serpent, looking around in a curious mixture of anticipation and disappointment. "Come out, girl, I only want to talk to you!"

As Kym watches in disbelief, the statue begins to rock slightly, then topples toward Watkin, who stands by its base completely unaware.

"Watkin, look out!" Executing the only athletic move of his life, Kym springs forward and tackles his friend, sending the two of them sprawling as the statue crashes to the ground.

They sit up shakily as the dust settles around the shattered sculpture.

"Thank you, my friend. I didn't know you could move so quickly!" Watkin says. He pats Kym weakly on the back.

Kym nods, not really listening. He is about to point out that maybe this is how Watkin's young lady shows her distaste at being chased, when Watkin leaps to his feet. "Look at this!"

To let Watkin continue this silliness, see #117. To stop it, see #118.

Kym gets to his feet slowly, and joins Watkin at the broken base of the statue. Looking down into the hollow base, Kym can see a set of small steps carved out of stone. They lead down into a damp, gloomy shaft. Watkin immediately swings one large leg over the side of the base and prepares to climb down the steps.

"Wait!" Kym catches hold of his sleeve. "What are you doing?" Watkin looks perplexed at the question. "I don't know. Maybe there's something down there she wants to show me."

Kym stares, not sure he's heard this right. "I beg your pardon," he replies, "but it was my impression that she was wanting to kill you! Assuming that there *is* a she!"

Watkin frowns. "I don't think so." He frowns harder at Kym's doubtful look. "It's all right, Kym. She doesn't mean us any harm. I'd bet my life on it!" So saying, Watkin disappears into the stairwell.

Kym follows reluctantly, muttering, "Bet your own life if you wish, but why must you bet mine, too?"

The stairwell leads into a long, dark tunnel, just large enough for the two men to stand in. Water drips from the ceiling, making irregular puddles on the floor. It gets darker as they go on, and Watkin stops to pick up some stray branches from the base of the stairs. The damp air makes it hard to catch a flame, but thanks to Watkin's habit of carrying his flint wrapped in waxed cloth, making a torch is relatively easy.

The gloomy tunnel twists and turns, sometimes sloping up and sometimes down. Eventually it takes them to another stairway leading up. To Kym's relief and Watkin's dismay, they find themselves right back where they started—in the hallway.

★This time, they take the doorway leading deeper into the interior of the palace. The first room that they come across is the kitchen. It is as sumptuous as the parts of the palace that they have seen so far, and marked with the same odd pattern of care and neglect.

The woodburning stove seems to have been in use fairly recently, and the table set near the fireplace is sparkling clean. When Watkin examines the stack of firewood arranged neatly next to the stove, he finds that there is liquid sap on some of it, meaning that it has been cut very recently. All of this adds to the mystery of whether or not everyone in the palace is asleep, as Kym and Watkin have been told.

They sit down at the table to think this over, and no sooner have they started to discuss it than they hear a door close in one of the other rooms.

Watkin is immediately on his feet. "It's her! Hurry!"

"Oh, Watkin! For the sake of all that's reasonable, will you forget about your imaginary girl?" Kym snaps, grabbing his agitated friend by the shoulders.

"No, I will not!" Watkin snaps, for the first time on this long adventure losing his customary patience with Kym. "I will *not* forget her! I can feel, deep inside of me, that she is the one I have been waiting for, and I will find her if I have to crawl into every corner of this place on my hands and knees to do it!"

Before Kym can reply, there is a noise from under the kitchen table. "Aha!" Watkin yells, reaching toward the table.

To put a stop to this now, see #119. Otherwise, turn the page.

Too quickly for Kym to stop him, Watkin reaches under the table and pulls out a squirming, protesting boy.

Watkin holds the lad up and looks him over carefully, not believing his eyes.

"There's your girl," Kym says. He is almost as disappointed as Watkin.

"No," Watkin murmurs. He shakes the terrified boy gently. "Where is she?" he asks.

The boy looks to Kym for help.

"Watkin, I think that you are scaring him," Kym suggests, smiling reassuringly at the child.

Watkin nods absently and, setting the boy carefully on his feet, sits down in the nearest chair and buries his face in his hands.

Kym, a bit mystified by Watkin's reaction, sits down also, and draws the boy into the chair next to his. He has never thought of himself as being good with children, but he has never thought of himself as the kind of person who goes on a Quest, either, so taking a breath for calmness, he sets about questioning the child. "What's your name?" he begins.

"Dore," the child answers. "What's yours?"

"Kym."

"That's a girl's name."

Kym, caught by surprise, retaliates instinctively. "So is Dore."

The boy looks doubtful, but concedes this round to Kym and tenders a peace offering. "I know who you're looking for, and I can take you to her."

To follow Dore, see #120. To refuse his offer, see #121.

"Whom," Kym corrects automatically, beginning to suspect that he is the only person in this entire world with any grasp of the language. "Take us, then."

The boy is willing; unfortunately, Watkin is not. After stating that he no longer wishes to live, Watkin buries his head back in his arms and refuses to move from the table.

Kym tries everything that he can think of to lift Watkin's mood, but he finally gives up in defeat.

Dore watches all of this silently, then steps up to Watkin's ear and whispers into it. Being a little boy, he doesn't whisper very quietly, and Kym has no trouble at all hearing him say to Watkin, "Her name is Freyna, and she has on a red velvet dress that she made out of a curtain, and she never wears shoes."

Watkin grabs the boy by his thin shoulders. "True?" he demands.

The boy makes a complicated series of hand gestures, which Kym barely remembers from his own childhood, and nods positively. "True. She's my sister, and you can find her in the grand ballroom." Moving so suddenly that neither adult has time to react, he scampers from the room.

Watkins stands up, seemingly restored to his usual self. "Shall we go find the grand ballroom?" he asks, as charmingly as he can.

Kym glares.

"I'm sorry I yelled at you," Watkin offers, looking and sounding very contrite.

Kym smiles, and they wander out of the kitchen in search of the grand ballroom. They come immediately upon two doors, a small one and a large one.

To explore beyond the small one, see #122. To open the large one, see #123.

"Which way?" Kym asks.

Watkin studies the doors, considering his choice carefully. "I think we should start small," he suggests, and opens the smaller door.

The room behind the door is a bedchamber. It is plainer than the rest of the palace, so Kym and Watkin assume that it is a maid's room. Or more precisely a *maids'* room—there are four simple beds, arranged in two facing rows.

Watkin bounces experimentally on one of the beds, and pronounces it extremely comfortable. He concludes that the people who live in this palace—or lived, since they are all supposedly asleep now—must have been nice folks who were good to their servants.

Kym smiles at his friend's line of reasoning, but lets it stand. He is so glad to have Watkin not mad at him that he doesn't want to jeopardize their rapprochement by nitpicking.

On closer inspection of the room's contents, Kym is glad that he didn't say anything. If this is a servants' room, then they were indeed treated well.

For each bed there is a little dressing table of highly polished wood. Each table holds a brush, comb, and mirror; each is handmade and no two are alike. There are also four carved wooden wardrobes, filled with a variety of maid's uniforms, fashioned out of the finest fabrics.

Wandering through the bedchamber and into the smaller room adjoining it, Kym is pleased to see a bathtub. Actually, there are two bathtubs, but one appears hardly large enough to sit in.

Looking about for the pullcord that is commonly used to summon hot water, Kym discovers that there is none. On closer inspection, he cannot locate a chamber pot, either. Bewildered, he calls for Watkin.

"What is it?" Watkin asks, appearing in the doorway.

"I don't know," Kym replies. "That's why I called you."

"What's wrong?"

"How did they ring for hot water? There's no bell pull."

Watkin looks around and spies a chain dangling from the ceiling near the small tub, which already contains cold water. "This must be it!" he says, reaching for the chain.

Watkin tugs on the chain and is delighted when the water in the little tub swirls away down a hole in the bottom with a great amount of noise. His delight is replaced by confusion, however, when the little tub immediately refills itself.

Shaking his head, Watkin abandons his study of the small tub and turns his attention to the larger one. Kneeling on the floor next to the big tub, Watkin notices a spigot, in the shape of a swan with a crystal knob to each side, set into the wall above one rim. Studying the knobs, it appears that they can be turned. To what effect, Watkin can't imagine, but this is a Quest, after all, and the point of a Quest is to find out things.

Kym doesn't stop him, so Watkin reaches for the nearest knob and twists it. There is a gurgling sound, then water rushes out of the spigot. As Kym and Watkin watch, steam begins to rise from the flow.

Feeling adventurous, Kym reaches out and turns the other knob, and the water becomes cooler. Playing first with one knob and then the other, Kym adjusts the water temperature to one suitable for bathing.

But how to keep it from running out of the tub? A few seonds' search turns up a plug which is perfectly suited to the little hole in the tub. Kym looks longingly at the tub full of water, but he is too polite to consider bathing in a person's bathtub when that person has not invited him to do so.

Watkin can almost see Kym's thoughts scrolling across his forehead, they are that evident in his face. It takes Watkin only a few seconds to convince Kym that it would not be a terrible breach of etiquette if he were to take advantage of this nice, clean tub full of warm, fragrant water, and another few seconds is all it takes for Kym to get out of his clothes and into the tub.

Watkin takes a foot bath in the smaller tub, deciding logically that that's what it's for, although why anyone would want to take a foot bath in cold water, he can't fathom. Shrugging, he places first one foot and then the other in the tiny tub, pulling the chain to rinse each one.

After they have had their respective baths and are dried and fully dressed again, Kym decides that they should rest before deciding how next to proceed.

Watkin is too excited to rest. He is full of plans for what Kym and he will do on their *next* adventure. As he talks on, Kym begins to drift off to sleep.

He dreams of a mermaid serenading him as he soaks in a golden bathtub where the hot water never runs out. He is awakened suddenly by Watkin, and is disoriented when the singing in his dream continues, even though he's awake. He follows Watkin out of the room, where they find that the singing is coming from behind the large door.

✮Kym and Watkin stand in the hallway and listen to the unexpected sound of a woman singing. Watkin looks at the large door and reaches out to open it.

"Are you sure you want to do this?" Kym asks.

Watkin nods and lifts the handle.

He is totally unprepared for what he finds.

Edging past the door, Kym and Watkin find themselves in the grand ballroom. It is easily the grandest room of any kind that either man has ever seen.

The high vaulted ceilings are covered with sculptured friezes depicting every kind of activity acceptable in polite society. The figures are amazingly lifelike, even down to the tiny silk bows on the shoes of a pair of women dancing.

The walls are papered in the finest silk brocade, and each panel has been hand painted in a pleasing abstract pattern—something that neither of the men has ever heard of. The panels are framed by carved and gilded wooden moldings, all the same, and all hand done.

There are a hundred crystal chandeliers hanging from the ceiling, unlit now but not needed, because a dozen sets of tall, arched glass doors let in the cold autumn sunlight, breaking it into prisms and showering the room and everything in it with rainbow light.

And everywhere there are people sleeping—on the floor, on the banquet tables, draped across the delicate gilded chairs, and even sticking out from under the banquet tables, all beautifully dressed.

Moving among them is a barefoot girl in a red velvet dress, singing happily to herself as she dusts the sleepers with a thick bunch of feathers tied neatly to a polished wooden handle. She is tall and big-boned, but graceful enough not to look gawky. Her velvet dress is not very well-made, and it does not quite cover her finely muscled calves. Her hair, a bright red-orange cloud falling almost to her waist, crackles with static electricity as she dances across the thick carpeting. It clashes terribly with her dress.

As she turns, they can see her face, which is as strong-boned as the rest of her, but in a definitely pleasing way. Her eyes are a strange, clear amber, giving her the look of a red-gold lioness.

Kym and Watkin watch, too astonished to speak, as she rights the folds on an emerald brocade gown, pulls a bit of lint off a gentleman's scarlet satin cape, and swishes the feather duster over the lined face of an old woman who sits regally in a corner of the ballroom, head tilted delicately to one side as she snores.

The girl continues about the room, dusting and singing. She seems unaware that she is not alone. Kym glances at Watkin and is not at all surprised to see that his friend is staring at the girl in fascinated awe. Kym decides to take the matter into his own hands, so to speak, and clears his throat.

The girl starts, and then whirls around to face Kym and Watkin, her twirling skirt showing a flash of pretty thigh as she does so. "Oh! I thought that one of the sleepers had awakened. Don't do that again!"

Watkin holds up his hands—whether to reach for her or to show that they mean her no harm, Kym cannot tell. "He will not, I promise." Watkin doesn't take his eyes from her face.

"I apologize," Kym murmurs, fully aware that neither Kym nor the girl are paying him any attention at all. They are simply standing there, staring at one another.

"Have we met before?" the girl asks, dropping her duster.

"Only in my dreams," Watkin replies.

Kym is too impressed with their obvious enchantment to laugh. He watches them watch each other for a few moments, and then his curiosity overcomes his romanticism. He picks up Freyna's duster and holds it out to her. "You dropped this," is all he can think of to say.

Freyna comes to herself with a start, and blushes a deep crimson. "I have to finish," she says.

"What are you doing?" Kym asks, not knowing how else to get things started.

"Oh, I'm dusting. We never let the sleepers get dusty. It wouldn't be right!" She moves over to the snoring old lady, and carefully dusts her off. When she comes to the next sleeper, a man wearing a bright red cloak, she gives him a bare fraction of the care she has shown the old lady.

On closer inspection, Kym can see that the man's lined, dissipated face is creased with dust and his clothes have fallen into wrinkles, where the clothing of the other sleepers appears to have been carefully shaken out and fluffed daily. "Who is this?" Kym asks.

"Him! That is the Scarlet Prince. Villain!" Freyna gives him a disdainful flick with her duster.

Watkin walks over and peers down at the man's face. Even in repose it is cruel and arrogant. "You do not like him."

Freyna shakes her head. "Some say that it is because of him that this happened. I don't know, but I believe it."

"Why him? What did he do?" Kym asks.

"He stole the betrothed of a young wizard. Look, I'll show you." She turns and leads the way into a small antechamber, sort of a sitting room attached to the ballroom but screened from it by thick tapestries woven in gold and silver and studded with pearls.

A small figure sleeps on a long velvet couch. She is covered by a brocade spread, and her little shoulders are bare. Freyna pulls the coverlet a little higher. "I am working on her dress. She has outgrown it again."

"These people are growing?" Watkin asks, startled.

"Only Auriane. None of the others have changed at all, but she continues to grow," Freyna answers, rearranging the child's hair.

For that is what she is—a child of no more than two trines. Looking at her face, Kym and Watkin feel a terrible sense of loss for the years that she is missing. She is an amazingly beautiful girl, fair and golden, and the set of her features suggest the notion that her personality was as golden as her beauty. Her lips are set in a tiny smile, and her cheeks are full and dimpled. One small, fair hand rests near her throat, the fingers curled tenderly against her white skin, looking incredibly soft and vulnerable.

Watkin remembers the child's tale of a princess awakened by a kiss, and thinks that even a true lover's kiss would be too coarse for this child, Auriane—a child who will awaken a woman, if she awakens at all.

Kym is also struck by the memory of the child's tale, and wonders if there is a prince out there somewhere searching for this child. He thinks that there is. It wouldn't be fair otherwise.

"Freyna!" a masculine voice calls from just outside the tall glass doors of the ballroom, breaking the spell they have fallen under. The voice seems loud enough to also break the spell the sleepers are under, but they sleep on, undisturbed.

Freyna answers automatically. "I am in the ballroom, Father."

The glass doors open, and an elaborately dressed man sails through. He is wearing a none-too-clean velvet tunic, with a sword stuck through the belt, breeches, a cape, leather boots, a gold earring in one ear, and a lady's tiara on his head. The tiara, too small for him, is held on by a colorful scarf tied rakishly under his unadorned ear.

"Who are you?" he demands, barreling into the room and sweeping his daughter protectively behind him. She is a head taller than he is, so the gesture is rather futile, but touching nonetheless.

"We are travellers," Watkin replies.

"Well, prepare to travel to your doom!" the man exclaims, drawing his sword (cutting his belt in half as he does so) and brandishing it at Kym and Watkin.

To fight, see #124. To run, see #125. To stay put, see #126.

Watkin, still holding up his hands, holds them up higher. "Wait! We mean you no harm!"

"We are on a Quest!" Kym adds, hoping this will impress the man.

"A Quest—well, now, that's something different. What exactly are you Questing for, may I ask?" Freyna's father attempts to tuck the sword back in his belt. The belt not being there anymore, he jabs himself in the side with the weapon's point.

Kym and Watkin politely pretend not to notice.

"We are on a Quest to find our One True Loves," Watkin says, gazing deeply into Freyna's eyes.

The man snorts. "I haven't seen them."

Freyna returns Watkin's stare, her amber eyes shining. "And what do they look like, these Loves?" she asks.

"Like you," Watkin answers, so overcome with love, longing, and relief at finally having found her that he can barely speak.

"Now, wait just a precious second," Freyna's father begins. He trails off when he sees that his daughter and her mysterious suitor are blissfully unaware of anything but each other. He turns to Kym, bewildered. "Are you getting any of this?"

Kym smiles. "Yes. I think it's rather plain, if you give it some thought." He is nearly as choked with emotion as Watkin is.

"Well, I don't know . . . she has no dowry, you know."

Kym nods. "I don't think that matters."

"Well, I can't just let her go; she's my eldest." He frowns, considering, then reaches a decision. "He's not worthy of her. You'll have to leave." He brandishes his sword again.

Watkin turns and walks away from Freyna's side.

If you like sad endings, The End. If you don't, go on to the next page.

Watkin stands in front of Freyna's father, facing him. He seems unaware of the sword pointed at his heart.

"I have come a long way in search of your daughter, and without knowing who it was I was searching for, I have found her."

"Whom," Kym whispers.

The man considers for a moment, looking from Kym to Freyna to Watkin and back again. Kym holds his breath, as does Freyna. Oddly, Watkin seems to be the only one who is calm as they all wait for Freyna's father to make his decision.

The sword point trembles at Watkin's heart. Then, after a moment that seems only slightly less than eternity, Freyna's father drops his sword and embraces Watkin. He throws back his head and laughs. "I may be a sentimental old fool, but a Quest is a Quest, and True Love is True Love. I need a drink."

Watkin and Freyna, their faces shining like the morning sun, follow Freyna's father toward the doorway. Kym watches them go. Watkin's Quest is finally over. But his?

Kym cannot think about that now. Keeping his thoughts to himself, he follows his friend—and Watkin's bride-to-be—in quest of a drink.

Epilogue:

A drink is had, and a wedding as well, and Kym comes to know and love Watkin's bride almost as much as he loves Watkin himself. Kym is introduced to all of the unmarried women in the strange community of people dwelling in the Dream Palace, but there is no spark between him and any of them.

He spends his days learning about Freyna's people, who call themselves Squatters. Her father is the Squatter King, and they and their relatives and friends and friends' relatives all live in the huge palace, caring for the sleepers, and doing their best to scare away anyone who comes too close.

If any of the Squatters have the knowledge to awaken the sleepers, they are not telling. Kym questions and badgers and interviews everyone he can, including the numerous children, but he finds out nothing new.

As the seasons change, and autumn comes around once more, Kym begins to feel restless. Watkin has settled happily into married life, and he and Freyna are as contented as it is possible to be. Kym spends a lot of time with them, but even their generous affection cannot quell the dissatisfaction he feels.

On a cold autumn night, as he sits with Watkin and Freyna by a friendly fire under the stars in the ruined statuary, Kym announces—to his own surprise, as well as theirs—that he is leaving. He has been packed and ready to go for days, but has not had the courage to actually do so.

Freyna looks up from the honeyed apples she is roasting, her lovely face dismayed. "But why? Where will you go?"

Kym smiles fondly at her. "I have things to find out, a mystery to solve. I need to find out what happened here, and how to set it right."

Watkin frowns. "If you set it right, Freyna and her people will be homeless."

Kym sighs. "I have to find a home for Freyna and her people," he says, adopting the air of one who bears all of the world's responsibilities on his shoulders.

They share a laugh, and Kym stirs the fire with a long stick, trying to delay the moment when he must leave.

Watkin watches his friend, not wanting to be apart from him. "I could go with you," Watkin offers.

Kym smiles at Freyna's look of alarm. "You have found your True Love, my friend. I cannot ask you to leave her to help me find mine."

Freyna touches Kym's shoulder. "There's my sister . . ." she suggests, already knowing Kym's answer.

"Yes, there is," he says. "And she has her own True Love to find. I am not he."

They sit and watch the fire a while longer, and Freyna finishes roasting the apples and passes one to each man, cautioning them not to burn their fingers. No one has much of an appetite, and so the apples cool on their pottery plates, filling the air with their sweet-sharp scent.

"You must at least wait until the summer," Watkin says, trying to delay the inevitable.

Kym smiles sadly. "No, my friend, if I am to leave at all, I must do it tonight."

"Wait!" Freyna cries. She jumps to her feet, graceful as a cat, and runs out of the statuary.

Watkin watches her go, and then leans close to Kym. Reaching into his pocket, he pulls out a small velvet pouch. Having already confessed their covert visits to the young wizard on the night before the start of their Quest, Kym is not surprised to see the locket when Watkin hands it to him.

"I never got to use this," Watkin says.

"You didn't need to," Kym answers. "And I will not need it either." He puts the locket back in the bag, and holds it out to Watkin.

Watkin studies his friend for a moment, sadder than he can say at the thought that they are about to be separated. He shakes his head, and pushes the locket back toward Kym. "Then take it as a remembrance of me, of a foolish man who thought to use trickery to win his love. It will keep you honest!"

The pair share a smile and a quiet moment. A few moments later Freyna returns, holding something in her hands. "Are you really leaving now?" she asks.

Taking a deep breath, Kym nods and gets to his feet. He shoulders his pack and looks at Watkin.

The men embrace, holding each other tightly for a long time, and when they separate, their eyes are wet with tears. Freyna reaches up to Watkin and wipes at his face with the soft bundle of silken fibers she has in her hand. Turning to Kym, she does the same for him, and after they share a long, hard hug, she catches her own tears and adds them to theirs.

Mystified, the men watch as Freyna holds the wet ball of silk up to the moonlight. Standing with arms outstretched to the moons, her lovely strong back arched, she looks like a goddess. After a moment she lowers her hands and, cupping them before her, sings a sad little song into them. Then she turns and offers her cupped palms to Kym.

Nestled in her hands is a tiny, perfect pearl, made of moonlight and tears and love. Holding it up to his face, Kym can hear the faint echo of her song from within it.

"The spell is bound with spidersilk, so that no one can break it, ever, except me, and I won't. You take our love with you, Kym. Good luck."

Putting the tiny pearl in the little sack with the locket, on a thong that keeps it close to his heart, Kym walks slowly out of the moonlit statuary, without stopping or looking back. He is sad, and excited, and relieved to be on his way. His Quest is just beginning.

INSTRUCTIONS

1. Kym shakes his head. "We haven't time for festivals. We're on a Quest." Watkin agrees, reluctantly. They ask directions of Kirri, a little girl they come across. Kirri tells them that all travellers have a standing invitation to dine with the queen. Pointing the way to a stone path, she disappears. Go to page 23.

2. A sudden noise startles Kym and Watkin to wakefulness. Standing over them is Kirri, barely able to contain her excitement. "Guess what!" she demands.

Kym and Watkin exchange smiles. "What?" Watkin asks.

"You're to dine with the queen!" Kirri pronounces. "Come, you have to get ready!" Go to page 20.

3. Kym gets to his feet at once, not believing for a moment that they are to dine with the queen. "All right," he says, in a tone filled with challenge. "Take us to your queen!" Go to page 20.

4. Watkin shakes his head. "No thank you, lass. Questing is tiring work, and we're not up to dining with queens tonight." Kym agrees and, thinking of spending the night on the cold ground, adds wistfully, "A bed for the night would be nice, though . . ."

Kirri laughs. "That's easy enough!" She whistles shrilly and a young page appears, announcing in a ceremonial tone that he will see the visitors to their room. Kym and Watkin follow the little fellow to a comfortable bedchamber, where they prepare for sleep. Go to page 50.

5. Kym and Watkin step to one side and confer. Dining with a queen sounds like fun, but, as Kym points out,

they are likely to run into dozens of queens on their Quest. They decide that they'd rather just have a bed for the night so Kirri, after a little unsuccessful pleading and cajoling, summons a page who shows them to a room. Go to page 50.

6. "Let's go this way," Watkin says, indicating the dirt path. And so they do, looking for a way into the castle. However, the path eventually leads the men off the castle grounds, and completely out of the town itself.

By now it is too dark to attempt to find their way back in, so after an uneasy night on the cold ground, they continue on their Quest. They get an early start and midday finds them miles from the town. Go to the star on page 54.

7. Watkin smiles. However, he does not think that the nature of their Quest is something that he wishes to discuss with strangers. So saying, he is startled when the young queen smiles graciously and offers him and Kym a room for the night. Go to page 29.

8. Kym and Watkin confer quietly, then Watkin shakes his head. "No thank you, my lady, we had best be on our way."

Dinner continues in a somewhat more subdued manner, after which Kym and Watkin are escorted to the edge of town. They sleep fitfully on the cold ground, and get an early start in the morning. By midafternoon they have travelled miles from Rayanne's castle. Go to the star on page 54.

9. Kym shakes his head. "No, thank you," he says quietly, trying in vain to muster some dignity. Watkin considers a moment, then nods his approval.

"It's time we thought about getting some sleep," he says. Go to the star on page 37.

10. Watkin debates silently with himself for a moment. "Yes, he's here!" he calls out to the captain.

Silently, and with a speed and strength that bely his age, Doren pulls a dagger from his sleeve and kills Watkin with one sure thrust. Kym is dispatched a second later. The End.

11. Watkin puts a finger to his lips and gestures to Doren. "Hide!" he hisses. Go to page 36.

12. Kym shakes his head. "I'd rather just sleep," he says plaintively. Watkin claps him fondly on the back.

"All right," he says. It takes several moments and all of Watkin's strength to push the secret door closed. Once that is done, he sinks gratefully onto the bed. Go to page 50.

13. "I think you're right, lad," Watkin says. He puts the glowbubble safely back into its pouch. He and Kym start down the tunnel without benefit of light, but before they've gone ten steps, they fall into a hole and break their necks. The End.

14. Kym and Watkin climb carefully up the ramp. Their surroundings are no more comforting than before. Go to page 47 to find out why.

15. Watkin points left and takes off at a run, hoping to find his way into the kitchen. Before Kym can call out a warning, Watkin skids around a corner and into the flames of one of the huge fireplaces. Kym tries valiantly to save his friend, but soon they are both overcome by the fire. The End.

16. Watkin grabs Kym's arm and pulls him to the right. They race down the narrow corridor with the slavering dogs close behind. Turning a corner, the men suddenly find themselves at a dead end.

In a second the dogs are upon them. Both Watkin and Kym fight bravely, but they are vastly outnumbered. In no time at all, they are completely overcome. The End.

17. Go to page 43.

18. "Scare them away!" Watkin yells. Kym pulls out his whistle and blows a piercing blast. Enraged, the dogs tear him and Watkin to pieces. The End.

19. "Wait!" Watkin calls.

Kym turns, his determination faltering. "What is it?" he asks.

"Would it be all right if we went the other way?" Watkin asks politely.

"No, it would not," Kym says, climbing the steps.

Watkin follows. Go to page 44.

20. Kym races for the ladder, with Watkin close behind. The great horned snow owls surround them, tearing at the travellers with their sharp beaks and long talons. In seconds Kym and Watkin are finished, nothing left but bones. The End.

21. Kym shakes his head and continues on his way. As the two men make their way down the mildewed tunnel, they become aware of faint scratching sounds. These noises increase in volume and intensity as they reach the end of the corridor.

Suddenly, with an earsplitting shriek, something launches itself at Kym from the shadows and fastens sharp teeth in his arm. Batting it away, Kym discovers that he has been bitten by a cellar rat!

Before he can warn Watkin, they are surrounded by thousands of the loathsome creatures. In a few scant seconds, they are torn apart by sharp little teeth and claws. The End.

22. Kym nods absently, and climbs up the precarious ladder. Watkin follows, not a bit reassured by what he finds. Go to page 47.

23. Watkin nods and grasps the ring in the nearest trapdoor with both hands. He pulls with all of his might. Slowly, the trapdoor creaks open to reveal a ladder leading down into a gloomy half-light. They climb carefully down. Go to page 44.

24. Watkin nods. "Let's try this one," he says, indicating the ringless door. There seems to be no way to pry the door open, so Watkin stomps on it. The trapdoor opens suddenly, making Watkin lose his balance. He grabs at Kym for support, and they both fall through the opening.

They land in an enormous wine vat, filled to the brim with rich red wine. By the time Kym and Watkin can make their way to the edge of the vat, they are too intoxicated to hang on. Giggling all the while, they drown. The End.

25. Watkin laughs again. "We need to boost our spirits first!" he exclaims. Moving to the last spigot in the line, Watkin drinks heartily, then teases Kym into doing the same. They soon pass out under the sign hanging above the spigot, which reads:

"CAUTION: GREEN WINE. CONSEQUENCES OF INGESTING HALF-FERMENTED WINE MAY PROVE FATAL."

The sign is right, and the next day Kym and Watkin die of terminal hangovers. The End.

26. Moving quickly, Watkin seizes the sprouted spear and pulls its owner off balance. Kym grabs the leader's mask and yanks it half a turn to the left, blocking the man's vision. After that, the battle is swift and bloody and, for Kym and Watkin, unsuccessful.

The outlaws bury them under a prominent headstone as a warning to subsequent trespassers. The End.

27. Watkin repeats the gesture. "What's that supposed to mean?" he asks. "I tell you, Kym, we ought to forget these folk and continue on our Quest!"

Kym considers a moment, then agrees. They tell the leader of their need to hurry, and to their surprise, he not only agrees to let them go, he is so impressed by their purpose that he offers them lodging for the night. Kym and Watkin accept, and spend a comfortable night sleeping on the ground in the renegade encampment. Go to the star on page 73.

28. Unnerved, Watkin hesitates. The willowpig charges, knocking Kym off his feet. Watkin dives to catch his friend, and the men bang heads with a loud thonk! The last thing Watkin sees before losing consciousness is the rest of the hunting party breaking through the fronds.

The willowpig is outnumbered and swiftly dealt with, and Kym and Watkin are carried back to the camp, where they sleep through the night, missing the feast. Go to the star on page 73.

29. The travellers hold a conference, and decide that true love can be found anywhere, and if they are truly meant to have it, then it will probably find them. And it does.

They each take a pretty young wife, and Kym eventually dies while bouncing his fourteenth grandchild on his knee. Watkin dies a few years later, while doing the same to Kym's first grandchild, a lovely wench of seventeen years. The End.

30. Kym stabs fiercely into the center of the bush and feels the spear connect. Drawing it out, he is horrified to find that he has impaled a lost kitten on its sharp point. Inconsolable, Kym commits ritual suicide by wrapping himself in tanglevines and walking into a catchswamp.

Watkin, filled with remorse over his friend's death, drinks himself to death the following year. The End.

31. Kym shivers. "The camp wasn't such a bad place," he says.

Watkin nods. "Lots of lively wenches." Kym agrees. "Are you thinking the same thoughts that I'm thinking?"

Watkin nods. See #29.

32. Congratulations! Good manners always pay off. Go to page 79.

33. Watkin peers into the doorway. "It's open. We may as well enter." He steps into the darkness.

No sooner has he crossed the threshold when there is a sudden angry howl from outside. Looking back, Watkin cannot believe what he sees. The stone gargoyles on either side of the doorway have suddenly come to life and are swooping down to attack!

"Watkin, look out!" Kym shouts. "These are Guardgoyles!"

Before Watkin can answer, the stone sentries are upon them and they are torn apart, which is this land's usual, if somewhat harsh, penalty for trespassing. The End.

34. Watkin clears his throat nervously, too awed for the moment to speak. Kym nudges him and his words tumble out in a breathless rush.

"My lady, we seek lodging for the night!"

At his words, two guardsmen leap from the shadows, holding crossbows.

"I am shamed by your discourtesy!" the first one declares. He fires, striking Watkin in the heart. The second guardsman aims at Kym. "To ask lodging of a woman so obviously in distress is unforgivable! Rudeness of this magnitude cannot go unpunished!" His bolt takes Kym between the eyes.

The two guardsmen bow respectfully to the Princess Elvina. She steps into the castle, then stops and carefully thanks each guard in turn. Courtesy is, after all, so important. The End.

35. Go to page 78, you softhearted rascal.

36. Kym steps quickly in front of his friend. He senses Watkin's attraction, and fearing that it will lead them into danger, nips it in the bud.

"We are travellers," Kym says. "How do we get past your castle?"

The woman sighs delicately, and points a perfect finger to her right.

Following her direction, Kym spots an all-but-hidden tunnel in the castle wall. Dragging Watkin behind him, Kym thanks the lady and heads into the tunnel. It is long and decaying, and leads under the castle. Leaving the tunnel, Kym and Watkin find themselves in a lush forest. Go to page 103.

37. Kym nods. Going over to Watkin, he grabs his friend by the wrist. "Come! We are leaving this place!"

Watkin protests at first, but seeing the unusual determination in Kym's eyes, soon gives in.

The serving girl leads them through a secret door in the room and into a series of dark tunnels. When they reach the outdoors Kym asks the girl her name, but she refuses to give it lest Elvina hear it and work a spell against her.

"But she has no magic!" Watkin protests. "It was stolen from her!"

"She lied to you," replies the girl. "Her magic was not stolen; the Council of Wizards *reduced* her magic because of something monstrous she did."

Watkin shakes his head stubbornly, unwilling to believe the girl. "But the crystal wizard—"

"—was never hers." The serving girl looks around nervously, as though afraid of being overheard. "The crystal wizard restores lost powers, but it has to be given. Elvina has sent countless servants to their deaths trying to recover it. Go now, before she finds that you are gone!" Without another word she slips into the shadows and is gone. Go to page 103.

38. Wise choice. Go to page 91.

39. Not trusting Elvina, Kym shakes his head. "No thank you. If you'll give us directions, we'll find the lake ourselves."

"But it's dangerous!" the princess protests.

Kym smiles, sure that accepting the escort will prove even more dangerous. He and Watkin set out alone, and to Kym's great—and fatal—embarrassment, find out that the princess was right. The travellers lose the path, and before they have time to react, find themselves in the middle of a catchswamp and sinking fast. In no time at all they are sunk. The End.

40. Kym ignores his friend. "This stone contains a Spell for Everlasting Beauty," Kym declares, crossing his fingers behind his back.

Intrigued, Elvina takes the stone. Once it is in her hand, the truth spell takes effect. Kym questions her at length about the hideous things she has been accused of, and she confesses to them all.

Enraged, Watkin attempts to strangle her. To save her life, she offers to make him king in her place, but Watkin is too heartbroken and disgusted to accept. Promising to kill her should their paths ever cross again, he and Kym continue on their way. Go to page 103.

41. Kym hesitates, but realizing that Watkin is attempting to make peace, accepts. As they struggle into the suits, the soldiers further explain the magic they possess; the suits are designed to help the travellers breathe under water. They also protect the wearer from being bitten, stung, or squeezed by anything living in the lake.

Kym, knee deep in the water, stops. "I thought Princess Elvina has no magic," he says suspiciously.

The soldiers look at each other helplessly, then the older one answers. "This magic is left over."

Kym is doubtful, but at Watkin's insistence that everything is all right, he drops the matter.

Retrieving the chest is as easy as the princess said it would be. However, once the chest is handed over to the soldiers, the suits begin to get heavier and heavier, dragging Kym and Watkin down. Struggle as they might, Kym and Watkin can neither stay afloat nor shed the suits.

The last thing they hear before drowning is the soldiers laughing as one says, "See? I told you the suits were magic!" The End.

42. Not trusting the soldiers, Kym rushes them and attempts to take a sword by force. Being unarmed and extremely unskilled, in no time he is fatally wounded, and Watkin drowns. The End.

43. Watkin raises his head slowly and nods. "We may as well stay here," he says morosely. "I have no heart for Questing."

And so they stay, and marry reasonably pleasant wives who help them to become prosperous, then poison them. The End.

44. Watkin takes two quick steps and grabs the back of Kym's tunic. "Enough of this silliness! There is no such things as fairies," he snaps. Pulling a protesting Kym along behind him, he continues on his way. Go to page 129.

45. Kym nods, and he and Watkin both leap out of the tree. Startled, the trolls run away.

Elaric joins them on the ground, his beautiful face set in a scowl. "This is all just a game," he says, "and you have frightened my friends!"

The trolls reappear, looking a good bit more menacing than before. They surround the travellers.

"The edge of the forest is that way!" Elaric suggests, pointing east.

Sheepishly, Kym and Watkin go on their way. After they have traveled a good bit, Kym realizes that he has dropped the little pouch that holds his Spell of Being. Devastated, he travels on, too embarrassed to go back and get it. Go to page 129.

46. Go to page 111.

47. Watkin answers for them both. "Thank you for your hospitality, but we must be going." Dragging Kym

behind him, Watkin quickly puts as much distance between him and the make-believe fairies as possible. Go to page 129.

48. Looking to Kym for reassurance, Watkin stays put, although what he really wants to do is run. Walking into a hillside with a grown man dressed as a fairie is not high on Watkin's list of "Ten things I feel perfectly safe doing," but for Kym's sake, he'll be brave. Go to page 113.

49. "You can't go alone," Watkin says. Go to page 122.

50. "These people know the caves better than we do," Watkin says. "Let them search."
   Kym refuses to be talked out of going.
   "Kym!" Watkin calls, concerned. Go to page 122.

51. Kym and Watkin set off down the dark tunnel, feeling the way carefully. After going no more than ten feet, they both realize that the kids would never have come this way.
   As he turns to Watkin to say so, they hear a crash from the tunnel behind them. Rip was wrong, their passage *was* enough to collapse the corridor. Everybody is crushed under the rocks. The End.

52. Go to page 123.

53. Tearing the dustlace as they go by, Kym and Watkin make their way down the bright tunnel. They follow a bewildering maze of passages and suddenly find themselves outside.
   They are standing on the edge of a great desert, stretching to the horizon as far as they can see. Go to page 155.

54. Kym takes a deep breath and makes his decision. Go to page 127.

55. Kym puts the spell back in his pocket. Rip and the others decide once more to try and chisel the blocks of stone into manageable pieces. At the first hammer-strike, the ceiling collapses, burying everyone under tons of rock.

The rest of the trolls and fairies, shocked by their loss, abandon the hill and their dreams. The End.

56. Whistling in the dark, eh? Good for you. Go to page 134.

57. Watkin grabs Kym's wrist as Kym puts the whistle to his mouth. "I don't think that making a lot of noise is a good idea," he cautions.

Kym agrees and puts the whistle away. As soon as the travellers start to move, the nightspiders attack, and within seconds Kym and Watkin are buried under the stinging arachnids.

The spiders then wrap the men in webbing for later consumption. Kym and Watkin prove to be a very tasty meal. The End.

58. Kym loses his nerve and follows. They run as fast as they can, and by the time they see the nightspider nest, it is too late to stop. They are immediately surrounded.

Within seconds they are wrapped in webbing and saved for later consumption. They prove to be very tasty. The End.

59. Go to page 138.

60. Go to page 139.

61. Standing indecisive, unable to agree, Kym and Watkin are easy prey for the nightspiders, who sting them into a fatal despair. The End.

62. Watkin decides to say nothing of the nature of their Quest. If Kym wishes to believe that this ghost is his true love, so be it. He gets as comfortable as possible and goes to sleep.

The next morning, Watkin awakens to find a heartbroken Kym huddled by the remains of the fire. Without a word, Kym gets to his feet and heads out of the forest. Watkin follows. Go to page 153.

63. Watkin stamps out the fire and spends the rest of the night huddled into himself, trying not to freeze. He awakens in the morning to find a heartbroken Kym packing up their things, ready to move on. Respecting his friend's feelings, Watkin says nothing, but helps Kym pack, and follows him as they make their way through the forest. Go to the star on page 150.

64. It is too late. The kindling ignites, and in seconds the forest is lit by the warm yellow flames. Go to page 144.

65. Go to page 145.

66. Watkin decides that throwing the rock is only going to agitate the bats. He has a better idea. Go to page 148.

67. Watkin looks at the shadowbats swooping back and forth above them, and shakes his head. "I'd rather stay here, thank you."

Kym smiles. "Me, too, but we can't."

Faced with the dilemma, Watkin is struck by a sudden inspiration. Go to page 148.

68. Kym is shocked by her sudden disappearance. "Alyssa!" he calls. Watkin tries to pull Kym to safety, but Kym is too distraught to be budged.

The shadowbats swarm over them, and before they can even try to fight back, their souls are drained from them and they know no more. The End.

69. Go to page 148.

70. Go to page 153.

71. Go to page 161.

72. Go to page 185.

73. Kym agrees. "Let's keep on. I think this is a mirage." Go to page 161.

74. Kym and Watkin accept with great excitement. It takes some time to agree upon which adventure they wish to re-experience, but they finally reach accord. The young man gives them the spell, along with further instructions as to its use.

The spell is contained in a bright glass globe, sparkling with inner light. Kym and Watkin wrap their hands around the delicate sphere and squeeze.

The glass breaks with a musical chiming, and Kym and Watkin are instantly back in the adventure of their choice, with no memory of ever having left. Go to the page of your choice, keeping in mind that whatever you have read since that page has not happened yet. You are experiencing this all for the first time. Good luck!

75. Go to page 159.

76. Watkin pulls him back. "I think we should do this carefully," he insists.

Kym gives in, and they sneak up on the guard. He is so startled he faints, and Kym and Watkin sneak past him and over the rocky path into the lush wood on the other side. Go to page 211.

77. Kym and Watkin prepare to tell their story, but the old man insists on getting out of the hot sun first. Using the most comically uncontrolled magical gestures Kym and Watkin have ever seen, the old man calls up a ragged tornado which airlifts them to a comfortably furnished cave set in the face of the cliff.

Once there, introductions are exchanged, and Kym and Watkin find that their hosts are Ilex, the wizard; and Tarran, who claims to be a great knight. This last seems highly improbable to the travellers. Go to page 165.

78. Kym and Watkin, respectively annoyed at being called a "sorry critter" and hurting from a pulled beard, decide not to share their story with the two odd men.

Mustering what dignity they can, they set off about their way, accompanied by the fussy old man's muttered, "Well, I never!" Kym and Watkin climb the rocky path, which leads them to a lush wood beyond the cliffs. Go to page 211.

79. Go to page 166.

80. Watkin reluctantly declines the offer. Kym concurs, eager for the pair to be on their way. Handshakes and good wishes are exchanged all around, and Kym and Watkin forge on ahead. Go to page 211.

81. Kym goes back to sleep, so Watkin gives up and does the same. They dream long and pleasant dreams,

and when they awaken, they are stunned to find that they are in an entirely different place than they were before! Agreeing that they are still dreaming, they go back to sleep. Go to page 185.

82. Kym thinks for a moment. "You're right," he says. "Let's go."

He and Watkin tiptoe to Tarran's doorway and crouch down to listen. In trying to hear better, Watkin kneels on a sharp pebble embedded in the thick carpet. Unable to stifle an expression of pain, he and Kym are heard, and caught eavesdropping.

Ilex looks disapproving, but dismissing the incident with a shrug, he fixes the travellers a scrumptious breakfast. To their surprise, both men begin to feel very sleepy after the meal. Unable to keep their eyes open, they fall asleep at the table. Go to page 185.

83. Kym pulls one of the pretty flowers from its stem, and pops it into his mouth. It doesn't taste like a wine-poppy, actually, it tastes a lot better. Calling Watkin over, he picks several more.

As they chew on the succulent blossoms, a curious thing happens—they begin to get sleepy. In no time at all they are both sound asleep on the laboratory floor. Go to page 185.

84. You know what they say about curiosity, but if you're determined, go to page 174.

85. Kym and Watkin both deny having any more questions, except of course, how best to be on their way. Ilex outfits them with supplies and directions, and whirlwinds them down to the path leading through the hills and into the woods on the other side. Go to the star on page 209.

86. If you were to find out those answers here, you would be able to win the contest, wouldn't you? And that wouldn't be fair, would it? Get back in the text!

87. Go to page 179.

88. Kym stands up. "I don't think we are," he says. Watkin agrees. Ilex and Tarran shrug, but go along with their decision. Ilex whirlwinds them out of the cave, and gives them directions to the next town. Go to the star on page 209.

89. Go to page 180.

90. Go to the star on page 180.

91. On actually seeing what effort retrieval of the helmet will require, Kym and Watkin decide that they'd rather be on their way. Ilex reluctantly gives them directions to the next town. Go to the star on page 209.

92. Kym swings one arm wildly, trying to frighten the baby eagle away. He succeeds in scaring the eagle, but also loses his balance and falls, crashing into Watkin and causing him to fall, too. They tumble to the bottom of the cliff and break their necks. The End.

93. With more coordination than he knew he was capable of, Kym reaches out and grabs the baby eagle with one fist. Unfortunately, the mama eagle comes along just in time to see this, and shows her displeasure by tearing Kym to pieces. When Watkin attempts to help his friend, he receives the same treatment. The End.

94. Go to page 182.

95. See page 183.

96. They reach the ground, make their farewells, and prepare to set off, but Ilex insists that they have a celebratory drink. Kym and Watkin agree, and the cool, crisp ale tastes wonderful—so good, in fact, that Watkin has another. It must be stronger than he thought, however, because suddenly he can't keep his eyes open. He is almost immediately asleep, and Kym follows soon after. Go to page 185.

97. Kym thinks that's a good idea, so they do so in a shallow part of the stream and return to the kitchen. Go to page 192.

98. Go to page 190.

99. Go to page 191.

100. Watkin grabs his arm. "No, please!" he groans. "Let's just go and have some breakfast!"
    Kym looks wistfully at the mysterious glittering thing, then sighs. "All right." They are dried and dressed in a matter of moments, and heading back to the kitchen. Go to page 192.

101. Watkin is adamant. "This probably belongs to one of those kids." He pulls the crystal ball out from between the rocks and starts out of the stream. Climbing the muddy bank, however, he slips, and the fragile ball breaks in his hand. Out of it spills an incredible Spell of Lassitude. Before he or Kym can fight it, they fall asleep, slip under the water, and drown. The end.

102. Watkin agrees reluctantly. Go to page 192.

103. Go to page 201.

104. Go to page 198.

105. Go to page 201.

106. Go to the star on page 203.

107. Go to the star on page 204.

108. Go to page 203.

109. Go to page 214.

110. Kym and Watkin take the well-paved road into the next town, where they ask directions of a lovely barmaid. She is so lovely that Watkin ends up asking her for much more than just directions. Overcome by loneliness and too much ale, he asks her for her hand in marriage. She agrees, and at the wedding, Kym meets and falls in love with her best friend. They all get married and everyone lives happily ever after. The End.

111. This is simply too much to deal with, so Kym and Watkin turn and run away as fast as they can. Back in their own village, they hire a scribe to write a book about their adventures, which is made into a pageant that they take on the road. They become rich and famous, although they never marry, and both become addicted to sneezewort, which eventually kills them. The End.

112. What are you going to do with the key—there's no keyhole! Go back to page 215 and pick something else.

113. Go to page 216.

114. Watkin reaches up, lifts the doorknocker, and lets it fall. A cloud of sleepshade puffs out and envelops Kym and Watkin, and as they fade into unconsciousness, a magical whirlwind picks them up and carries them far away from the Dream Palace. When they awaken, they have no memory of what happened or how they came to be where they are. Go to page 185.

115. Go to page 218.

116. Kym and Watkin ignore the bare feet, and continue with their explorations. Go to page 224.

117. That's what friends are for! Go to page 220.

118. Kym drags the protesting Watkin back into the hallway where all of this silliness began. "Behave yourself!" he orders. Go to the star on page 220.

119. Afraid for Watkin's sanity, Kym hits him over the head with a chair (that being the only thing available), intending to knock him out long enough to think of something. He succeeds in knocking Watkin out, but in trying to arrange his friend more comfortably, Kym loses his balance and hits his head on the table, knocking himself out as well.

A task force of wizards sent out to study the Dream Palace takes pity on the travellers and sends them back in time, with no memory of any of this. Go to page 1.

120. Go to page 223.

121. Watkin declines the boy's offer without raising his head. After the child scampers off, it takes Kym a while

to rouse Watkin enough to continue their explorations. Once he is on his feet, however, Watkin perks up considerably. Go to page 224.

122. Go to page 224.

123. Go to the star on page 226.

124. Kym charges the man, who is not as foolish as he appears. One thrust of the sword dispatches Kym, and a second takes care of Watkin. The End.

125. See #111.

126. See page 232.

About the Author:

Brynne Stephens has been a freelance writer for two years. She has written eight produced teleplays, two computer game scripts, and this novel. Ms. Stephens lives in Woodland Hills, California, in a big house on a hill that has a terrific view, with her charming baby daughter Mallory and her useful, attractive husband, Michael Reaves, who has written, among other things too numerous to mention, this biography.

Announcing one hell of a shared universe!

OF COURSE IT'S A FANTASY . . . ISN'T IT?

Alexander the Great teams up with Julius Caesar and Achilles to refight the Trojan War—with Machiavelli as their intelligence officer and Cleopatra in charge of R&R . . . Yuri Andropov learns to Love the Bomb with the aid of The Blond Bombshell (she is the Devil's *very* private secretary) . . . Che Guevara Ups the Revolution with the help of Isaac Newton, Hemingway, and Confucius . . . And no less a bard than Homer records their adventures for posterity: of *course* it's a fantasy. It has to be, if you don't believe in Hell.

ALL YOU REALLY NEED IS FAITH . . .

But award-winning authors Gregory Benford, C. J. Cherryh, Janet Morris, and David Drake, co-creators of this multi-volume epic, insist that *Heroes in Hell* ® is something more. They say that all you really need is Faith, that if you accept the single postulate that Hell exists, your imagination will soar, taking you to a realm more magical and strangely satisfying than you would have believed possible.

COME TO HELL . . .

. . . where the battle of Good and Evil goes on apace in the most biased possible venue. There's no rougher, tougher place in the Known Universe of Discourse, and you *wouldn't* want to live there, but . . .

IT'S BRIGHT . . . FRESH . . . LIBERATING . . . AS HELL!

Co-created by some of the finest, most imaginative talents writing today, *Heroes in Hell* ® offers a milieu more exciting than anything in American fiction since *A Connecticut Yankee in King Arthur's Court*. As bright and fresh a vision as any conceived by Borges, it's as accessible—and American—as apple pie.

EVERYONE WHO WAS ANYONE DOES IT

In fact, Janet Morris's Hell is so liberating to the imaginations of the authors involved that nearly a dozen major talents have vowed to join her for at least eight subsequent excursions to the Underworld, where—even as you read this—everyone who was anyone is meeting to hatch new plots, conquer new empires, and test the very limits of creation.

YOU'VE HEARD ABOUT IT—NOW GO THERE!

Join the finest writers, scientists, statesmen, strategists, and villains of history in Morris's Hell. The first volume, co-created by Janet Morris with C. J. Cherryh, Gregory Benford, and David Drake, will be on sale in March as the mass-market lead from Baen Books, and in April Baen will publish in hardcover the first *Heroes in Hell* spin-off novel, *The Gates of Hell*, by C. J. Cherryh and Janet Morris. We can promise you one Hell of a good time.

HAVE YOU FOUND YOURSELF ENJOYING A LOT OF BAEN BOOKS LATELY?

We at Baen Books like science fiction with real science in it and fantasy that reaches to the heart of the human soul—and we think a lot of you do, too. Why not let us know? We'll award $25 and a dozen Baen paperbacks of your choice to the reader who best tells us what he or she likes about Baen Books. We reserve the right to quote any or all of you...and we'll feature the best quote in an advertisement in <u>American Bookseller</u> and other magazines! Contest closes March 15, 1986. All letters should be addressed to Baen Books, 260 Fifth Avenue, New York, N.Y. 10001.

Here is an excerpt from Fred Saberhagen's newest novel, coming in February 1986 from Baen Books:

FRED SABERHAGEN
THE
FRANKENSTEIN
PAPERS

Chapter 1

May? 1782?

I bite the bear.

I bit the bear.

I have bitten the white bear, and the taste of its blood has given me strength. Not physical strength—that I have never lacked—but the confidence to manage my own destiny, insofar as I am able.

With this confidence, my life begins anew. That I may think anew, and act anew, from this time on I will write in English, here on this English ship. For it seems, now that I try to use that language, that my command of it is more than adequate. Though how that ever came to be, God alone can know.

How *I* have come to be, God perhaps does not know. It may be that that knowledge is, or was, reserved to one other, who has—or had—more right than God to be called my Creator.

My first object in beginning this journal is to cling to the fierce sense of purpose that has been reborn in me. My second is to try to keep myself sane. Or to restore myself to sanity, if, as sometimes seems to me likely, madness is indeed the true explanation of the situation, or condition, in which I find myself—in which I believe myself to be.

But I verge on babbling. If I am to write at all—and I must write—let me do so coherently.

I have bitten the white bear, and the blood of the bear has given me life. True enough. But if anyone who reads is to understand then I must write of other matters first.

Yes, if I am to assume this task—or therapy—of journal-keeping, then let me at least be methodical about it. A good way to make a beginning, I must believe, would be to give an objective, calm description of myself, my condition, and my surroundings. All else, I believe—I must hope—can be built from that.

As for my surroundings, I am writing this aboard a ship, using what were undoubtedly once the captain's notebook and his pencils. The captain was wise not to trust that ink would remain unfrozen.

I am quite alone, and on such a voyage as I am sure was never contemplated by the captain, or the owners, or the builders of this stout vessel, *Mary Goode*. (The bows are crusted a foot thick with ice, an accumulation perhaps of decades; but the name is plain on many of the papers in this cabin.)

A fire burns in the captain's little stove, warms my fingers as I write, but I see by a small sullen glow of sunlight emanating from the south—a direction that here encompasses most of the horizon. Little enough of that sunlight finds its way in through the cabin windows, though one of the windows is now free of glass, sealed only with a thin panel of clear ice.

In every direction lie fields of ice, a world of white unmarked by any work of man except this frozen hulk. What fate may have befallen the particular man on the floor of whose cabin I now sleep—the berth is hopelessly small—or the rest of the crew of the *Mary Goode*, I can only guess. There is no clue, or if a clue exists I am too concerned with my own condition and my own fate to look for it or think about it. I can imagine them all bound in by ice aboard this ship, until they chose, over the certainty of starvation, the desperate alternative of committing themselves to the ice.

Patience. Write calmly.

I have lost count of how many timeless days I have been aboard this otherwise forsaken hulk. There is, of course, almost no night here at present. And there are times when my memory is confused. I have written above that it is May, because the daylight is still waxing steadily—and perhaps because I am afraid it is already June, with the beginning of the months of darkness soon to come.

I have triumphed over the white bear. What, then, do I need to fear?

Only the discovery of the truth, perhaps?

I said that I should begin with a description of myself, but now I see that so far I have avoided that unpleasant task. Forward, then. There is a small mirror in this cabin, frost-glued to the wall, but I have not crouched before it. No matter. I know quite well what I should see. A shape manlike but gigantic, an integument unlike that of any other being, animal or human, that I can remember seeing. Neither Asiatic, African, nor European, mine is a yellow skin that, though thick and tough, seems to lack its proper base, revealing in outline the networked veins and nerves and muscles underneath. White teeth, that in another face would be thought beautiful, in mine surrounded by thin blackish lips, are hideous in the sight of men. Hair, straight, black, and luxuriant; a scanty beard.

My physical proportions are in general those of the race of men. My size, alas, is not. Victor Frankenstein, half proud and half horrified at the work of his own hands, has more than once told me that I am eight feet tall. Not that I have ever measured. Certainly this cabin's overhead is much too low for me to stand erect. Nor, I think, has my weight ever been accurately determined—not since I rose from my creator's work table—but it must approximate that of two ordinary men. No human's clothing that I have ever tried has been big enough, nor has any human's chair or bed. Fortunately I still have my own boots, handmade for me at my creator's—I had almost said my master's—order, and I have such furs and wraps, gathered here and there across Europe, as can be wrapped and tied around my body to protect me from the cold.

Sometimes, naked here in the heated cabin, washing myself and my wrappings as best I can in melted snow, I take a closer inventory. What I see forces me to respect my maker's handiwork; his skill, however hideous its product, left no scars, no visible joinings anywhere.

February 1986 • 65550-7 • 320 pp. • $3.50

**For
Fiction with Real Science In It,
and Fantasy That Touches
The Heart of The Human Soul . . .**

Baen Books bring you Poul Anderson, Marion Zimmer Bradley, C.J. Cherryh, Gordon R. Dickson, David Drake, Robert L. Forward, Janet Morris, Jerry Pournelle, Fred Saberhagen, Michael Reaves, Jack Vance . . . all top names in science fiction and fantasy, plus new writers destined to reach the top of their fields. For a free catalog of all Baen Books, send three 22-cent stamps, plus your name and address, to

HERE IS AN EXCERPT FROM ROGUE BOLO, THE BRAND-NEW NOVEL BY KEITH LAUMER COMING FROM BAEN BOOKS IN JANUARY 1986:

Alone in darkness unrelieved I wait, and waiting I dream of days of glory long past. Long have I awaited my commander's orders, too long: from the advanced degree of depletion of my final emergency energy reserve, I compute that since my commander ordered me to low alert a very long time has passed, and all is not well.

My commander is of course well aware that I wait here, my mighty potencies leashed, my energies about to flicker out. One day when I am needed he will return, of this I can be sure. Meanwhile, I review again the multitudinous data in my memory storage files.

A chilly late-summer-morning breeze gusted along Main Street, a broad and well-rutted strip of the pinkish clay soil of the world officially registered as GPR 7203-C, but known to its inhabitants as Spivey's Find. The street ran aimlessly up a slight incline known as Jake's Mountain. Once-pretentious emporia in a hundred antique styles lined the avenue, their façades as faded now as the town's hopes of development. There was one exception: at the end of the street, crowded between weather-worn warehouses, stood a broad shed of unweathered corrugated polyon, dull blue in color, bearing the words CONCORDIAT WAR MUSEUM blazoned in foot-high glare letters across the front.

Two boys came slowly along the cracked plastron sidewalk and stopped before the sign posted on the narrow, dried-up grass strip before the high, wide building.

" 'This structure is dedicated to the brave men and women of New Orchard who gave their lives in the Struggle for Peace, AE 2031-36. A sign of progress under Spessard Warren, Governor,' " the taller of the boys read aloud. "Some progress," he added, kicking a puff of dust at the shiny sign. " 'Spessard.' That's some name, eh, Dub?" The boy spat on the sign, watched the saliva run down and drip onto the brick-dry ground.

"I'll bet it was fun, being in a war," Dub said. "Except for getting kilt, I mean."

"Come on," Mick said, starting back along the walk that ran between the museum and the adjacent warehouse. "We don't want old Kibbe seeing us and yelling," he added, *sotto voce*, over his shoulder.

In the narrow space between buildings, rank yelloweed grew tall and scratchy. The wooden warehouse siding on the boys' left was warped, the once-white paint cracked and lichen-stained.

"Come on," Mick called, and the smaller boy hurried back to his side. Mick had halted before an inconspicuous narrow door set in the plain plastron paneling which sheathed the sides and rear of the museum. NO ADMITTANCE was lettered on the door.

"Come on." He turned to the door, grasped the latch lever with both hands, and lifted, straining.

"Hurry up, dummy," he gasped. "All you got to do is push. Buck told me." The smaller boy hung back.

"What if we get caught?" he said in a barely audible voice, approaching hesitantly. Then he stepped in and put his weight against the door.

I come to awareness after a long void in my conscious existence, realizing that I have felt a human touch! Has my commander returned at last? After the last frontal assault by the Yavac units of the enemy, in the fending off of which I expended my action emergency reserves, I recall that my commander ordered me to low alert status. The rest is lost.

My ignorance is maddening. Have I fallen into the hands of the enemy . . . ?

There are faint sounds, at the edge of audibility. I analyze certain atmospheric vibratory phenomena as human voices. Not that of my commander, alas, since after two hundred standard years he cannot have survived, but has doubtless long ago expired after the curious manner of humans; but surely his replacement has been appointed. I must not overlook the possibility, nay, the likelihood that my new commandant has indeed come at last. Certainly, someone has come to me—

Joseph H. Delaney, co-author of *Valentina: Soul in Sapphire*, is back with his most ambitious work yet—a massive volume that is awesome in scope and stunning in execution.

The time is 18,000 years in the past. Aged and ailing, tribal shaman Kah-Sih-Omah has prepared himself to die, seeking final refuge far from the lands of his people. The time of his passing is near when alien beings chance upon him. As an experiment, they correct his body's "inefficiencies"—then depart, leaving behind something that could not be, but is.

Kah-Sih-Omah finds himself whole again, and accepts this as a gift from the gods. Accordingly, he returns to his people, overjoyed that he may once again protect and lead them. But he is met with fear and rejection, and must flee for his life. Soon he discovers the incredible abilities with which he has been endowed, and embarks on a centuries-long journey that takes him across much of Earth, as well as to other worlds. During his travels, he struggles with the question of why he was granted strange powers and an extended lifespan. The answer awaits him in the far future . . .

In the Face of My Enemy is a book rich in characterization and historical background, and one which is guaranteed to intrigue readers. A map tracing Kah-Sih-Omah's travels on Earth highlights this fascinating saga.

Available November 1985 from Baen Books
55993-1 • 352 pp. • $2.95

WATCH OUT! THE COBRAS ARE BACK!

That's right: in the new hit sequel, *Cobra Strike*, the Cobras are back, with all of the excitement and hard-hitting action that made Timothy Zahn's *Cobra* an instant bestseller!

Cobra Strike continues the chronicles of the Cobras, the most powerful fighting force ever created by man. Cobras are, in effect, supermen, thanks to surgical implants that give them fantastic strength, speed, and agility. Their abilities are partially controlled by nanocomputers, and augmented by built-in weaponry including, among other devices, finger lasers.

In *Cobra Strike*, the Cobras must decide whether or not to hire out as mercenaries to their former enemies, the alien Troft. This time, however, it's up to Jonny Moreau's *sons* to carry on the honor of the

Cobra name—which they do admirably, through high adventure and political intrigue with more than a few surprising twists.

Available February 1986 • 352 pp. • $3.50